THE GROUP

A Clint Smith Thriller

Bob Doerr

TotalRecall Publications, Inc.
1103 Middlecreek
Friendswood, Texas 77546
281-992-3131 281-482-5390 Fax
www.mousegate.com

ISBN: 978-1-59095-569-7
UPC: 6-43977-45692-2

Library of Congress Control Number: 2016937339

Printed in the United States of America with simultaneous printings in Australia, Canada, and United Kingdom.

FIRST EDITION
1 2 3 4 5 6 7 8 9 10

To the sheepdogs who protect the sheep.

Award Winning Author: Bob Doerr

grew up in a military family, graduated from the Air Force Academy, and had a career of his own in the Air Force. Bob specialized in criminal investigations and counterintelligence gaining significant insight to the worlds of crime, espionage, and terrorism. His work brought him into close coordination with the security agencies of many countries and filled his mind with the fascinating plots and characters found in his books today. His education credits include a Masters in International Relations from Creighton University. A full time author with ten published books and a co-author in another, Bob was selected by the Military Writers Society of America as its Author of the Year for 2013. The Eric Hoffer Awards awarded *No One Else to Kill* its 2013 first runner up to the grand prize for commercial fiction. Two of his other books were finalists for the Eric Hoffer Award in earlier contests. *Loose Ends Kill* won the 2011 Silver medal for Fiction/mystery by the Military Writers Society of America. *Another Colorado Kill* received the same Silver medal in 2012 and the silver medal for general fiction at the Branson Stars and Flags national book contest in 2012. Bob released an international thriller titled *The Attack* in May 2014, and more recently, *Caffeine Can Kill,* his sixth book in the Jim West mystery series. Bob has also written three novellas for middle grade readers in the Enchanted Coin series: *The Enchanted Coin, The Rescue of Vincent,* and *The Magic of Vex.* Bob lives in Garden Ridge, Texas, with Leigh, his wife of 42 years, and Cinco, their ornery cat.

The Book

Someone is killing off the world's rich and famous. The murders are sophisticated, requiring precision and skill. The international community is in an uproar but has no leads in its attempt to find the assassins. The victims were members of the Bilderberg Group, an international, loose knit group of the uber rich that meet annually. While the attacks have not had a direct impact on the U.S., Theresa Deer, Director of the Special Section, a small unit whose existence is known by only a handful in the U.S. government, sees this new age League of Assassins as a national threat. She sends her hunters out. Clint Smith finds their trail in Switzerland where his discovery almost leads to his own death. The hunt leads him to Mallorca, Spain, where he witnesses a helicopter attack on a villa where a number of attendees from the Bilderberg conference were holding a follow-on meeting of their own. Smith picks up the trail a couple weeks later in Las Vegas, NV, and in his hunt finds out that he is no longer the hunter. He has become the prey.

Chapter 1

Eileen Custer sat by herself at an outdoor table of the Café Rey. She sipped a latte and watched the Mercedes parked in a private lot across the street. At the moment, one of her jobs included making sure nothing happened to the Mercedes while her client ate his dinner with his two guests in the members only club next to the lot. Her employer, the Moore Group, paid her handsomely for these plush assignments.

After six years in the U.S. Army, Eileen had jumped at the chance to join the company. The Moore Group, an international security firm, specialized in armored vehicles for the world's rich and eccentric. It also had a sizeable personal security services division, and a smaller branch that offered training to foreign governments and companies. Eileen belonged to the personal security part of the company.

Eileen hadn't yet regretted her decision. The pay more than doubled what she had made in the military. The people with whom she rubbed elbows, at least those associated with this client for the last four months, definitely ran in higher circles than anyone she had ever been around before.

She looked over at her boss, L. P. Stewart, the team chief for the small group traveling with the client on this trip. This stopover in Paris had been kept off the public agenda, so only the two of them escorted their client, Mr. Galen McPherson, to the dinner meeting. Tomorrow, McPherson's private jet would take them on to Basel, where he would join dozens of other world billionaires for a meeting of the Bilderberg Group. Stewart and Eileen would join up with the other five members of the security team already in Basel.

Stewart signaled to Eileen. She sprang up and hurried across the street, dodging two cars in the process. She reached the Mercedes a few seconds before the others and held the back passenger door open for McPherson. Stewart climbed into the driver's seat at the same time as McPherson started to get into the car. Stewart's door shut. Eileen checked to see if McPherson's legs were in and out of the way and started to close the door when it occurred.

It seemed to happen all at once. In that half-second, Eileen's mind had trouble putting it together, but her instincts told her that it was bad, really bad. The blast, the flash of light, and the heavy, armored door smashing into to her seemed to happen instantaneously. Then, as she lay there, stunned and unable to move, the smell of smoke and the awful heat overcame her. Her world went dark.

CHAPTER 2

Clint's phone rang when he had reached the farthest point of his hike. He struggled briefly with his backpack to get to the phone. The glare of the morning sun as it rose above the Gulf of Mexico made it nearly impossible to see who was calling.

"Hey," he said into the phone. Clint saw little need to identify himself. A call from this number could only be answered by one of his fingers first touching the screen. No one else's fingers would do.

"You out exercising?"

Clint recognized Buzz' voice. He dealt more with Buzz than he did with Theresa Deer, his boss, and most of his contact with both came via the phone. Although he had never seen an organizational chart, he believed Buzz was Deer's deputy. He liked Buzz, even if he couldn't remember the guy ever telling him his last name.

"Sort of. What's up?"

"Someone's killing off the rich and famous. You're booked out of Houston tomorrow afternoon for a flight to Paris. Is that going to be a problem?" Buzz asked.

"No." Truth be told, Clint Smith needed to do something. The last three months of inactivity had gotten old.

"Okay. You should have the tickets and some background in a little. She'll probably call you tomorrow before the flight."

"Should I plan on a long stay or a brief one?" Clint knew as soon as he asked the question it was a dumb one.

"Your guess is as good as mine. Be safe, my man." Buzz terminated the call.

Clint started jogging south back to the city. The sand along this part of South Padre Island could be difficult to walk in, much less run in. He didn't mind. Finally, he had something to do.

Three sea gulls took off in flight about thirty yards ahead of him and circled wide before coming back to the same spot after Clint ran past them.

He had once sensed that not all of the hunters felt the same about Buzz as he did. Buzz was a desk guy, not an operator, and there always seemed to be that superiority bias that many operators in many professions had about themselves. The military had been no different, and he knew that field agents with federal law enforcement and security agencies often looked down at their headquarters' staffs. Clint figured everybody had a place, and where you were was less important than how well you did your job. In Clint's mind, Buzz did his job very well.

In fact, considering the size of the staff of Special Section, Clint stayed impressed with how much Buzz did. He wondered if the small size of Section kept it so efficient. If it did, the rest of the government could sure learn something from the example. But then, the rest of the government didn't know about its existence.

Clint followed the beach around a bend of the shoreline, and the tall towers of the new condos built a little north of the city came into view. His mind went back to his job and how little he really knew about the organization he had joined after leaving the military a little over three years ago. While he had heard Buzz and Ms. Theresa Deer refer to it as Special Section and sometimes simply Section, he had never seen any paperwork acknowledging that title or anything else. He knew Section was situated in a basement suite of three offices in the U.S. Marshal Service Headquarters building in Washington D.C. The placard on the door did not refer to it as Special Section but rather as

Advanced Research and Analytics, or something similar.

Only a few at the very top of the U.S. Marshal Service knew that the handful of people in the small basement suite of offices didn't work for the Marshal Service. These few had only been told that the individuals working there had an extremely sensitive, interagency mission and required a covert location to do their job. Since the need for the office originated during the reorganization of U.S. security agencies following 9/11, the Marshal Service had been happy to help out without too many questions.

Clint had only visited the offices a couple of times. These occurred before he had been given his first operational assignment. For cover purposes, Clint, like the rest of the hunters, carried the badge and credentials of a U.S. Marshal. Deer believed, therefore, that they should be familiar with the Service's headquarters building and location within the city.

Deer had instructed him that even his fictitious tie to the Marshal Service had to be kept confidential. The credentials gave him some legitimacy if confronted by the police at a crime scene or some similar situation. Even in those situations, he was to disavow any Marshal Service interest in the matter, extricate himself as quickly as possible, and immediately inform Deer or Buzz of his use of the credentials.

Clint understood the need for secrecy. If what he did became known to the public, Special Section would be shut down in a second. No one in the government would admit to knowing about the unit, its mission, or anyone in it. People could go to jail, and he could be one of them.

For all the respect he had for Buzz, Clint's opinion of Deer reached another level. One could almost describe it as awe. He knew little of her background other than she was once an operative with the CIA. How she managed to get things done amazed him. She had once told him she was simply a parasite operating off everyone else's information. Section didn't have any collectors, so Clint knew any information to which Deer's team gained access came from other sources, either through agreement or through covert hacking into somebody else's networks. However, Deer's ability to siphon through the trillions of gigabytes of data with the help of a few super computers, and come up with the relevant information that she did, impressed the hell out of him.

He jogged up the stairs to his sixth story apartment and took the old backpack out to the balcony. Clint kept the main compartment in the backpack filled with sand, and he didn't need it spilling inside his home. There always seemed to be sand on the floors anyway, but it seemed prudent to keep the pack on the balcony. Despite being on the Gulf of Mexico side of the narrow island, his balcony gave Clint an unobstructed view of the bay. The few friends that had visited the condo had asked him why he preferred the bay view. His answer was simple. He tried to not be awake during sunrises and seemed to always be awake at sunsets.

The information from Buzz had arrived on his laptop. The first email came with the fictitious return address of a fictional friend.

"Hey C, how's the writing? Thought this might be a fascinateing plot line for a book – Brent." The email contained two links. One was to an article in the online version of the Financial Times. The other sent him to a Wikipedia site.

The Times article claimed a brutal terror attack resulted in the death of a Galen McPherson, one of the richest men in the world. The article didn't contain many specifics other than saying that the cause of death was believed to be from an explosion. A second, unidentified individual died in the blast, and a third person was critically injured.

Clint had never heard of McPherson. He clicked on the second link. An article on the Bilderberg Group appeared on the screen. Reading through it, Clint thought of a number of conspiracy theories he had heard of in the past. The article described the Bilderberg Group as a secretive group of the world's most powerful people who have met annually since 1954. The Bilderberg Group considered those invited to the annual meetings and the topics discussed to be official secrets which they had continuously refused to release to the media.

Clint doubted a non-governmental entity could forbid the press to report any information they wanted to release to the public. He also doubted this group could keep their activities very secret. Unaccounted for leaks from anonymous sources made the world go round. Still, he found the article interesting. Already aware of a number of so-called secretive organizations that allegedly ran most of the world, such as the Trilateral Commission, the Free Masons, the Illuminati, and the Opus Dei, Clint supposed he could now throw the Bilderberg Group into that mix.

Neither article mentioned McPherson's connection with the group, but Clint knew there had to be since Buzz sent both articles to him. He wondered why Deer might be interested in either McPherson's death or the group. Special Section only got interested in something when Deer became interested, and Deer only got interested in something when someone posed a significant and imminent threat to the United States.

He knew better than to concern himself with the details at this point. Besides, a trip to Paris sounded better than doing nothing for the next few days. He decided to plan for a weeklong stay in France.

Before he would do any preparation, though, he needed to shower and shave. He wouldn't be leaving until the next morning, but while drying off he thought he might as well get organized for the trip. After taking a total of five minutes to pack, one didn't spend a third of one's life bouncing around the world without knowing how to pack, Clint decided he deserved to treat himself to some pecan waffles at the Grapevine Café.

Two restaurants on the island served a great breakfast, and Clint bounced between the two. He had favorite servers at both and tried to get a table in their sections. At the Grapevine, he found a table in Flor's area. She waved at him when he entered.

"The usual?" she asked as she walked by taking coffee to another table.

"Yes, ma'am."

Clint guessed Flor's age to be somewhere between sixty and seventy, but she showed no signs of slowing down. When she brought him his waffle with a side of sausage, she stood next to him and studied his hair.

"You're getting some grey hairs in that shiny black hair of yours," she said.

"A sign of maturity," Clint said.

"A sign you need to find a woman and settle down. Did I tell you about my niece, Rose?"

"Which one is she?"

"The tall one. She's six feet tall. She needs a tall husband. What are you six two, six three?"

Clint nodded while he took a bite of waffle.

"You check her out on that Facebook. You like her, and I'll arrange for her to come up here."

"Where does she live?" Clint asked.

"Mexico City. She's driving my sister crazy. Lives at home. You look at her on that Facebook. Rose, Rose Escobar. I'll bring her up here. Maybe it could be free waffles for a long time for you." Flor walked off to take care of another customer.

Flor had teased him before about being single, but this was the first time she tried to set him up. He grinned to himself as he finished his breakfast. Bribing him with waffles, he'd hold out until she threw in the sausage. Perhaps it was time for that trip to Paris.

Deer didn't call until Clint turned his Lincoln MKZ north onto Texas Highway 77 the next day.

"We've got an interesting situation developing, Clint," Deer said in her normal pre-mission, abrupt style. "The attack on McPherson was no normal hit. A person fired what I believe was some sort of shoulder fired missile from two hundred yards and sent it through an open door of an armored Mercedes. We have reason to believe the missile utilized laser guidance. High tech and a bit overkill for your normal hit in Paris."

"Sounds like it," Clint agreed. "Any idea who or why?"

"No specifics, but we're working through some unpleasant probabilities. I need you in Basel. Once you're in Paris, check into your hotel and do what you want for the day. On Thursday morning, you're booked on a train to Basel. Don't check out of the hotel in Paris. Details on the train and where you'll be staying in Basel will be sent to you once you arrive in Paris."

"Do I have a target in Basel?" Clint asked.

"Not yet. The group you read about is having one of their annual meetings right now in Basel."

"Am I going?" Clint asked. He thought he heard an actual laugh come from the other end of the call.

"You wish," Deer said. "I need you there because I don't like what I see developing. Let's leave it at that for now."

"Okay," Clint said, and the call ended.

CHAPTER 3

He spent his one day in Paris sightseeing. He had visited Paris a handful of times in the past, yet he still found himself drawn back to the Notre Dame, the Sacre Coeur, and the artist area along the Seine.

An early morning knock on the room door minutes before he left to catch his train answered his questions about what to do with the hotel room key when he left for Basel and whether to leave any clothes in the room.

"Good morning, Clint. I'm Dolly. Ms. Deer said I could use your room while you were gone." The woman who stood in front of him had a large red suitcase next to her. She looked like she had slept in her clothes and hadn't combed her hair in twenty four hours. The airline baggage claim ticket still clung to her suitcase.

"Long flight?" Clint asked, at loss for what else to say at the moment.

"I hope you don't mind," Dolly said.

"No, not at all. I won't be here," Clint said as he stepped back and opened the door wider for her.

She mumbled something to herself that Clint thought sounded like "My loss," as she entered the room.

"It's good to finally put a face to a name," Clint said. "Nice to meet you."

Usually when he had phone contact with Special Section he talked with Buzz or Deer. On a few occasions when they weren't available he had talked to Dolly. The times he had been to the offices, he had only seen Deer and Buzz. He had seen a couple of other desks that appeared to belong to someone, but the desks were vacant when he was there.

"Nice to meet you, too. Ms. Deer said I deserved a vacation, and that my being here will keep any questions from being asked why the hotel room is vacant all week. I'm to tell anyone who asks that you're traveling around France doing some research for your book, and that you'll be back in a day or two."

"Good idea. I guess you don't have any idea how long I'll be gone, do you?" he asked.

"No more than you. This won't be a total vacation for me. I speak French. Deer wants me to do a few simple things while I'm here."

"Well, you be careful," he said. Clint thought she would blend in with the locals. In fact, she could blend in well in any western city. Dolly's appearance could best be described as bland or nondescript. He didn't think she was ugly by any means, but there wasn't anything about her appearance that would make anyone look twice at her.

"You, too," she said when he left.

The train rolled into Basel, Switzerland, at three o'clock in the afternoon. Clint had never been to Basel before, and at first glance, he thought he would rather have stayed in Paris. If he had to sit around and wait for things to happen, Paris offered a lot more options to fill his time. Basel didn't appear tiny, but Clint thought it looked like a peaceful small city and a place where a tall American stranger roaming the streets might draw someone's attention.

The train had few empty seats, so when it came to a stop at the Basel station, Clint avoided the rush and took his time getting off. He wouldn't be competing for taxis or buses. His hotel was within easy walking distance of the train station.

Hotel Euler faced the square where all the city buses and trolleys merged to drop off or pick up passengers at Basel's main train station. It took less than five minutes for Clint to walk to the hotel. The lobby appeared empty, and no one manned the reception counter. As he reached the counter, a woman with thick glasses and grey hair pulled tight behind her head in a bun, walked out of an office and greeted him. With typical Swiss efficiency, she checked him into the hotel in seconds.

"The bar will open shortly," she pointed at a small bar tucked into the corner of the room. "Breakfast is served from six. You can find coffee and tea in your hallway by the elevator."

Clint looked around the small lobby and noticed the half dozen tables scattered about. He took his room key and proceeded to his third floor room. Like the hotel in Paris, this one seemed to be privately owned, not very big, but classy. The location of the hotel would require a long hike to get to the old center of Basel, but that pleased Clint. He considered leaving his suitcase unpacked and taking a walk when his phone rang.

"How's the hotel?" Buzz asked.

"Looks fine. Been here before?"

"Who? Me?"

"Yes," Clint said.

"No. It looked pleasant on the internet, but that's not why we picked it. You've got eight bodyguards at the hotel with you right now. Two of them are with the Moore Group. That's the same company that had the protection detail on McPherson."

"Why are they still here?" Clint asked.

"These two have a different client. It's a big organization, but these two must be aware, interested, curious, whatever the right word might be, about the assassination. The other six should be, too, even though they work for other companies. Deer thinks it might be interesting to hear what they are saying about the incident. We might learn something that hasn't made the police or news wires."

"Why aren't they with the rest of their teams?"

"Simple hotel space. These guys are lower in the food chain.

They didn't make the cut to stay in some of the nicer places nearer the action. There are other small pockets of security personnel spread out in a number of smaller hotels throughout the city. Deer liked your location," Buzz said.

"It's good. I can step out of my hotel and catch public transportation to just about anywhere."

"Is the noise going to keep you awake?"

"No," Clint said. He had slept through a lot worse. "Any theories yet, about McPherson's death?"

"Yes. Nothing we can pass on yet. At this point we just need you there. Try to establish rapport with some of the security guys but don't be inquisitive. We have no suspects, only theories. Can't hurt you to have a couple of contacts over there if you need some help," Buzz said.

"You think these guys would moonlight for a few bucks?" Clint asked.

"Don't know, but they wouldn't be the first to take on a short term second job for some extra money, if they thought their boss wouldn't know about it. We have reason to believe some of them are planning to meet for drinks there at the hotel at five."

Buzz said goodbye, and Clint decided to take that walk. He went out the front door and turned left. Carrying a brochure from the hotel, he figured he could make his way to the old town square without getting too lost. The walk would be good exercise and allow him to get a feel for part of the city.

Clint found himself again trying to figure out Deer's interest in the Bilderberg Group or even McPherson's death. Since he started working for her, all his targets had been bona fide threats to the U.S. and its citizens. The murder of McPherson did not seem to meet the criteria that got Deer interested. He knew the uber-rich had a status of their own, but he didn't like thinking that an attack on one of them held the same importance as a terrorist team bent on dispensing Saran gas in the DC metro or bombing a string of embassies. There must be more to it, and he knew that if and when Deer felt like letting him know, she would. Meanwhile, he would do his best to enjoy Basel.

He reached the town square in thirty minutes. The old Ratskeller dominated the square. A tour group looked like it was waiting to go in. Rather than fight the crowd, Clint decided he could check it out later. He found a vendor selling hot pretzels.

Clint made it back to the hotel a little before six. Buzz' info had been correct. Five men sat around a small table near the bar drinking beer. They spoke English, and all looked like they spent half their life in the gym. Clint nodded at one of them who looked up at him as he walked past. The nod wasn't returned. Clint went straight up to his room where he spent about ten minutes before returning to the bar. He didn't need to go to his room, but he wanted the group to know he was a resident there and not someone who might have come off the street to eavesdrop on them. They would be a suspicious group. It came with the turf.

Clint leaned against the bar and ordered a beer. An old man worked behind the counter, and a young woman in traditional garb worked the floor. Her outfit could have come off the set of The Sound of Music. It fit her well, though, and most of the men at the table didn't mind staring at her.

A middle-aged couple speaking French entered the bar and sat at a table across the room. Clint watched as the waitress went to their table and took their orders in French. She returned to the bar and passed on the order in what sounded like German.

"How many languages do you speak?" Clint asked.

"Only a few," she said in English. "You have to be able to speak English, French and German. A lot of us can speak Italian, too, but not me."

"I'm impressed." Clint noticed a couple of the men at the table watched him. He recognized the look in their eyes. They didn't like the competition.

"Where are you from?" she asked.

"Texas."

"Ah! A cowboy," she said. Her smile widened. "I'm Polly."

Clint had discovered in the years he had spent overseas that where he said he was from could bring different reactions from people. Saying he came from America or the United States lumped him in with everyone else and received a reaction based on an existing bias. Some people liked America and others didn't. However, he learned that if he claimed he was from California, New York, or Texas he could get a totally different reaction. No other states got similar reactions, other than Florida if he was traveling in South or Central America. Hollywood had made California famous, and, perhaps in an indirect way, had made Texas and its history with cowboys famous. New York City made New York famous. Clint once read that a survey among a remote native tribe in Africa found that, despite not knowing the names of the countries that surrounded their own country, most of those surveyed had heard of these three American states.

Clint didn't deny being a cowboy. "This is a beautiful city. Are you from here?" he asked.

"Near here," she said.

She started to say more, but the bartender placed two drinks down on the counter and mumbled something. She smiled at Clint again and walked off to deliver the drinks to the couple across the room. On her way back to the bar, one of the men with the security group motioned for her. She stayed with the men for a while laughing and talking. When she returned to the counter, she gave a little twirl of her finger and said beer. Clint figured they had ordered another round of beer.

"Are you here with the conference?" Polly asked after she

had delivered the round of beers.

"No. What conference?"

"Some big one. A lot of rich people are supposed to be attending it. I haven't seen much about it in the news."

"I'm strictly a tourist," Clint said. His comment must not have inspired her. She left him to stand by herself at the other end of the counter.

About twenty minutes later, Clint watched his third beer flow out of the tap. The couple had left, and only two of the original group of security personnel remained at their table. These two stood up and started to leave.

"One for the road?" Polly asked the two men. She had moved behind the counter to cover for the bartender who had gone somewhere a few minutes before.

The two looked at each other.

"Can we get something to eat here?" The taller of the two asked. He also looked a little older than the other guy.

"Pizza," she said.

"Might as well," the shorter one said. "It'll save us some money."

"Ok. You got pepperoni?" the taller one said.

"Sure," Polly answered. She started to walk off.

"Can I have one, too?" Clint asked. "A small one."

"They're all small," Polly said. She opened a tiny freezer and pulled out three small pizzas wrapped in cellophane. One at a time, the pizzas went into a microwave.

Clint saw the two men make a face at each other like they doubted their decision to eat at the bar. When the pizzas came, the two men remained at the counter, rather than go back to their table.

"I've had better," Clint said to the two men after taking a couple of bites of his pizza.

The tall man ignored him, but the shorter man leaned away from the bar. "Have you eaten anywhere else in Basel?" He asked with his mouth still full of pizza.

"Not yet, I just got in this afternoon," Clint said.

"Everything is expensive here. The dinner that cost me seventy dollars last night wasn't very good either," the man said.

"My name's Clint." He offered his hand.

"Mark, Mark Yancey, nice to meet you. Are you here for the conference?" The two shook hands.

"That's what Polly asked me, too, but no, I'm here as a tourist only."

"My silent friend here is Ray."

Ray finally made eye contact. Clint didn't see any hostility in Ray's eyes, but Ray only nodded at him. Clint didn't push him by offering a hand to shake.

"Other than the restaurant last night, have you found any places to eat that you'd recommend?" Clint asked.

"No," Mark said. "We only got in yesterday morning. Been too busy to scope out the city."

"What brings you here?" Clint asked.

"Our client. Where he goes we go." Mark bit into his pizza.

"Ever been on one of these river cruises up the Rhine?" Clint asked to indicate that he had little interest in the conference or Mark's client. "I hear one starts out of here and goes all the way to Amsterdam."

"No. Never even heard of them," Mark said.

Ray looked at Clint and rolled his eyes. "Sure you have. They advertise them on television. My wife and I even get their damn flyers in the mail."

Mark shook his head.

"He doesn't get out much," Ray said to Clint and went back to watching Polly in the mirror.

"Are they expensive?" Mark asked. Obviously, the cost of things made an impression on Mark.

"I think so, but like you said, everything else over here is expensive, too," Clint said.

"How long are you going to be in Basel?" Mark asked.

"I was thinking to use it as a base while I took a series of day trips throughout the region. If that works out, I may be here up to a week."

"We'll only be here another day or two," Mark said.

"Where's home for you?" Clint asked.

"Chicago."

"Great. Been there a few times. A super city. Cubs or White Sox fan?"

"Cubs, of course," Mark grinned.

The conversation continued while the three finished their pizzas and beers. Ray only added a few sentences to the entire conversation. Clint didn't learn anything significant, but he hadn't thought that he would. He would run into them again.

His jet lag still bothered him, so when Mark and Ray went upstairs, Clint went outside to get some fresh air.

CHAPTER 4

The night air felt cool and moist. A low cloud covered Basel half absorbing and half reflecting the lights of the city. The rattle of trolleys disrupted nature's peaceful ambience. Clint started walking but had only gone a few steps when his phone rang.

"Got a few minutes?" Deer asked him.

"Sure," Clint said. He spied a park bench across the street and in front of what looked like a museum.

"We have an interesting situation developing. It may be nothing, and hopefully it won't amount to anything that you'll need to get involved in."

Deer paused, and Clint figured she was trying to figure out how to explain why she needed him to be there.

"Okay," he said as he sat down on the bench.

"This Bilderberg Group plays a very important function. While it's a target of criticism by numerous conspiracy theorists, the group's annual conference provides a forum for many of the world's most powerful to get together and share ideas. Within the large group, there has always been and will always be factions. That's typical anywhere you put a lot of people together. What worries me, and it's not just me, is that one of the factions may be taking more aggressive steps to get their way."

"Do you know who and why?" Clint asked.

"No. It's not beyond reason to think it's not even someone in the group."

"Which means what?"

"Someone close to one of the factions, but who chooses not to be, or maybe can't be a part of the group, may have a vested interest," Deer said. "McPherson's murder was the second recent murder of a powerful member of the group."

"Who was the other target?"

"A South American very much into oil and iron. He was killed two weeks ago on his front porch by someone who was good enough to hit a target a mile away. One shot to the head."

"Doesn't sound like your average terrorist," Clint said. He thought the killer had to be a trained sniper.

"Not at all. No average terrorist took out McPherson either.

"But why change the method? The guy could have just as well shot McPherson."

"If you have access to a team of assassins, it makes a lot of sense to use different ones," Deer said without explanation.

"I guess so," Clint said. He couldn't help but wonder who had a team of assassins. "How do we fit into all this?"

"We may not, but there are a number of reasons why we might want to."

Clint wanted to ask what the hell that meant, but thought it might be smarter not to ask. He wondered if Deer had her sights on the team of assassins rather than the factions within the Bilderberg Group.

"I've met a couple of guys from one of the security teams." Clint said.

"Good. Most of them will be leaving in a couple days. I don't think anything will happen there, but if you need a weapon, a key to a locker at the train station will be delivered to you in the morning."

"Thanks."

"There's a gym about six blocks from the hotel that a lot of the guys use. I'll send you the address. I also want you to rent a car and keep it handy."

"I'll do that first thing in the morning," Clint said.

"Interpol has sent a team there, and the CIA has increased the size of the team that normally covers these meetings. The community is spun up over these murders. It gives us more to read, but so far nothing of any value. That's about it for now. Anything you need?"

"Not that I can think of."

After the call, Clint walked a few blocks before returning to his room. Although no rain fell while he was outside, the patches of fog and the light mist that seemed to float in the air made his hair wet enough that a drop of water rolled down into his face as he entered the hotel lobby. He wiped it off with the back of his hand.

"Why the tears?" Polly asked from the bar as he walked in.

She didn't have any customers, and Clint knew she was only teasing him.

"Want a night cap?" she asked.

"Thanks, but not tonight. I have an early day tomorrow." Clint might or might not get up early, but he had taken the walk to shake off the effects of the alcohol and the jet lag. He also didn't feel like any more small talk.

The next morning turned out to be drizzly and slow. No new instructions came from Deer and nothing exciting happened. He received a small package that had been dropped off at the front desk. Inside the package, he found the locker key along with three pair of black socks. With the assistance of the hotel staff, Clint rented a Volkswagen Passat.

Clint spent two hours at the gym Deer recommended. He saw a half dozen other Americans there who he thought might belong to security teams in Basel to support the conference. He thought a few of the Europeans in the gym might also be part of security contingents from their own countries.

Only one woman worked out in the gym. She arrived with two men shortly after Clint started his own exercise regimen. Clint couldn't help but stare at her when she entered. He noticed almost every other set of eyes in the gym watched her, too. To say she was pretty was like saying Bill Gates was rich.

Her looks went way beyond pretty. The word "striking" came to Clint's mind. He watched her over the next hour. She easily kept pace with her two male companions. Not that she lifted weights as heavy as they did, but she worked at her level as hard and as fast as they did.

"They call her 'The Princess'," said a large bald man, who paused next to Clint in his walk across the gym.

"I'd be afraid to call her names," Clint said.

"Ha! Do you know her?" the man asked.

"No."

"They don't call her The Princess to tease her. She looks like she could be the twin of a princess, who, by the way, is now the Queen of Spain. You know how we all get nicknames. The story is that while the nickname flattered her, she worried that because of their similar appearances the real princess might not like it. Her client, a Spanish billionaire, actually cleared it with the royal family."

"Interesting. I didn't know any of that," Clint said.

"Well, I've been doing this a long time. Keep your head down man," he said and continued his walk to the showers.

Clint imagined that most of the people working out in the gym thought that he, like them, belonged to someone's security contingent. Few billionaires travel internationally without a security team of some sort. A handful of senior government representatives from various countries were also attending the conference. Many of them most likely brought security teams, too.

While Clint ran on the tread mill, he imagined what conversations between billionaires sounded like. He thought it could be like the rest of us but with more expensive toys. Instead of, "I hear you have a new car," they might say, "I hear you have a new yacht." Maybe instead of talking about buying a house, they talk about buying an island. He wondered if the old rich had more or less empathy for the masses than the new rich. He didn't have the answers, and he didn't really care, but it gave him something to think about while he worked out.

The Princess walked by, and Clint smiled at her. She smiled back and kept walking. Clint's mind turned to thoughts of Doctor Barbara White. He thought a lot about her these days. He had never considered settling down, but Barbara had changed that a little. Barely a day went by where he didn't find himself thinking of her. He wondered if maybe she had similar feelings, and because of them, she had accepted the temporary posting in Africa with the group Doctors Without Borders. He worried about her over there.

After the workout, Clint headed back to Hotel Euler to shower. When he entered the lobby, he had to walk around three men engaged in an animated conversation. They spoke in English and appeared to be pleased about something. Clint recognized two of the men as being part of the group that sat at the table with Ray and Mark the night before. He stopped for a second near the reception desk and looked back at the three men.

"Their friend is going to be okay."

Clint looked back at the registration desk. He didn't think anyone had been there when he turned to look at the men. The same receptionist who had checked him in now stood behind the counter.

"Their friend?" Clint asked.

"Yes. One of them wanted me to know, too." She made a face and lifted her shoulders like she didn't know why. "The woman injured in the rocket attack in Paris, she's going to be okay."

"Was that the attack that killed that millionaire guy?"

"Yes. That's what they said."

"I guess that is good news," Clint said.

"I think one of the men works with her." She nodded her head at the group, but Clint didn't know at which one she nodded.

A car pulled up out front of the hotel, and two of the men departed. The third man headed down the hall to the elevators. Clint followed him. They entered the elevator together, and Clint thought the man would say something to him, but he didn't. They both got off on the third floor but went separate ways down the hall.

Clint spent the rest of the day sightseeing. He checked out the hotel bar at six and again at nine, but other than seeing a few other tourists stopping by for a drink, the place remained empty. He imagined the security details kept everyone busy. No calls came in from D.C.

He walked out of the hotel at half past nine. A crowd of people started coming out of the train station down the block. Clint leaned against the railing that ran across the front of the hotel. The fresh air felt good, but every now and then a hint of diesel exhaust from the buses that ran in front of the hotel ruined everything.

Clint walked a short distance to get away from the buses. The sound of two men arguing in hushed voices caught his attention. The voices came from somewhere nearby in the darkness. Clint moved closer to the voices. When he reached a spot where an alley ran between the Hotel Euler and an adjacent building, he could see two men in the alley.

Despite the poor lighting, he thought one of the two might be Mark Yancey. He didn't recognize the second man, who jabbed a finger into Mark's chest.

"If I find out your guy was behind it, I'll break every bone in your body," the guy said to Mark.

"Come on, Steve, you know," Mark said, before they both noticed Clint standing at the end of the alley.

"What are you looking at?" The man growled the question at Clint.

"I thought I heard you out here, Mark. I promised to buy you and Polly drinks tonight. She's waiting. Let's go," Clint said.

Mark took a step toward Clint, but the man grabbed his arm. "He ain't going anywhere until I'm done."

The man, taller and heavier than Mark, reminded Clint of all the bullies he had encountered in his life.

"Don't be silly," Clint said, while he started toward them. He didn't like the confined space in the alley. It would limit his movement, and he had no doubt that this guy, Steve, or whatever his name was, knew how to fight. Clint held both palms up in front of him in a gesture to indicate that he didn't mean any trouble.

As expected, the guy ignored Clint's gesture and charged. Clint already knew what he had to do. He didn't want to really hurt this guy, but he had to subdue him quickly. If he didn't, they both could get hurt a lot.

Clint took a step backwards and tried to act like he was both surprised and afraid. The guy obviously wanted to get his hands on Clint. At the last second, Clint stepped aside to his right like a well-trained matador. If he wanted to do real damage, Clint would've kicked the guy's knee. Rather, he hit Steve on his left temple with a straight right as he surged past. The guy fell and skidded face first on the pavement. Clint wondered if many would agree that he chose the more humane thing to do.

"Holy cow! Where did you learn how to do that?" Mark said.

Clint ignored the question. "Help me get him up. We'll take him into the bar with us and make sure he's okay."

"Might be safer to leave him here. Steve's been drinking and has quite the temper."

"No. Help me out," Clint said.

They each took an arm and lifted Steve to his feet. He hung limp, so Mark and Clint each strained to support him under a shoulder and half-carried, half-dragged him to the hotel lobby. Once inside, they positioned him into a large, cushioned chair.

Polly came over to help.

"He'll be okay," Clint said. "Can you bring us two beers and a glass of water?"

"Of course," she hurried back to the bar.

Mark and Clint sat at the closest table to Steve. Polly returned with the water first. Clint picked up a paper napkin and dipped it into the water. He got up and wiped the dirt and debris off Steve's face. A few droplets of blood oozed out of a scrape on the end of his nose. Clint cleaned the scrape.

"What do you think?" Clint asked, once he returned to the table.

"If you didn't kill him, he should be coming around any minute."

He did. At first Steve moaned. His right hand reached up and touched his face. His eyes blinked.

Clint noticed Polly still stood next to them. "Should I call a doctor?" she asked.

"I don't think so," Clint said. "He tripped on a step out front."

The bartender called her to come get the two beers.

"What was the argument over?" Clint asked.

"The idiot has some idea that the guy we're here supporting might have had something to do with the attack that killed McPherson," Mark said.

"What?" Clint asked, no reason not to feign ignorance.

"It doesn't really matter. The point is my client and McPherson don't, I mean they didn't like each other, but I've never gotten any feel that their dislike for each other was deep rooted enough to cause them to resort to violence."

"What's he doing here, if he worked for McPherson?"

"Steve's here supporting a different client. The company he works for also provided security for McPherson. The guy who was killed along with McPherson was a good friend of his," Mark said.

"Why would he expect you to know anything about the killing?"

"You got me," Mark said, shaking his head. "I think it's simply the alcohol."

Steve coughed a couple of times and looked around like he was trying to figure out where he was.

"How are you feeling?" Clint asked.

"What the hell?" Steve said and rubbed his head. "What happened?"

"You were being an idiot, Steve," Mark said.

Steve looked at him. Some recognition showed up in Steve's eyes.

"How'd we get here?" Steve asked.

"You charged at me and tripped. You hit your head pretty hard on the pavement," Clint said. "We were worried about you and brought you in here."

Polly returned with the beers. "Are you okay?" she asked.

"I think so," Steve said.

"Your friends carried you in here, but they didn't buy you a beer." She grinned at him.

"Cheap bastards. Bring me one, please," Steve growled.

Polly returned to the bar. Steve stood up and, for a moment, appeared like he might collapse back down into the chair. He looked at Clint. "Did you hit me?"

"No, you just fell."

Steve rubbed the side of his head. "Who are you?"

"Clint Smith." Clint stood up and held out his hand.

"Steve Windsor," he said, as he accepted Clint's hand. "Who are you with?"

"No one. I'm only visiting the area. I met Mark last night here in the bar. When I heard him in the alley, I got curious. I didn't mean to make you mad."

"Oh, yeah." Steve seemed to remember something and turned his attention to Mark. "You seriously don't think your client had anything to do with it."

"Honest, I don't. You know Arnold," Mark waited for Steve to acknowledge that he did. Steve nodded his head. "Well, Arnold has very good rapport with our client, and after we all got news of it, he said the client was quite shook up. We've increased security and have been in touch with Interpol daily. I know the two families have never gotten along, but that's been going on for at least a couple generations. They might steal business from each other, but there's never been any violence between them."

"Well, if the cops don't get this guy first..." Steve let his voice trail off.

"You heard that Custer is going to pull through," Mark said.

"Yes. Didn't know Eileen very well, but I'm glad she's going to be okay. I heard that the door did most the damage to her when it blew off, but at the same time, it saved her life."

"Damn," Mark muttered.

"You guys must live dangerous lives," Clint said.

Both men looked at him. Their eyes called him naïve, but the two refrained from saying anything.

CHAPTER 5

Clint woke up the next morning feeling refreshed and finally acclimated to the time zone. He grabbed a cup of coffee and a pastry before jogging to the gym. He thought about Steve and Mark while he ran. Despite the confrontation, the two men seemed comfortable with each other. Clint didn't learn anything substantive from the two. Steve appeared to have been motivated more by anger than any evidence he had that Mark's client had anything to do with McPherson's death. He found it interesting that the two of them referred to the people they were protecting as "client" rather than by name. Maybe it was all part of the security culture these days. He had heard the term "Principal" used before during actual protective service operations in an attempt to conceal the dignitary's identity from eavesdroppers. Maybe this casual reference to them as clients served as another layer of protection.

For the most part, Clint observed the same people at the gym. He even lucked into seeing the Princess again. Like the day before, she took to her workout with enthusiasm. At one point, their eyes met, and Clint offered one of his well-honed smiles. This time, however, the smile wasn't returned.

Leaving the gym, Clint checked his phone and noticed that he had missed a call from D.C. He called the number and Buzz answered.

"You got your car?" Buzz asked.

"Yes. What's up?"

"A long shot, but Deer wants you to drive over to Wilmont. Don't check out of the Euler, but there's a Gasthof Gruner in Wilmont. Check in there for one night. You need to leave Basel before noon. Deer will call you while you're in route to explain. She's trying to identify a piece of the puzzle."

"How far away is that?" Clint asked.

"Maybe an hour, an hour and half."

"Okay. I guess you'll know when I'm on the way." Clint hung up and decided to swing by the train station before leaving Basel.

The box that contained the 9mm Beretta also contained a pair of new hiking boots. He found the pistol hidden inside one of the boots and two loaded clips in the other boot. Back in his room he transformed what appeared to be an elbow brace and an extra belt into a shoulder holster. He decided to take the boots.

The drive to Wilmont took Clint in the direction of Neuchatel and into the mountains. He found the Gasthof Gruner on the side of a steep incline about a half mile outside the village. Someone long ago had carved a small parking lot into the mountainside next to the hotel. Clint took a second to admire the view after he got out of the Volkswagen. The scene looking down into the valley was breathtaking, and he thought the picture of the old Gasthof with the mountain behind it should be made into a postcard. The smell of pine with a hint of smoke drifted in the clear air.

The call he had expected on the drive finally came.

"What's the view like?" Deer asked.

"Breathtaking," Clint answered. He knew that she knew exactly where he was.

"There's someone staying at the Gruner whom I need to get a look at."

"Who is it?"

"That's the problem. I don't know. I need you to check in and hang close to the Gruner. The guy I'm trying to identify is staying there. It's a complicated story, but there is a link with the phone the person is carrying that intrigues me," Deer said.

She paused.

Clint thought she was trying to decide how much more to say. "What can I do?" he asked.

"Should be very simple. He or she should go somewhere this evening for dinner or drinks. Once I can pinpoint where he is, I'll need you to go there. At a set time that you'll know, I'll call the number to the phone. I'll need you to take a picture of whoever answers the phone."

"That may not be easy, especially if he's in a crowded bar or restaurant."

"Look around," Deer said. "Don't think you could find a crowd anywhere around there."

He looked around and realized that she was most likely correct. "Good point. I'll be waiting for your call."

Clint checked into the hotel. He saw a stack of picture postcards next to the register that made him grin. The postcards reflected the same view of the hotel that he had admired from the parking lot.

The old man who checked him in looked like he hadn't shaved in a few days. He also smelled like he had been hitting the schnapps since breakfast. The room key came attached to a large wooden square that made it impossible to fit into a pocket.

"When you leave, we will keep your key in its slot," the old man gestured to the row of cubby holes behind him.

"Do you have internet here?" Clint asked.

"No, but we have hot water," the man almost giggled when he said this like it was an old in-house joke. "There's a very nice hiking trail right behind the hotel."

"Thanks." Clint looked around the small lobby. He didn't see a bar or a restaurant. From the number of slots to store the room keys, he figured the place only had a dozen guest rooms. At least they accepted his credit card.

His room didn't have a television, so he decided to check out the trail behind the hotel. He put on his new hiking boots and left the hotel. Clint had no trouble finding the trail, but he soon realized that hiking it was more akin to mountain climbing than hiking. The steep slopes and slanted footing made going even a short distance more of an effort than he was in the mood to do. After twenty minutes, he turned around and made his way back.

The call came in at quarter after five.

"Our person just left the hotel and went into the village. He's been there for ten minutes, so my guess he's meeting with someone and may be there for a while. I'll send his GPS coordinates to your phone. Try to get to wherever he is as soon as you can. If he's in a private residence or someplace else you can't access, let me know. Otherwise, get his picture and send it to me immediately. Then delete it."

"Will do," Clint said.

He considered walking to the village. It would take around fifteen minutes. However, if he had to move from the village to follow the guy somewhere else, he might need the car. The place turned out to be easy to find. Situated at the end of the short road that seemed to be the town's main street, a wooden building with a steep sloped roof sat off the road by itself amidst the trees and next to a steep drop off on the side of the mountain.

A circular sign that Clint thought lit up at night advertised a Bavarian pilsner. He saw five cars parked on the side of the building away from the drop off. He decided to drive the Volkswagen a hundred yards back toward the center of the village and park near an old church. He took a picture of the church with his phone before making his way to his target.

When he entered the building, he first thought the place was closed. The foyer and large restaurant space off to his right showed no signs of life. After a second, he heard voices coming from somewhere down a hallway that ran straight ahead of him. He headed down the hall and discovered a fair-sized room that served as a bar. He entered it, and everyone stopped talking.

All eyes stared at him. Clint looked at the young man behind the bar for some signal to indicate whether he should come in farther or go away. The man waved him in. Everyone else went back to their conversations, but Clint noticed that everyone now talked quieter.

"I hope I'm not interrupting anything," Clint said to the bartender.

"Ah, American, my English is not so good," the bartender said.

Clint ordered a beer and sent a text to Deer to let her know he was set. He studied the people in the room. One man stood off by himself and tossed darts at a dartboard. Two men leaned against the bar and discussed something in French that had them both laughing. Two other men sat at a table not far from the bar and were also speaking to each other in French.

His phone buzzed, and he received a text that said five thirty. That gave him only a few minutes to find the best place in the room to get a good angle at everyone. Looking around he decided there wasn't one place that would work. Staying at the bar gave him a good vantage point at three of the five. If one of the remaining two turned out to be his target he would have to move around to get the picture. He didn't think it would be hard. He had already eliminated the bartender from being his target.

When the call came, Clint thought his luck couldn't be better. The man sitting at the table facing him reacted. First, he reached into a pocket of his sport coat and pulled out a phone. Clint could almost see him tense up when he realized the phone in his hand wasn't the one making the chirping sound. The man reached into a small leather briefcase that sat on the table. He pulled out the phone, and Clint snapped his picture.

Clint transmitted the picture to Deer. He knew it was a

good one when he took it. He deleted the photo and put the one of the church on his screen. When he looked back up the man was putting the phone back into his briefcase, but he stared right at Clint. The two men at the bar didn't seem to be paying any attention to what was going on, but the man playing darts watched the two men at the table. Clint saw the dart player's eyes move from the table with the two men to him.

Clint took a sip of his beer and tried to ignore the hairs on the back of his neck. He turned to the bartender and showed him the picture of the church on his phone.

"What's the name of the church here in town?" Clint asked.

The bartender looked at the phone and gave it back to Clint. "I don't go to that one. I don't know its name."

"That's okay." Clint said, although he thought it strange that the man didn't know the name of the nearby church. He looked at the couple at the table.

The man who had the phone still watched him with a blank look on his face. The man suddenly turned his head toward the guy throwing darts. Clint didn't hear him say anything, but the dart player gave an almost imperceptive nod and started walking toward the door that Clint had come in through a few minutes before. As he passed the table with the two men, the man sitting with his back toward Clint stood up with him.

Clint took another sip of beer and looked down at his camera. He kept the two men in his peripheral vision as they left the bar. The two men at the end of the bar stopped talking. They looked around the room as though they, too, sensed something wasn't right. Clint felt uncomfortable with his situation. He paid the bartender for the beer and walked out of the bar. He didn't like leaving half of his beer behind, but he didn't want to be in the bar if the two men who left returned with reinforcements, or if they went to get some weapons.

Clint went out of the front door and looked around. He didn't see the two men. He walked to the corner of the building, and using the corner of the building to conceal himself, he looked out at the parking lot. He saw the two men right away. They leaned against the nearest car and appeared to be waiting for something. Clint went to the steps that led off the porch right in front of the entrance.

As he reached the steps, he caught a flash of something charging at him from the front door. He turned his head to see what it was, when one of the two men who had been standing at the bar ran into him like a linebacker trying to blindside a quarterback. Behind his first attacker he saw the second man coming at a less reckless pace. This second man had a knife in his left hand.

Clint didn't try to resist the first man's attack. He leaned away from the man when they collided limiting any damage from the initial impact. He rolled in the direction the man's rush took him and pulled his attacker over him as they tumbled in the air and over the steps. When they made contact with the ground, his assailant landed underneath him, and Clint's knee went into the man's solar plexus. Clint put as much of his weight that he could into the blow without damaging his own knee. The air went out of the man. Clint smashed the base of his palm into the man's nose and heard it crack.

He jumped off his attacker as the man's partner slashed at his back with a knife. The blade missed him. Clint took a couple quick steps toward the cliff to avoid the man's straight on attack. He tried to circle the man, but the man moved to keep Clint's back to either the cliff or the building. Clint had ample room to maneuver, but he knew time wasn't on his side.

He had hoped these two men weren't allied with his target. He figured the other two were. At any moment those two would stop waiting by the cars and come see what was going on. The odds would only get worse. Since he couldn't get around the man and his knife, Clint decided he had to go through him. He considered pulling his pistol, but decided to do so only as a last option.

Clint didn't doubt there were men better at close-in fighting than himself, but he also realized the chances that this man was one of them had to be very, very small. Clint had done a lot of amateur fighting as a teenager and in college. The fighting was the competitive type, controlled and in a ring, not the hoodlum type on the streets. His skills were further honed in the military. Since leaving the military, Clint had routinely trained in additional martial arts skills with some of the best instructors in the country.

He knew the knife changed the odds a lot. Any mistake could be fatal. He feigned three attacks in quick succession to get the man off balance, and started to make a serious move into the man when he heard a switch blade pop open in the man's right hand. Clint stopped himself in time. The man's trick might have worked. Clint's focus on the man's left hand and any attempt he made to neutralize that hand or its knife would have left the man's right hand open to plunge the hidden knife blade into him.

Clint decided to reconsider the use of his pistol. He took a step back and saw the two men come running around from where they had been by the parked cars to the front of the building. One of the two men threw something at him. The item flickered in the late afternoon sun. Clint ducked as the dart flew by him. Unfortunately, he was getting closer to the drop off, and the three men pressed in closer.

Moving back and side-to-side in an attempt to not be an easy target for another dart, Clint reached into his jacket for the pistol. As his hand touched the pistol, something buzzed by him and tore a piece of material off the left shoulder of his jacket. Simultaneously, he heard the crack of a handgun being fired from the front doorway. He also saw the dart player start to throw something at him. His odds had become dismal.

Clint started to sprint diagonally at the edge of the cliff and away from the shooter on the front porch. He needed to get past the man with the knife, but didn't have the angle. After eight or nine steps, he realized the man would cut him off. Any contact with him would slow him down enough for the other two to reach him. He saw a large boulder that jutted out several feet from the steep cliff wall maybe fifteen feet below him. Below the boulder, he saw a section of the slope that wouldn't be too severe to climb down. He didn't think he had another choice and jumped.

In mid-flight he realized he had jumped too far. He landed on the boulder but on the outer edge. He slid off and dropped another ten feet into a layer of small rocks that slid with him as he continued his tumble. He clawed for a grip that might slow or stop him from sliding. In the mini-landslide he had started, everything he grabbed moved with him. He went over the next ledge.

This last drop would have caused some serious injuries, if it hadn't been for a cluster of tall fir trees that broke his fall before he dropped ten feet from the ledge. At first, the small soft branches at the top of one tree seemed too good to be true. However, as he fell through the top branches into the sturdier ones below, the branches started to hurt him. They also repelled him away from the tree and finally into the lower branches of a second fir tree.

He stopped falling. Clint remained still for a moment to be sure he had stopped and to take mental inventory for any damages. He hurt or stung all over, but he didn't sense any significant damage. He pulled his hand away from his face, where he had placed it soon after entering the tree to protect his eyes. Only a few feet separated him from the ground. More horizontal than vertical, it took a moment for Clint to untangle himself from the tree.

The fall had ripped his slacks and jacket. His new hiking boots had a nasty gash through the leather by his right ankle. If he had only been wearing shoes, his ankle would have been sliced open. Both hands revealed dozens of small scrapes and cuts. He wiped the blood off his fingers on his right hand and with the two fingers that weren't bleeding, he patted at his face. His jaw felt bruised, but the fingers didn't find any blood. His right temple throbbed, and he found blood near his sideburn. He wiped his fingers and checked his right ear finding more blood. None of the spots disclosed a significant amount of blood.

Convinced that he suffered no major wounds, Clint looked for a way to get back to the village and to his car. The vertical rock wall next to him rose at least twenty five feet. He couldn't climb it, but at least it hid him from his pursuers. They had to think he had been seriously injured, if not killed, by the fall. If he had broken a leg or worse, spending the night up here in the cold could kill him.

Fortunately, neither his phone nor his pistol fell out during the fall. He checked his phone. It worked, but he had no signal. He wanted to make sure Deer received the picture, but that would have to wait. With less than an hour of daylight left, he hoped it wouldn't take him that long to find a way back up to the village. If he could find a trail, he could be there in five minutes, but could he find a trail?

The ground dropped off sharply to his left and again opposite the cliff wall, so unless he wanted to climb further down, he had only one direction to go. He started walking. The terrain remained level and widened to the point where he didn't feel like he was walking on a ledge. He could no longer see the ridgeline, and thick clusters of bushes and trees blocked much of his view. He stayed close to the cliff wall on his left and watched for any place where he thought climbing might be possible. His ribs and back hurt where they had collided with some of the larger tree branches during his fall, but nothing felt broken, so he maintained a pretty good pace.

After about fifteen minutes, he realized that the cliff wall had gotten shorter. In another five minutes, he stopped walking and climbed a couple feet up the wall to peer over the ledge. He had made it. The village sat a mere hundred yards away. The road back to his hotel was even closer.

CHAPTER 6

Clint decided to stay concealed until dark. He didn't expect the group of men to be out looking for him, but he hadn't expected the reaction he got from Deer's phone call to the guy either. He wondered who the guy was.

He checked his phone again and saw that he still didn't have a signal. He was certain he had a signal in the bar when he sent the picture to Deer. The thick trees or maybe what was left of the vertical wall of earth and rock that he now sat against had to be blocking the signal. He thought about the picture he took of the man in the bar. The photo had captured sufficient facial features to allow Deer to do whatever she needed. The face didn't mean anything to him. He hadn't encountered any of the group before and hoped he wouldn't see them again.

Clint wondered how Deer would go about identifying the man in the picture. He often thought about how she did things. He had no personal motivations or interest in judging her. It simply fascinated him that she could be so effective with such a small staff and fulfilling a role of which virtually everyone she dealt with in the community was unaware. Clint knew that in her cover position as the chief of a small inter-disciplinary analytical group within the U.S. Marshal Service, she had a great deal of access. However, in D.C. and especially when dealing with our foreign allies, it could take weeks if not months to receive responses to requests for information.

Deer did have access to her own set of super computers, which she and Buzz referred to as Abigail. However, Clint didn't believe Abigail had all the answers. Buzz and Deer had both inferred to him that if they didn't have ready access to the information they needed, they had the capability to find it in another agency's database or emails. While not being anything near a computer wizard, Clint still imagined that access entailed hacking into some of the most secure networks in the world.

Darkness came quickly when it did come. The bruising in his back and side made standing up painful. A couple of young lovers leaned together against a tree not far from where Clint had parked the car. He watched them while he approached the Volkswagen, but they were more interested in each other than anything happening around them. A storekeeper swept the sidewalk in front of his store on the opposite side of the street.

He drove by the Gasthof Gruner rather than going back inside. He hadn't left anything in the room and had already paid for the one night stay. Deer had told him that she believed the man with the phone had a room there. Clint figured his buddies did, too. He didn't need to see any of them again, and if they somehow learned that he rented a room there, his not returning might reinforce their belief that he had died.

The call from Buzz came ten minutes later. Clint grinned. He expected the call.

"Heading back already?" Buzz asked.

"Yes. The call created quite a fuss. I suggest future, similar plans to do anything like that be scratched."

"You okay?"

"Barely," Clint said. "There were five of them, and Deer's call made them very suspicious of my being there. My departure involved some conflict and an embarrassing retreat over the side of a mountain. More importantly, tell me you got the picture."

"Yes, we did. I put it into the system right away. Nothing back yet, but that just means he's not in one of the main databases. We should have something by tomorrow."

"Good. If you have to work late tonight, Buzz, I hope it's not just for me."

"We have a couple of problems elsewhere, too. Besides, it's still early here. I should be out of here in a few hours," Buzz said.

"I wish I had taken pictures of everyone. The four guys with him definitely worked for our target. The guy in charge is sharp. He didn't answer the phone and immediately figured out he was being set up."

"Don't worry about it. The photo of the main guy is what she wanted."

"One thing you could check. I think I broke one guy's nose and maybe one or two of his ribs. Might be some report of it," Clint said.

"Not likely if he went to a local doctor or clinic, but you say you got into an altercation with these guys?"

"Altercation? That's putting it mildly. Even had a round rip my jacket."

"Maybe an anonymous tip to the police will help us pick up a few things. Were there any witnesses?"

"A bartender. He might have seen something. Also, I had to register at the hotel. The guy I busted up may be registered there."

"I think Deer has already considered that, but I'll pass all this on to her," Buzz said.

"Any new threats to the Bilderberg Group?"

"No. Everything's quiet. You heard that the security team member injured in Paris is going to pull through?"

"Yes. Some of the guys at the hotel were talking about it this morning. That's good news."

"Doubt if she saw something, but you never know," Buzz said.

They ended the call, and Clint drove the rest of the way to Basel in silence. The terrain reminded him of Colorado. He maintained a condo near Dillon Lake but didn't use it very often. He used an agency to rent it out most of the year.

Usually, tourists rented it a week at a time, but every now and then he had families rent it for an entire month. Even with the rental fees and taxes, the condo had paid for itself the last six years. He had hoped to get Barbara to stay with him for a week at the condo during ski season. Now that she had extended her stay in Africa, he didn't know if that would happen.

He parked the car in the hotel's small lot, brushed off what was left of the dirt and trees on him, and entered the hotel. A different group of men sat at two tables pulled together in the middle of the room. Polly and the same old man worked the bar again.

"Clint, what happened to you?" she asked. She approached him and looked at his face. Her eyes went on to inspect the rest of him.

"It's rather embarrassing. I fell down a mountainside."

She nodded. "You need to stick to the trails. Two years ago, we had a guest who broke his arm in a fall."

"Believe me, from now on I will. I'm going up now to shower. I'll be back down in a little bit. You'll still be here?"

"Yes, until we close at eleven."

Even though Clint knew he ached in a lot of spots, the extent of his bruising surprised him. His right thigh, his ribs, and an area on his back below his left shoulder all sported large patches of discoloration. On the bright side, none of the cuts to his face and hands were deep. While these scratches looked nasty, if he kept them clean they would pose no problem. The hiking boot, on the other hand, was a total loss. The gash almost went all the way through the side of the boot.

Clint spent an extra minute or two in the shower soaking in the hot water. By the time he closed his hotel room door behind him, he felt rejuvenated.

He heard the woman's loud voice in the lobby when he stepped out of the elevator. She leaned against the counter at a spot where she was closest to the table where the five men sat.

She wore a grey business suit and had a briefcase on the floor next to her. A thin man dressed more casually in jeans and a sweatshirt, probably in his late thirties like her and looking rather pale and uncomfortable, stood next to her. He avoided eye contact with the men at the table, while the woman stared at the men.

"I don't understand how any of you can justify to yourselves what you do," she said in a voice a little louder than necessary.

"We've told you, lady. We like what we do and have no problems with who our clients are. Now would you leave us alone?" Clint didn't recognize the man who spoke.

The woman noticed Clint and studied him for a moment.

Clint ignored the woman and approached Polly. She appeared to be keeping her distance from everyone. "Know who she is?" he whispered.

"No. She's been here about five minutes and has been bothering those men the whole time. She has her eyes on you now."

"I know. Think it's safe for me to order a beer?"

"Ha! I'll protect you," she called to the bartender for a beer.

Clint moved to a nearby table. The woman approached Clint, and Polly made her escape. So much for protecting me, Clint thought.

"So, who are you here with?" the woman asked.

"Myself. Why?"

"Which of the grotesquely rich are you protecting?" she asked.

"I don't have a hell of an idea what you're talking about."

She stared at him for a second and considered his answer. "Can I sit down?"

Normally, Clint would have said no, but her anger at the rich and her presence in Basel interested him. She had also recognized the men at the table as being part of a security team.

"Sit," he pointed at the chair opposite him.

She sat down, but her male accomplice remained at the

counter. Polly approached Clint with his beer and raised an eyebrow at him.

He intended to make some remark to Polly like, "Where were you when I needed you?" The woman, however, started talking to Clint right away.

"My name is Mary Marvel. I'm a reporter doing a story on the Bilderberg Group," she offered her hand.

"I'm Clint," he accepted her hand. Her grip was limp, almost too much so to be real. "What does your story have to do with me or anyone else?" He looked over at the group of men. They didn't seem to have any interest in him or Mary Marvel.

"Are you serious that you're not here protecting one of the attendees at the conference?" she asked him.

"I'm not here protecting anyone, and I don't know about any conference." He took a sip of his beer while she thought about what to ask him next.

"What happened to your face and hands?"

Clint looked at his hands. "I was hiking the trail and fell. Almost killed myself!"

His fall didn't interest her, nor did it draw any sympathy. "You haven't heard about the Bilderberg Group?"

"Not that I can recall. What is it?" Clint asked.

"A secretive group of the world's richest. Mostly men." She said men in a way that Clint wondered if she was against the group more for being comprised of the rich or because of its mostly male status.

"The world is full of exclusive country clubs and powerful families. What about this group has your interest?"

She looked at him suspiciously. "What are you doing here in Basel?"

"Tourist. I kid myself saying it's research for a book I'm writing, but I've been working on the manuscript a long time now."

"I've written some stuff. I mean besides the articles for the newspaper. If you want to write about something, you should write about the Bilderberg Group."

"I thought that's what you're doing here?" Clint said.

"I am, but I'm doing an expose, an exclusive about how the rich are manipulating and exploiting the world while the common people and governments sleep. Some governments get involved, but they do so behind closed doors and in secrecy. I've tried to get into the meetings, but they won't let me get near it."

Clint couldn't blame them, but he kept his thoughts to himself.

"It's the people behind those doors who decide what goes on in the world. They manipulate governments, exploit child labor, add chemicals to our food, pollute our environment, and manipulate the world stock markets for their own aggrandizement."

"I don't mean to be argumentative, but if their meetings are held in secret, how do you know they are doing any of this?" Clint asked.

"Get real. What do you think they're doing? If they had nothing to hide they would hold the meetings in the open."

"Good point," Clint said, while he really wanted to say: and let people like you in there to harass them?

She nodded. "Sorry I mistook you for a member of one of the security details. You look like one. You know any of these guys?" she motioned with her hand at the group of men at the table.

"Not them. I met a couple last night who might be, but I'm not sure. We mostly talked about Basel and how expensive everything is here."

"That's for sure. I'm spending good money to be here and can't get anyone to talk to me. You would think one of those guys would at least tell me who they're here with." She looked like she might spit at the group at the table.

"Who's your friend at the bar?" Clint asked.

"He's my partner."

"He's not having any luck either?"

"No, but he's not a journalist like me. It's more of a vacation for him. We're traveling together. You sure you're not pulling my leg?" she asked.

"What?"

"You're not really a security guy?"

"Sorry, but I'm not."

"Well, you still need to learn about the Bilderberg Group. Everyone's in complete ignorance while these men exploit us." She stood up without a goodbye and returned to her partner at the bar.

"Poor guy," Clint said to himself.

Polly approached him with her back to the couple at the bar. She wore a big smile. "You handled that pretty well," she said.

"Where were you when I needed you?"

"I could hear everything she said. You may have noticed that she's not exactly a quiet woman. What's this group she's so worried about?"

"I don't know. Just another conspiracy theory would be my guess. If it's not the Catholic Church, it's the communists. In the U.S. today, it's the Tea Party. Everybody has to blame somebody for their predicament," Clint said.

"I'm glad I already have enough to worry about. No time to pick up any new causes, unless it involves abandoned puppies," Polly said.

"Me, too."

Polly headed over to get refills for the group at the table. Clint observed Mary's partner paying for the drinks the two had. He wondered if the good money she had complained about spending for this trip had really been her partners. It could be why she brought him along.

He sent Buzz a text that read, "Mary Marvel???"

CHAPTER 7

No call came in from D.C. the next day. Clint walked most of the city taking in the sights and working off the stiffness from his fall down the mountainside. In the late afternoon, he took the Volkswagen for a short drive in the country. Only an older European couple occupied the bar in the Hotel Euler when Clint entered it at seven in the evening.

"Still here?" Polly asked him.

"Where's everyone?"

"They all checked out this morning."

"It'll finally be peaceful here," he said.

"I don't like it peaceful. Too boring."

Clint smiled. Polly said they all checked out. He imagined she and the rest of the hotel staff, not to mention the entire hotel industry in Basel, knew who had come to town as part of the conference.

"Uh-oh. You spoke too soon," Clint said.

Polly turned around and saw Mary Marvel step into the hotel lobby. Her partner strolled in right behind her. She came straight at Clint.

"So, you're still here," she said to Clint. She ignored Polly's presence.

"What's up?" Clint asked.

"A lot. What's your last name?"

"Why?"

"Because I learned something today that's going to blow the socks off everyone."

"About my last name?" Clint asked.

"No. Shouldn't you have left today with everyone else?"

"Well, Margie--"

"It's Mary. So you really weren't here to protect one of attendees? Did you look up the Bilderberg Group?"

"You ask too many questions, but no and no. If they're gone, shouldn't you be, too?" Clint tried to keep the irritation out of his voice.

"I didn't know they were leaving."

Clint felt like telling her if she was nicer someone may have told her. "So what did you learn that was so important?"

She looked at him like she couldn't be sure if she told him that he wouldn't blab it to the rest of the world. "Someone is killing off the members."

"What?"

"I received an anonymous text last night," she paused for a moment, considering what to say. "It said I should check out the murders of two Bilderberg members. Did you know that someone has murdered two members in the last month?"

"No. Someone doing your work for you?"

"Don't be an ass. I don't think they should be murdered. I think they should be taxed out of their wealth, and the money should be used to clean up the environment and help the masses. Some of them belong in jail, but I don't believe in the death sentence either."

"Think one of the guys that you met here in Basel sent you the text?" Clint asked.

"That's what I think. I have a large number of contacts elsewhere, but I'm working the Bilderberg expose pretty much as an exclusive, so they wouldn't know I'm interested in the group right now. The text was sent only to me. It wasn't a twitter tweet to the whole world. It seems logical someone here wanted me to know it." Her lips tried to form a smile when she said the last sentence.

"Why would anyone want to kill off any of the members?" Clint asked. He noticed Polly had hung close to listen to the conversation.

"Probably for the same reasons I don't like the group. I told you, the members of this group are destroying the world."

"So what can you do with the information?" Clint asked.

"Dig into it. I've already started. My boss is excited, really excited." This time the smile came through.

"Well good luck to you," Clint said. "I think your friend is waiting for you." He looked at the man at the counter of the bar.

"Here," Mary said, while she held out a business card. "If you need any advice on your writing, give me a call. He's with me on this trip, but maybe not the next one." She joined her partner at the counter.

"Did she just hit on you?" Polly asked wide-eyed.

"I hope not," Clint said.

"A strange woman," Polly said. "What did she say about two murders? I didn't see anything on the news about anyone murdered here in the last few days."

"I'm not sure, but I don't think the murders took place here. I think she was referring to the guy killed in Paris a couple of days ago and someone else."

"So, are you going to call her?"

"Give me a break," Clint said.

Polly laughed and returned to a spot behind the bar where she had a stool to sit on. She picked up a tablet and started to read.

Clint sent a text to Buzz. "Did you send a text to Marvel?" He waited for about thirty seconds before a reply came back. "Yes. Why?" Clint finished his beer and walked outside where he dialed Buzz' number.

"What's up?" Buzz asked.

"Mary Marvel told me about the text. I thought right away about you all. She's thinking one of the guys here gave her an anonymous tip."

"That's what we hoped. We've had no success on the

picture, or on anything else. Marvel is already burning up the wires trying to look for leads. Her efforts have started a whole lot of other news service wire inquiries."

"Too bad for her exclusive. Do you think the press will uncover something that you can't?" Clint asked.

"Wouldn't be the first time. They're like a million army ants looking for a bug. At a minimum, they might cause some activity by our target that we can pick up on. Right now, everything is invisible."

"I thought you had a link with the phone and the guy I took a picture of?"

"After a lot of digging we came up with one link, and that was only to the phone number. We're not sure what the link meant. The picture was supposed to help us, but so far it hasn't." Buzz sounded tired.

"Want me to go back and ask the guy?"

"No. We have reason to believe the phone is no longer being used, and we no longer know where it is. Hold on for a second." After a ten second pause, Buzz returned to the phone. "We need you to head back to Paris in the morning. Plan on staying just one night there."

"Anything else?"

"Not at the moment."

Clint returned to the hotel.

The train ride back to Paris seemed even more crowded than the one to Basel. Clint wondered if some of the passengers had worked at the Bilderberg conference. He felt certain that a meeting as high powered as this one required a large support staff. Due to the secrecy involved and the wealth of the members, Clint thought the attendees might have brought in their own people.

He studied the passengers around him, but didn't see anyone wearing a ball cap or golf shirt with the Bilderberg logo, if there was such a thing. Maybe they had tee shirts saying "I

Survived Bilderberg 2015". Somehow, he doubted it. He dozed off about an hour outside Basel and dreamt about life as a billionaire.

Clint grabbed a bratwurst at the Paris train station. He guessed the French venders sold them in the station for the German travelers. He hadn't seen a bratwurst vendor in Paris proper. When he reached his room at the hotel, he found a note from Dolly. He unfolded the piece of paper and read it.

"Sorry, but I had to leave this morning. I would've loved to have stayed and had dinner with you, but the boss booked me on a flight home this afternoon. I enjoyed the room. Thanks, Dolly"

It didn't bother him that she was gone. In fact, if he had been asked, he would have voted for her to be gone, too. It made his life much simpler.

His phone got his attention. This time Deer spoke to him after he answered it. "I need you to check out tonight and take the night express train to Barcelona. From there you're booked to Valencia. Once there, you're to take a ferry to Mallorca. You still have your boots from the train station?"

"Yes," he knew she didn't really mean the boots, but rather what came with them.

"You shouldn't have any issues with the train or the ferry. A few members of the group left Basel and are meeting tomorrow for a day or two in Mallorca. We're picking up some parallel traffic that we can't pin down that's also talking about the gathering in Mallorca."

"What do I do when I get there?"

"I'm still working on that. I need to verify a few things, but that shouldn't take long."

"Ok," Clint said. The call ended. He didn't feel like getting back on another train, but he knew the high speed, express train wouldn't take that long and going first class would at least allow him to be comfortable and get some rest. He hoped getting from the train terminal in Valencia to the ferry wouldn't be a hassle.

Despite his pre-dawn arrival in Barcelona, Clint discovered that he had less than an hour to make the connection to the express train to Valencia. The transfer from that train after its arrival in Valencia to the late morning ferry to the island of Mallorca turned out to be a well-oiled operation. Dozens of taxis waited on the passengers from the train, and Clint noticed several of them on the same route his taxi took to the ferry terminal.

For most of the ferry ride, Clint stayed in a lounge chair on one of the decks and enjoyed the sun and the view. When he did move about the ferry, he didn't see anyone he recognized from Basel or from elsewhere in his past.

Mallorca appeared on the horizon about an hour before the ferry reached the island. He also saw some smaller islands in the distance. Clint hadn't been to Mallorca, but he knew some things about the island. Mallorca was one of a handful of islands that belonged to Spain and sat a couple hundred miles off the Spanish coast in the Mediterranean Sea. It belonged to the same group of islands that included Minorca and Ibiza. Both Mallorca and Ibiza were famous for their beaches and tourism.

The size of Palma, the capital of Mallorca, surprised him. As the ferry went through its docking procedures, Clint studied the skyline of the city. He had been expecting a sleepy Polynesian type of an island. This was more like sailing into Honolulu.

Per instructions he'd received in a text while on the train, Clint took a taxi to Hotel Escargot, which he was surprised to discover had nothing to do with snails. The hotel got its name from the original owner of the hotel. The building seemed a little seedy and run down. On his way to the Escargot, he passed a number of larger, nicer hotels. After seeing his room, he considered switching to one of them after the first night. He knew, though, that Section had a reason for putting him here, and at least the sheets appeared to be clean. His phone vibrated in his pocket.

"I'm here," Clint said into the phone.

"We know," Buzz said. "Sorry about the accommodations, but a number of the same security personnel who were in Basel are now there on the island with you. Spanish security has increased its coverage of the main hotels. The local police already keep your hotel under scrutiny for obvious reasons, so the national boys won't waste their time with it. Believe it or not, the Escargot has a fair amount of legitimate middle class tourist business. It's a good location, and the price is right."

"Ok, ok, I'll stay." He didn't wonder what the obvious reasons were. The women that leaned against the lamp posts on the adjacent street corners had already given him an idea about the neighborhood.

"We knew you wouldn't be thrilled to stay there. Sorry. You should be able to rent a motorcycle across the street. It'll be the easiest way to work your way around the island. We're sending you the coordinates to where a few members of the Bilderberg group are meeting tonight and tomorrow. It's a private villa overlooking the southwest shore. We want you to get familiar with the area. They'll be security all around the place so try to avoid contact."

"No problem. I'd rather not have to explain to them why I came from Basel to Mallorca," Clint said. "Has Deer given you a reason why she has me here? I mean, I know she has concerns about something happening to another member of the group, but what does that have to do with us?"

"It's a legit question. I don't have the answer. I can tell you that protecting the group is not what she's concerned about. I don't mean she doesn't have any concern for their safety, but it's the people targeting them that have her interest. Like the guy you took the picture of. No one knows who he is. There are almost no leads on either of the two murders. None of the usual suspects appear to be involved."

"Still, I'm not a collector or an analyst. If something happens here, I won't be able to get involved. I'm not hunting somebody."

"I know," Buzz said. "She knows it, too. She has no expectation for you to do anything. I know she's working out something in her mind, and I think she wants to keep you close to the action in case something pops. Just don't ask me what's supposed to pop."

"Hey, I'd rather be here than back home doing nothing, and I've always wanted to visit Mallorca. I won't get bored. After I get off the phone, I'll check out the area you're interested in."

"Ok, stay in touch."

Clint rented the motorcycle and a helmet without difficulty. The small Suzuki wasn't something he would want to take out on an interstate back home, but in the tight environment of the island it seemed appropriate. He decided to go from one end of the island to the other and get a feel for the traffic and the bike. He ran into several spots of congestion and heavy traffic in the city. Once outside of Palma, however, traffic lightened up, and it didn't take long before he was speeding along hillsides overlooking the Mediterranean Sea.

In his younger life, he had owned a motorcycle for a couple years but was never at home enough to make it worthwhile to keep. Although the Suzuki didn't compare to his old bike, he enjoyed being out in the open air and zipping around the numerous bends in the road. To the west, the sun started to approach the sea. Clint figured he had about an hour of daylight left and decided to drive by the villa where a handful of Bilderbergers were supposed to be meeting.

It took him another twenty five minutes to reach the villa. The route took him around the southwest end of the island. In the distance, he saw dozens of sail boats, fishing boats, and luxury yachts docked in a small bay. The small town of Puerto Andratx wrapped itself around the bay. A number of nice houses sat high up on the hillsides overlooking town and the bay. The villa he sought was not one of them, but he slowed to admire the view before continuing down the road. He drove past a scenic golf course. Nearby, he saw a sign to Flor de Sal which the sign described as a deluxe beach club.

Clint found the villa situated on the southern coast about ten kilometers east of Puerto Andratx. The vast open grounds around the villa gave it an appearance of being in an isolated part of the island. Three men guarded the gated entrance to the villa, and a thick hedge lined the road on the side of the villa making it difficult to see into the property. He rode by the entrance without slowing. When he got to a spot on the winding road high enough to look back at the villa, he saw that the main house sat several hundred yards off the road. A white stone or cement wall surrounded the house, and a wrought iron gate controlled access there, too. A guard sat in a chair outside that gate under an open umbrella that provided shade.

Clint couldn't make out many details to the main house. He saw an unoccupied swimming pool in the backyard and what looked like a path that led to the beach. Three people patrolled the beach. A large rectangular building sat off to the side of the main house. Two cars were parked in front of it. Clint figured the building served as a garage, a maintenance shed, or a supply building. Maybe all three.

Movement quite a distance to the left of the house caught his eye. He looked over and saw what he believed to be two more security personnel walking along a path. Clint studied the area to the right of the house. It took a second before he saw two individuals sitting beneath a clump of trees. While he studied the villa, he saw a police vehicle drive up to the entrance and stop for a minute before driving away in his direction.

Clint had seen enough and decided to get something to eat

in Puerto Andratx before heading back to his hotel. He retraced his route and sped by the villa's entrance without giving it a glance. As he entered the small town, he saw a sign that he believed said fish market in Spanish. He didn't have any interest in seeing the market but thought there might be a few restaurants in the area. He found one adjacent to a pier where several boats had tied up.

He parked the bike and started to remove his helmet when he heard someone speaking in French. He turned his head and saw two men leave the entrance to the restaurant and walk in his direction. He recognized the person carrying a bag as the dart player, one of the five men who had tried to kill him in Switzerland.

CHAPTER 8

Clint left his helmet on and leaned over as though he was checking something out on the motorcycle. The two men walked by ignoring his presence. A few yards away they turned left and followed a sidewalk that led to the pier. Clint watched them as they boarded a fishing boat and disappeared.

Their presence here could not mean anything good. Clint entered the restaurant and found a small table by a back window where he could watch the fishing boat. He wanted an opportunity to take a picture of the dart player, or better yet, get him alone somewhere. He could still sense the heavy metal dart flying by his face. He ordered a beer and a fish plate that he couldn't fully translate from the menu. It turned out to be good anyway.

He had eaten most of it when the fishing boat left the pier and turned in the direction of the villa. Clint hadn't planned on responding to the boat's departure, but its quick turn to the east intrigued him. He swallowed the last of his beer, placed a wad of cash on the table, and left.

Clint had trouble keeping track of the boat as the sun had set and the terrain he travelled through often blocked the view to the sea from the road. The boat maintained a due east heading close to the shore line. The speed of the motorcycle made up for the constant bends in the road as it weaved through the hills next to the sea. Not far from the villa, Clint saw a small wooden sign that contained the single word "playa" and pointed down a narrow dirt road.

He decided to take a chance and turned onto the dirt road. After a short distance, the road took a steep drop and turned parallel to the shoreline where it became more of a walking path than a road. He imagined visitors to the beach must park their cars on the beach. Clint could still see the boat despite the evening darkness. He slowed down.

The breeze off the sea buffeted him as he followed the boat for another two minutes. He came to the end of the road at about the same time he realized that the fishing boat had stopped. The ground ahead of him took a steep climb for about thirty yards and seemed to be made mostly of large boulders and rock. He turned the bike around and placed his helmet on the seat.

Curiosity, more than any sense of mission, drove Clint to climb the rocks and see what might happen next. It didn't take long to climb to a high point in the terrain. He had a good view of the surrounding area and saw that he was on the edge of the villa's property. Not far from him, he saw the clump of trees where he had earlier observed a couple security personnel sitting in the shade. Lights lit up the villa, and despite the distance, he could see what looked like a dozen or so people mingling in the backyard around the pool.

The wind picked up, and Clint wondered if a storm might be heading his way. The sky over the sea looked darker than it did straight overhead. The last of the early evening light had faded away. Shapes in the darkness looked more like shadows. Clint thought the men on the boat must be observing the villa from a distance. He couldn't think what else they would be doing at this time of night.

Clint looked around for any security personnel. In the dark he didn't see anyone. A few droplets of rain blew in with the wind, and Clint considered leaving. Movement near the shoreline caught his eye. He stared at the rocky beach about a hundred yards closer to the villa than where he knelt. To his surprise, he saw a rubber raft and four armed men. The men had pulled the raft onto shore, and now out of it, they headed straight inland from the water.

Suddenly, Clint heard someone shout a command that sounded like halt. Gunfire erupted. Some shots came from the weapons of the security personnel, but most came with a muffled sound that Clint could barely hear over the wind. He probably wouldn't have heard them at all if they hadn't continued repeatedly after the louder guns finished shooting. He saw someone scrambling toward the beach and the confrontation. About forty yards right in front of him, the person stopped, crouched, and fired. The quieter weapons responded in such rapidity that Clint knew the attackers must have automatic weapons of some sort.

The person in front of him gasped loud enough for Clint to hear it and dashed toward some larger rocks closer to Clint. Rather than make a retreat back to the raft, now that they had been spotted, the attackers closed in on the security person. Instinctively, Clint moved closer and positioned himself behind a section of rock. He knew he shouldn't get involved and didn't plan to.

Two things happened that made him change his mind. The first came as a benefit of the view of the area he had from his position slightly above the others. He saw one man move cautiously closer to the security guard firing repeatedly to keep the guard's head down. Two other attackers sprinted to get around to the guard's flank where they intended to surprise her. This brought them close to Clint.

The second thing occurred when the security person crawled to a spot that brought her closer to Clint. He finally saw her face. Even in the darkness he could see that she was Princess, the same woman he had watched work out in the gym in Basel only days before.

No one had seen Clint. If he wanted to leave, now was his last chance. He knew he couldn't stay where he was and simply watch them gun down Princess. He would have to turn his back and leave before that happened. He had no doubt that would be the guidance from Buzz or Deer.

The two men crept among the rocks a mere fifteen yards to the right and slightly in front of Clint. They closed in on Princess who crouched twenty yards directly in front of Clint. Preoccupied with the head-on assault by the one gunman, she didn't seem to be aware of the other two. The two men rose in unison to fire at Princess. As they did, Clint shot the closest man. The man fell to the ground. In the heat of battle, the second man never registered Clint's presence. The gunman maintained a focus on Princess and fired a short burst at her with what looked like an AK-47. Clint fired two rounds into the man's left side that struck him under the armpit. The man crumbled to the ground.

Clint heard three rapid shots as the man hit the ground. He knew they came from Princess' weapon. Did she think he was one of her attackers? It would be a reasonable assumption. He held onto his pistol, but raised both hands even with his shoulders and with the palms facing Princess. When he looked at her, though, he realized the last shots were at the third attacker who had charged her when the other two men stood up to fire. He no longer saw the man. Her aim must have been good.

She looked at Clint. Despite the darkness, something must have registered as she quickly scanned the area again before looking back at Clint.

"I think we got them all," Clint shouted.

She took a few steps toward him with her pistol pointed at him.

"Who were they?" she asked.

"Don't know exactly. I saw one of the men, whom I recognized and knew as not very nice, get on a fishing boat in Puerto Andratx. When the boat headed in this direction, I followed it out of curiosity. The boat is out there." Clint pointed to the boat.

"I saw you in Basel," she said almost as a question.

"Yes. I'm on your side, but I shouldn't be here. I need to leave, or I'll lose my job for getting involved. My client doesn't like any notoriety." Clint knew she thought he was working for another security team, and he imagined a number of the group's wealthy members could be difficult to work for. Clint could already see people running in his direction from the villa.

"I don't think I can let you go. There's too much to explain."

"There's no time. You need to check on your two partners. One of the attackers may also still be alive and getting ready to shoot us as we stand here. Let me go. After all, I did save your life."

"I know. I'm in your debt, but it will look worse for you if you run off," she said.

Clint considered turning his back and walking off. He didn't believe she would shoot him. He also knew he wouldn't be charged with anything by the Spanish if he stayed, but his career with Special Section would be over.

Before he could answer, an explosion rocked the villa. The flash lit up the sky, and Clint saw the dark form of an attack helicopter hovering above the sea a few hundred yards from the shoreline. The helicopter fired several rockets at the villa, and Clint saw tracer rounds race from the helicopter. He couldn't tell what damage the helicopter had done due to the smoke and dust that filled the air around the house. As quickly as it appeared, the helicopter seemed to vanish in the darkness.

Princess stared at the villa. Her back now to Clint, he turned and scrambled over the rocky hill to his motor bike. He slipped on the helmet and sped away from the scene. Clint knew that at that moment, about every local policeman and federal agent operating on Mallorca would be heading in his direction. He didn't know how fast they would close off the roads.

About five minutes after he got back on the paved road, he

realized he should have ditched his pistol and ammunition in the sea. He hoped that calls to the police emphasized the attack came from the sea and by a helicopter. That might limit how aggressive they would be about stopping a lone guy on a motorcycle. He didn't know the geography well enough to take side roads so he returned via the same route he had taken to the villa. This took him right past Puerto Andratx and a number of emergency vehicles rushing to the scene.

His luck held, and Clint made it back to Palma. He didn't head straight to his hotel. Rather he parked the bike near a wooden pier that extended some distance out from shore. The handful of lights that lit up the pier seemed inadequate against the darkness. Clint saw several people, mostly couples walking on it. A short distance out over the water, a young couple sat on the edge of the pier with their feet dangling over the side.

He took out his phone to call D.C. and saw that he had missed a text and a phone call. On the ride back, he hadn't heard or felt the calls come in.

Buzz answered. "Did you hear what happened?"

"What? No hellos or I hope you're okay?" Clint said.

"Don't tell me you were there?"

"In the flesh, and you may need to watch for any traffic talking about an unidentified person being involved."

There was a pause in the conversation, and then Clint heard Deer's voice.

"Are you okay?" she asked.

"Yes."

"Tell me what happened. The whole story."

Clint did. While he talked, he walked out to the darkest part of the pier and leaned against the railing. A couple walked by him arm-in-arm laughing about something.

He had reached the point where the two men were about to shoot Princess. "I really had no choice. I couldn't let them kill her right in front of me." He expected some form of chastisement, but it didn't come. "She saw me afterward, and we briefly talked. She thinks I'm a fellow bodyguard for one of the Bilderberg members. We never exchanged names. Before the conversation went too far, the helicopter appeared. I took advantage of its arrival to leave."

"When the gun fight erupted, one of the security people got word to the villa," Deer said. "All the key personnel had already moved to a safe room when the helicopter attack started. None of them were injured. It appears that one of those who got killed in your gunfight had part of a laser guidance system. Without it, the helicopter still managed to hit the villa, but missed what everyone believes would have been lit up by the laser. The villa uses a lot of propane, and the storage tank sits adjacent to one of the villa's walls."

That would've lit up the sky, Clint thought. "What terrorist group uses helicopters and laser guided missiles?"

"Now you know why this group has my interest. No one was on the fishing boat when they got to it."

"Was the man I took a picture of among the dead terrorists?"

"No. All four died at the scene. The Spanish have already released the photographs to Interpol and some allied services for assistance in identification."

"That's quick," Clint said.

"These days it only takes seconds to take a picture and send it out. Someone in Madrid made a wise decision not to sit on the pictures. There was nothing on the men to identify them."

"I'm going to ditch the pistol and ammunition."

"Do it. Tomorrow, I'll need you to fly back to New York." Deer didn't elaborate.

"Okay."

"Does she really go by the nickname Princess?" she asked.

"I guess so. That's what I've been told."

"So, should we now call you 'The Prince'?"

"No, thank you."

Like many phone conversations with Deer, the phone simply went silent and she was gone. No goodbyes, good lucks, or even a keep your head down. He realized they must not have been actively monitoring his location over the last hour or they would have known that he was near the villa.

Clint disassembled the Beretta and dropped the pieces into the sea while he walked out to the end of the pier. He removed the ammunition from the two clips and tossed them and the empty clips into the water. He didn't think anyone would ever find all the pieces to the gun or any of the bullets, and he only needed one day before he would be long gone from the island. He walked back to his rented motorcycle and drove it to the hotel.

The hotel looked quiet, but a bar across the street looked active. A neon sign above the front door flashed "Rojo's". Clint went over to it and stopped for a moment a few steps inside the entrance. The place smelled of cigarette smoke and sweat. Two distinct groups of people filled the bar. A large group of Germans, men and women, who looked like they had come straight from the beach hours earlier, bunched up on one side of the large room. Most of them appeared drunk. All of them seemed to be in a good mood as they sang a song in German that Clint didn't know.

Local workers, mostly men, occupied the other side of the room. They sat in small groups at different tables. At some tables the men laughed, and at others they had a more serious look. Clint walked up to the bar through an open space that seemed to be the unofficial boundary or the neutral zone between the two groups.

The counter at the bar extended at least twenty feet, but there were only three bar stools. A man sat in the middle one and chatted with a bartender. Two other men hurried around behind the bar making drinks. Three harried waitresses ran drinks back and forth from the bar to the thirsty crowd.

Clint leaned against the bar. The bartender talking to the lone man on the stool looked over at him.

"Cerveza, please," Clint said to the bartender.

"It's cerveza, por favor," the bartender said grinning. "English or American?"

"American and I knew that. My brain just didn't get to my mouth in time."

"That's okay. First time here?" the bartender asked.

"Yes."

"Then the first drink is on me."

It dawned on Clint that the man's thick red hair likely meant that he was Rojo, the bar's owner, or at least whom the bar might have been named after.

"Grab the stool and sit down," the customer sitting in the middle stool said. "No reason to stand. I'm Gabe." He leaned over a little and extended his hand.

Clint had to take a few steps toward Gabe to reach the hand, but he did. "Name's Clint. You from the States?"

"Yes. Nebraska. Omaha."

"A Cornhusker fan?" Clint asked.

"Of course," Gabe said.

"I hear they're getting a new coach."

"It happens about once every decade. You can't please everyone. I thought he was doing a good job."

The bartender returned with Clint's beer.

"Gracias," Clint said.

"Now you've got it. Where are you from in the States?"

"Texas. How about you?"

"Came over as a teenager with my dad when he and my mom got a divorce. Been living here ever since. This island was a lot better in the old days. Too crowded now. Too many people. Too many cars."

"I assume this is your bar," Clint said.

"Yeah. My dad opened it in the nineties."

"You do a good business."

"We stay busy on most nights. Close enough to the beach and a lot cheaper than the fancy bars along the boulevard."

"Hey Red, they're talking about it again," Gabe motioned to a small TV behind the bar.

Due to the noise in the bar, Clint couldn't hear the television. The bartender walked back to it and blocked Clint's view.

"What's going on?" Clint asked.

"A terrorist group attacked a fancy villa on the island. Apparently a number of people were killed."

"You're kidding."

"No. A big attack, too. Word is they used a military helicopter," Gabe said.

"A Spanish military helicopter?" Clint asked.

"No, no, probably some Arab group, but no one knows who yet."

"Anyone die?"

"Yes. Red, how many people got killed?" Gabe asked.

Red raised his hand indicating he was listening to the television reporter.

"Sounds like overkill. Who was being targeted?" Clint asked.

"Some millionaire. At least it's his place. No one knows why yet."

"Eleven people died. Sounds like four of them were the terrorists. The rest were members of the house staff and some bodyguards. No one is sure if the owner was the main target or one of his guests. He was throwing a party there, and a number of wealthy guests were in attendance," Red said looking back at Gabe. "Apparently when the shooting started, everyone went to a safe room in the basement of the house. The attack did a lot of damage to the house, but it didn't look too bad from the front. I guess no reporters have been allowed on the grounds, so the only pictures they're showing are from the road out front."

Clint imagined the news crew must have an elevated platform that they used to get any photos of the villa. He kept his thoughts to himself.

"Did they say who was responsible?" Clint asked.

"No. No one is taking any credit, and no one in the government is expressing any theories at this point. The knucklehead on TV has been talking about ISIS, Hamas, and a number of other nasty groups, but I don't think he knows what he's talking about. I'm just waiting for one of those jerks to say it was ETA."

"ETA?" Clint asked, although he knew exactly who they were.

"A Basque separatist group that was active in the sixties and seventies. It used to get blamed for everything."

"Never heard of them," Gabe said.

"Don't worry, they've been out of business for a long time," Red said.

"Did they say anything more about the helicopter?" Clint asked.

"No. It appeared out of nowhere and disappeared afterwards. Kind of frightening."

"Well, I guess those things can fly below the radar," Gabe said. "It could have come from some ship a hundred miles off shore. By the time anyone got around looking for it, the helicopter could already be hidden back on the ship."

"That's probably what happened," Clint said.

"She's dancing again," Gabe said.

Red looked over at the Germans. Clint followed his gaze. A woman, who looked to be in her mid-thirties and a little overweight danced by herself off to the side of the group. A couple of the men watched her, but most of the group ignored her.

"What is she dancing to?" Clint asked.

"Who knows, but watch her?" Gabe said.

"Why?"

"Give her a few moments and see if she takes off the robe," Gabe said. The words barely left his mouth, and the woman dropped her flowered robe to the floor.

"Last night she danced like that for a minute or two and then she took off her top," Red said.

Clint thought the poor woman didn't look all that great in the small bikini that she wore. He didn't think it would be much of an improvement if she removed the top. He looked around the room. Most of the Spaniards, men and women alike, were watching the dancing German. He wondered if most of them had been there the night before.

Clint looked back at the dancer. With a quick flick, she reached behind her back and the top of the bikini fell off. A couple of Spaniards cheered, but most of the Germans continued to ignore her. After about thirty seconds two German women approached the dancer, picked up her robe, and placed it back on her. They escorted her back to her seat and helped her sit down. No struggling, no shouting, nothing happened that would give one the impression that this was anything but an everyday occurrence. A tall, thin man leaned over, picked up the bikini top, and tossed it to one of the women.

"Last night, she tried to get back up after sitting there for a while, and that German man sitting next to her took a hold of her arm and pulled her back down. All done very matter-of-factly, like they go through this with her all the time," Red said.

"Do they come here often?" Clint asked.

"No. Last night was the first time they came here. Hope they return, as long as they don't break anything. They drink a lot."

"Can she get into trouble for taking off her top?" Clint asked.

"No, no way," Red said.

CHAPTER 9

The trip to New York occurred without a hitch. Buzz booked him into the Morgans Hotel, a small boutique hotel on Madison Avenue. The long flight had brought out all the aches and pains he had picked up in the last few days. He hadn't slept well on the train or at the Escargot in Mallorca. He even thought he might be coming down with a cold.

The text on his phone that came in after his plane landed in New York told him to hang loose for a couple of days. Hang loose, that was a term he hadn't heard in a while, but that was exactly what he planned to do. The cab that took him to his hotel pulled up to the curb in busy traffic. Clint looked around as the cab driver retrieved his suitcase from the trunk of the cab.

Clint didn't see a sign for the Morgans Hotel, but a door opened next to him.

"Checking in?" a young man holding the door open asked.

"Morgans Hotel?" Clint asked.

"Yes, that's us. A lot of people walk right by. We could use a bigger sign."

Despite its relative anonymity among the tall buildings and constant movement along Madison Avenue, Clint liked what he saw at the Morgans. Once in his room, he stripped, showered, and crawled into bed. The clock next to the bed claimed it was only five in the afternoon.

Clint slept until his phone rang at eight the next morning.

"As you can imagine," Buzz said, "the whole world is in an uproar over the attack at the villa."

"Good morning to you, too."

"Deer got herself invited to a National Security Council

meeting this morning. Not the principals, but their staffs and a bunch of deputies. The realization that someone is trying to kill a number of the world's richest has garnered a lot of press. What makes it even more significant to the NSC is that no one has a clue who is behind the attacks."

"So we have a new terrorist group?"

"Looks like it, but terrorist groups like to be known, and their attacks aren't usually conducted with such precision. These incidents are more like contract killings taken to a new level," Buzz said.

"Like the ancient League of Assassins or James Bond's SPECTRE or SMERSH? Sounds a bit silly, doesn't it?"

"Yes, but between our allies and ourselves, we have ample resources to get a lead on this. The fact that we haven't developed anything yet is very disturbing."

"Think a country is behind this?" Clint asked.

"No. Could be some rogue element of someone's military or intelligence service, I guess, but even that is highly unlikely."

"Why am I here, then?"

"We couldn't leave you in Mallorca, and anyone can blend in there in New York City. Actually, I think Deer wants you there so she can get you onto an airplane going most anywhere in a short notice."

"Did Marvel get to write her expose?"

"Your lady friend got steamrolled by the big presses. She did get a halfway decent article out, but it's hidden among the other billion similar stories out there right now. By the way, your other friend, the Princess, is being made out a hero over there. She's the one who called in the warning to the main group in the villa when the shooting started."

"Good for her. She deserves it."

"Publicly, they're claiming she killed three of the terrorists. There's no mention of you in the press. Privately, she came clean right away and said she had help. Other than saying she recognized you as another security guy and as being tall, dark haired with a flat nose--"

"Flat nose?" Clint asked.

Buzz laughed. "That's what she said."

"I told her I shouldn't be there. Maybe she was trying to protect me," Clint said.

"Don't worry about it. It's so low on their priority of things to solve it may never get looked at. The guests have all been asked to let the police know if one of their own bodyguards were involved. They all came back saying no."

"Good."

"I imagine none of them are anxious to be sucked any deeper into the investigation or have some security agency grilling their staffs. Even if someone had disobeyed instructions and hung around the villa, it's one of those things that worked out well from their perspective. They've all gone back to their respective countries or are going back today."

"Let me know what Deer hears at the meeting," Clint said, while knowing that no one would tell him anything unless he had a need to know.

"One more thing," Buzz said. "Did you know that she was shot during the gunfight?"

"Princess?"

"Yes. One round hit her on her left side at her hip level. Missed the bone and any major blood veins, but must have hurt like hell. Took some crazy amount of stitches to close up."

"Damn! One tough lady. It was dark, but I was fairly close to her, and I didn't see any indication that she was hurt."

After the call, Clint took advantage of the hotel's continental breakfast before heading outside. He'd been to New York several times, but never with much free time to do any sightseeing.

Clint spent his morning at a laundry mat and jogging in Central Park. While he ate two hot dogs he purchased from a street vender, he heard a couple who looked to be in their sixties discuss the Rockettes and the show they had seen the night before. They leaned against a wall of a building and shared a pretzel while they talked. Clint walked through a museum and went to the top of the Empire State Building. Later, he found an overpriced diner next to Times Square and had dinner. All in all, except for arriving with a suitcase full of dirty clothes, he felt like every other tourist.

At nine, Clint returned to the hotel and discovered that the morning's breakfast room had turned into a lounge for the evening. He enjoyed two local craft beers before heading up to his room. He felt refreshed. Most of his aches and pains had vanished, but he was also getting anxious. At any moment his phone could ring. He didn't only anticipate a call, he wanted a call, and resisted an urge to dial D.C. to ask what was happening.

During his stint with the military, he went on several missions in Southwest Asia. On many of these occasions, he had been a member of a team inserted into the desert that had to wait until higher command issued instructions to move out and fulfill the designated task. Those periods of waiting weren't unlike what he found himself doing now. He had to kill time while waiting for instructions that he knew would send him into danger. Over time, he found himself wishing that these periods of waiting would become shorter and shorter.

CHAPTER 10

Buzz sat at his desk and whistled an old song that he couldn't get out of his head. Unlike Clint who was anxious to get back on the hunt, Buzz felt like this new group offered him a challenge he hadn't faced in a long time. He couldn't remember another time where after three days no one had any idea who had committed a major terrorist attack. The fact that there were still two other unsolved, recent murders of Bilderberg members made the lack of leads more improbable.

Dolly's entrance into the office disrupted his concentration. "Welcome back. How was Paris?"

"Fantastic. I love Paris. I only wish she would've let me stay an extra night," Dolly said with a mischievous smile.

"You know she doesn't want any emotional bonds created with them," Buzz said.

"You've met him, right?"

"Yes."

Dolly smiled. "I don't know why we can't have any of their pictures here in the office. We don't even have any actual personnel records."

"You know why," Buzz said.

"I'd like to have an eight by ten glossy right here." She tapped a spot on her desk.

Buzz ignored her.

"You know I've met a couple of the others."

"I know."

"They aren't the same," she said while she turned on her two computers and fiddled with a small mirror studying her face. "Clint is....well, he's like the whole package."

"Deer thinks you did a good job in Paris."

"But still, no reward for me? She brought me back too fast."

"Get over it," Buzz said. "We've got a fascinating puzzle to work on today."

"I hate Mondays," Dolly said. Satisfied with her makeup, she put the mirror down, and poured herself a cup of coffee. "Hasn't anyone figured out who is behind the attacks?"

"No, and believe me, since the raid in Mallorca, everyone has been trying. There have been no claims by the group, no intercepts that might provide a lead, and nothing deduced from the four dead bodies. It's crazy. The Spanish are working the forensics of the attack and have allowed the FBI and CIA access."

"And?"

"They believe the helicopter originally belonged to the Russian military, and they think two of the dead terrorists are French and two were Serbian. One of the Frenchmen served time in prison in France and went by about twelve aliases. The last record anyone has of him was from 2011, the last time he was released from prison. When he left the prison, he simply disappeared."

"So someone has been building this team for some time," Dolly said.

"It looks that way. My guess is that over the last four or five years, somebody has organized a team of killers."

"For a cause or for hire?"

"I don't know," Buzz said. "Plus, I don't know who or where. For all we know this group may have already committed dozens of murders all over the world."

"So, our working theory is based on a possible what, without any idea as to the who, the where, or the why. This could be fun, but why is she interested in it? Do we have something that would indicate they are about to attack us?"

"Not specifically, but a lot of the Bilderberg members are

either Americans or have substantial business interests here. I think she's correct in assuming if this terrorist organization continues to focus on Bilderberg, then it's only a matter of time before something happens here."

"But that's stretching it a bit. That's not like her," Dolly said. "She's usually very protective of the hunters."

"I know." Buzz had seniority over Dolly because he had worked for the government a lot longer. However, they both started working for Deer when the office was first established. They got along well, and Buzz knew that Deer impressed her as much as she did him. "I've been working on another list of questions to send out."

They both knew the questions were intended to focus analysis and effort by other US government and foreign agencies. A lot of the recipients would ignore the questions, but usually a few would find one question or another worthy of pursuing.

"Want me to look at the search interrogatories you two have given Abby?"

Buzz almost grimaced at the word Abby. For some reason, Deer had personified the set of supercomputers they controlled by naming them Abigail. She felt it added a layer of confusion to what they did in case of any outside snooping. Buzz thought it odd at the time but accepted his boss' decision. Dolly's further familiarization of that name to Abby, however, had always bugged him.

"Sure."

"Oh, by the way, that female bodyguard in Mallorca was something else, wasn't she? Quite the looker, too. How much of what the press had is correct?"

Buzz had forgotten that Dolly had been out of the loop for the past few days. "Clint was there. He took out two of the bad guys. He saved her life."

"Has he been compromised?" Dolly asked. A worried look

crossed her face.

"Don't you want to know if he's all right?"

"Compromised would be worse."

Buzz knew she was right. "He's fine and luckily not compromised."

"Good. I don't suppose there's any file I could read?" Dolly asked already knowing the answer.

"Have you ever seen a file on anything any of the hunters do?" They both knew that was a rhetorical question. One of the office's golden rules was no paper trail. Volumes of documents and databases on the threats America faced, but not one sentence about the hunters or their operations.

"That Spaniard - he's not attracted to her, is he? I mean, what does she have that I don't?"

Buzz thought it best to ignore that question all together.

An hour later, Deer returned from a meeting. She signaled for both of them to join her in her office.

"It's a wonder they get anything done here in this city," she said when they both took seats in front of her desk.

Buzz had heard her say this many times before. Egos and politics trumped actual progress more often than not in Washington. Not so much at the working stiff level, but definitely when you got around senior staff and above.

"Anything get done?" he asked.

"Not much," Deer said. "A lot of finger pointing at each other regarding how this could have been missed and who's responsible for allowing this group to have gotten so far without being identified. Of course, that was all the unofficial chatter. Officially, it was all 'oo-rahs' and 'let's go kick ass'. I think I convinced Marge over at TSA to use their facial recognition technology to see if any of the dead attackers entered the country in the last two years."

"Good," Buzz said.

"It's only a matter of time," Deer said. "Something will

break on this. They can't stay invisible forever. I know you have questions why I've assigned four hunters to this. I don't have specifics I can give you. It's something I've seen developing out there over the past few years. No, not seen, I guess, just felt in my gut."

"Anything we can do to help?" Dolly asked.

"For a few years, I've seen snippets in the traffic that we've monitored that caught my eye. At the time, when one of these things popped up, it had nothing to do with what we were working at the time. It wasn't until I saw the third or maybe the fourth item that I started thinking that an unknown group of bad guys was stealing talent from other organizations, and was doing so very carefully."

"I imagine they steal each other's players all the time," Buzz said.

"Maybe, but it was the way it was being done. Like these people simply disappeared. I initially thought there might be another agency like ours out there eliminating some dangerous people. It didn't matter to me at the time, I just found it interesting."

"Can we retrace your steps?" Dolly asked.

"I don't see how. If we try a search using the keywords missing or disappeared, I don't think Abigail could cut it down to less than a few million hits. We need to come at it from a different angle."

"Even if your assumption is correct, and based on what has happened in the last few weeks, it certainly could be, what does that have to do with us?" Buzz asked.

"If I'm right, there's someone out there running a team of very talented killers. No one knows who they are, despite these assassins being able to attack people at will around the globe. If the CIA, or the Spaniards, or anyone can identify them, they can go after them, and we'll back off. My concern is that this group of killers will try to do something here, or against Americans elsewhere, and there won't be enough time or evidence for anyone to do something about it before it happens."

"These guys also appear to have a lot of talent and equipment at their disposal," Dolly added.

"Agreed. Their capability is impressive, but it's their ability to stay invisible that impresses me more." Deer took a sip of coffee. "There's been a small turf war in Las Vegas. At first glance, it looked like one mob group against another. That's what the FBI, state, and city cops are calling it. Only one shootout that happened in an abandoned building, but it was a bit odd. From all appearances, the coroner concluded seven people died. However, only four bodies were discovered at the scene," Deer said.

"Then how did he decide there were seven dead?" Dolly asked.

"Twenty feet from the four dead bodies, they found a pool of blood on the floor and brain matter along with blood splattered against the wall. Not far from that spot there was another pool of blood. It was so large that someone bled out at the scene. Coroner said a major artery must have been hit. A third area close by disclosed another pool of blood, except in this spot it appears a body laid in it for at least thirty minutes."

"So someone was sent in to remove the bodies?" Buzz asked.

"Yes. No bodies make it a lot harder to identify the dead, and for a reason that could only be to maintain secrecy, the dead bodies of one side of the shootout were removed. The shootout could have caused a greater war, but shortly after the gunfight someone paid off the man at the top. The FBI has intercepts that contain instructions sent by a mob boss in Chicago to his guys in Las Vegas telling them to back off. He told his people to let this group remain untouched, and that they'll be gone by the end of the year. The group and its members are never identified by name, at least a valid one." Deer took a sip of her coffee. "That's why I sent Dick yesterday to Las Vegas. I sent the FBI and Homeland Security a note last Friday voicing my concerns about the strange happenings in Las Vegas. They're all but ignoring it."

"Weren't there any leads on who these new guys might be in the intercepts of the mob's messages and phone calls?" Dolly asked.

"The only reference to them is as some new people. There's a reference to a Jack Kinslow and a Barry Mendes, but both names appear to be aliases. While the city investigation did look into those two and verified the two existed for a while in Las Vegas, they are no longer in the city, and the police couldn't find any trace of their existence prior to their arrival in Vegas. The FBI had no hits on either name when matched with the scant descriptive data they had. No one has any idea where they might be now. "

"Seems impossible," Buzz said. "I guess the assumption is that these two were killed in the shootout."

"Correct, and the level of interest in finding out more about them is non-existent. The police are understandably busy, and the FBI won't spend any time on an unidentified new organization that, as far as they know, has done nothing wrong," Deer said.

"Why do you expect this has anything to do with the bad guys we're looking for?" Buzz asked.

"They're invisible, they went straight to the top in Chicago via at least a two lawyer cut out, they seem to only want to be there for a couple months, and they had ready cash to pay off the people they needed to. Other than that, my gut tells me there's a connection."

"A two lawyer cut out?" asked Dolly.

"Although this is only what I believe happened from the research I've done, a wealthy private lawyer in Italy contacted a discreet law firm in Chicago to deliver the terms to the boss in Chicago."

"Do you expect the group to do something in Vegas?" Buzz asked.

"Yes. Yes, I do, and it shouldn't surprise you that quite a few Bilderberg members go to Las Vegas," Deer said.

"I would be surprised if they didn't," Dolly said. "Do you need me to go there?"

"You've had your vacation for this decade," Deer said. "I do need you to look into who among the Bilderberg might be going there next, and if any of them have any business interests there."

"The fact that this group left four bodies behind in Mallorca must be a big blow to them," Buzz said.

"I'm sure it is. I think the plan was for them to slip in, use the laser to guide the missiles from the helicopter to the propane tank, and leave without making contact. They probably used four individuals assuming that would be sufficient weaponry to overcome local security if things went wrong. The assault team was very well armed."

"I hear Clint saved the day," Dolly said. "I wish I could--"

"Don't go there," Deer interrupted. "He did. We're just very lucky he got away with it. Those four bodies and the dinghy they found on the beach will lead us somewhere. They have to."

"I imagine whoever was behind the attack is busy trying to make sure any trails that do exist are erased or at least well hidden," Buzz said.

"You can count on that. Luckily, every agency that has a finger in this will be trying to identify them. We'll not attempt to duplicate their efforts. We need to try to do some predictive analysis. Go through whatever we can out there and look for anomalies, especially if there is any reference to Las Vegas."

"Any instructions for Dick while he is in Vegas?" Buzz asked.

"No. I just want him there. Tell him to relax. He's good, but he's the least patient hunter we have."

"What should we do with Clint?" Buzz asked.

Deer thought about it for a few seconds. "Send him home for now. Tell him to stay in touch. This thing is far from over."

The meeting broke up. Buzz and Dolly returned to their desks in the outer office. He knew he didn't need to tell Clint, or any of the other hunters to stay in touch. They really had no choice. Whenever Section wanted to, they could get a fix on the location of any of the hunters. They didn't routinely monitor their locations, but had the ability to do so when they thought it necessary. They could also access historical data to see where a hunter had been.

Deer's information put an increased level of difficulty on the analysis that Buzz had already been looking forward to doing. That enhanced his already good mood for the day. He lived for these challenges. Deep down he had an additional, self-imposed goal. He wanted to come up with the answers before Deer did. He rarely did.

"Do you want me to call Clint?" Dolly asked.

"Let me do Clint, Dolly. Why don't you call Dick?"

"I haven't met Dick."

"How many of them have you met?" Buzz asked.

"Four. You know she doesn't like us to get to know them too well."

"My point exactly. I'll be happy to call both," Buzz said.

"What does Dick look like?" Dolly asked grinning. She knew that Buzz knew that she was teasing.

"I never know when you're joking around, Dolly. What happened to that boyfriend of yours? I thought you were swooning about some guy a couple of weeks ago."

"He went back to his wife," she said.

Buzz looked up at her, and she smiled. He hoped she was teasing him again.

"I'll call Dick," she said.

A few seconds later they both made their calls.

CHAPTER 11

Clint spent his first couple days back in South Padre working out, firing his old World War II era Colt .45 at the firing range, and fishing. He also killed some time cleaning the Colt and his Lincoln MKZ. He had planned to play golf in a Charity tournament on the fourth day back.

The phone call from Buzz didn't surprise him, but the contents of the call did.

"Something's come up," Buzz said.

"Good."

"No, it's not. One of our men was found in the desert a few hours ago outside Las Vegas."

"Sorry to hear that," Clint said. "Do we know what happened?"

"No, and that's not good. His phone went dead about two last night. When the calls wouldn't go through this morning, we ran a diagnostic. The best we can tell someone destroyed it next to a lake at a golf course. More than likely, the person tossed it into the lake."

"It's like mine, right?"

"Yes. We're not worried about the phone. We traced where it had been. Someone had driven it out into the desert and then turned around and went directly to the golf course. The spot where they turned around is where they found the body."

"Damn. Do we know what happened?" Clint asked.

"Only that he was shot in the back of the head at close range. We know that much from the preliminary calls from the police when they found him."

"He probably never saw it coming."

"I think so, too," Buzz said.

"How'd they find him so quick?"

"We made an anonymous call about seeing a body. It seemed like the quickest way to get someone out there to look around."

"Had I met him?" Clint asked. He only met a few of them during his first six months on the job when Deer sent him to talk to a few of the more experienced hunters. It constituted the only training that Section put him through. While the three he talked to gave him a few good pointers, he didn't consider it much more than an opportunity to gain a little insight as to what the job was like. He thought one of the three might have already retired from the job.

"No. His name was Dick Parrot. He was good, too, so it's a little spooky that someone got to him."

"What was he doing?" Clint asked.

"He wasn't supposed to be doing anything operational. He knew what was going on and that we thought that something may happen in Vegas, but he wasn't targeted against anyone yet."

"Could he have been compromised?"

"No, but we're looking at that possibility anyway. More than likely, it's something not at all related to the job. Somehow he must have pissed off the wrong person about something unrelated to us," Buzz said.

"What do you expect me to do?" Clint wondered why Buzz was so certain that he hadn't been compromised.

"We need you to head out to Vegas. You'll be on hold there like Dick was, so while there we'd like you to physically retrace his footsteps over the past four days. I don't know if we can learn anything from that, but she thinks it's worth the effort."

"You know, of course, that something he did over the last few days got him killed."

"We know. We've got a cover for you to use only if you're

pushed, and not with the cops. You're his brother-in-law sent there to find him by the distraught wife," Buzz said. "And no, he wasn't really married."

"I figured that. Do the police know who he is?"

"No. Actually, and not to be insensitive, the killer or killers did us a favor by removing all of his ID documents and credit cards. They probably took his wallet and disposed of that with the phone. We don't know if he had his credentials or gun with him at the time."

"Sooner or later the cops will figure out who he is," Clint said.

"Of course, we'll ensure he gets identified, if the cops can't do it. We'll give them a little while though."

"How should I go out there?"

"You're preference," Buzz said.

"Any guess how long I'll be there?"

"I'd say a week at least, Clint, and I'd bet longer. Dick was there in case a Bilderberger goes there. Deer is not letting go of this."

"When do you want me there?"

"In the next couple days, I wouldn't put it off any longer than that."

"Any special hotel once I get there?"

"Yes. He stayed at the Paris. We'd like you there, too. We think the pro outweighs the con. Listen, think about it, and give me a call back once you've decided how you're getting there. We can talk more then."

"One more thing," Clint said. "Any new developments on the Mallorca incident?"

"Not really. The community is chipping away at the identities of the four dead attackers. The raft and the boat they used are dead ends. At least, they found what they think was the boat, and it turned out to be stolen from a rural port in Greece ten days before the incident. No one's taken credit for the attack."

"Any update on the Princess' condition?"

"Yes, she's on sick leave but fine. We've seen a copy of her written report. Says the same thing she said that night. There've been no more attempts made to try to identify you. I think some powerful Spaniards are happy to have her be the sole hero."

"Good for her," Clint said.

"She still says you have a flat nose," Buzz said and ended the call.

It didn't take Clint long to decide to drive. He hadn't taken his car out on a road trip for months, and he thought the flexibility could be useful in Vegas. It also wouldn't hurt that there would be no flight or rental car records of his being in Las Vegas. He wondered if he could check into the hotel under an alias. An hour later, he was on the highway.

Late the next evening, the bright lights of Las Vegas appeared in the distance breaking through the desert's darkness. At the same time, a call from Buzz dashed his idea of checking in as someone else.

"We've done some basic backstopping for you. We've also checked you into a suite at the Paris. Nothing too fancy, just something I thought we owed you after Mallorca."

"Okay," Clint said.

"The credit card traces back to a small estate planning office in Alexandria, VA. Reservations are under your name. You can use whatever address you want as your own."

"Won't I need the card?"

"One fresh off the printer will be in your hands in the morning. It's been expressed mailed already to you via the hotel. There's some other stuff in the package that will give you some background. You just need to read pages seventy four and seventy five. Room is paid for until the end of the week. You might be there longer."

"Any new developments?"

"Not yet," Buzz said. "It turned out that the body was left just a short distance outside Clark County. That created a small jurisdictional dispute on handling, funding, and priorities. They'll work their way through it, but it has delayed the autopsy and efforts to identify him."

"Think his killers knew where they left him?"

"Yes."

"No amateurs," Clint said.

"You're right. We have no clue what Dick did to get himself shot. Best guess is that he went snooping where he shouldn't or stumbled across something and was caught by surprise."

"And yet, you want me to retrace his steps. Is now a time for me to start talking about a raise in my pay?"

"Ha! Maybe we'll enhance your employee benefits with a bigger life insurance policy," Buzz said. "Kidding aside, Clint, we know we're sending you on a trail that somehow resulted in another hunter's death. Our hope is that you'll be prepared where he wasn't."

Clint had been to Las Vegas a few times, but the size of the hotels still impressed him. He found the side street that led to the hotel's self-parking entrance and turned off Las Vegas Blvd. Once inside the garage, he parked in the first spot he found. He left his suitcase in the car and made the long trek to reception. The casino was buzzing with voices, laughter, and the sound of money fleeing from its owners' hands. He discovered while checking in that a thousand dollars had already been deposited with the cashier and credited on his Total Rewards card to be used at any of the gambling venues in the hotel.

"Their loss," Clint thought. He enjoyed playing Black Jack, and sometimes he'd find a poker room to play some Texas Hold'em, but he would be the last to claim that he had any special skill in either.

He walked around the shops and casino in the hotel to get a

feel for the layout before he retrieved his suitcase and found his suite. When he went to his room, he saw he had a view of the strip out his window. "The light bulb industry must love this place," he said to the empty room and wondered if anyone had ever attempted to count the number of light bulbs used along the strip.

He started to empty his suitcase when his hotel room phone rang, and a woman identifying herself as Jessica with guest relations wanted to ensure he was satisfied with his room. Clint wondered if Jessica had known he was in his room, or if guest relations kept trying until they reached someone in the room. He thought it might be worthwhile to talk to someone who worked security for the hotel. Perhaps, though, it would have been easier to simply have asked Jessica.

Despite the long drive, Clint didn't feel tired or hungry. He considered walking around to get a feel for the other nearby hotels and restaurants but decided that would be best done during daylight hours. He took the elevator down to the casino and located an empty chair at a bar with a video poker console.

"Someone's sitting there," the man to his right said when Clint sat down.

Clint started to stand up.

"No. She's gone," a waitress said to them as she walked up to Clint. "Please sit down." She looked at the man next to Clint and said, "You may wish she's coming back, but she said goodbye, and I saw her leave."

Clint saw a sheepish grin form on the man's face.

"Cocktails?" the waitress asked. The waitress had very short blond hair and a dark tan. Clint guessed she had him by about ten years.

"A Michelob."

The waitress nodded and walked off.

"Sorry," the man next to him said. "She's right. I was just hoping she'd come back. She was hot. I thought we were getting along pretty good, but then she up and left. I'm Oliver." He offered his hand.

"No problem, Oliver," Clint said. He shook the man's hand.

"On the bright side for you, she didn't win a penny off that machine. It ought to be ready to payoff good for you."

"Well, we'll find out," Clint said and activated the console.

Over the next twenty minutes, Clint managed to neither win nor lose much money. He noticed that Oliver played sparingly and spent most of his time watching Clint play. The guy kept looking around like he was looking for someone, too.

"There she is," Oliver said tapping Clint on the shoulder.

Clint looked to where the man pointed and saw an attractive woman in a tight, dark blue dress. She had shoulder length brown hair. She appeared to be looking for someone.

"I think she's part Chinese," Oliver whispered. Without another word, he hopped out of his chair and walked over to the woman.

Clint tried to ignore the man and the woman, but when he took a sip of beer, he saw them in the mirror in front of him. She didn't appear particularly pleased to see him again. Her body language definitely signaled, "I'm not interested." Clint thought Oliver had to either be clueless or very determined.

As Clint watched, another man approached the two and grabbed Oliver by the arm. This new person had a mean look to him. He shook Oliver as he dragged him away from her.

"Let me go!" Oliver said. He tried to pull his arm free and got shoved hard against the end of a row of slot machines. "You..." Oliver started to say something but wisely shut up as his assailant shoved a finger into his face.

"Roy! Let him be, please," the woman said.

"I'll take him back to the bar," Clint got off his bar stool.

All three sets of eyes turned to look at Clint. He saw fear in Oliver's eyes, anger in the eyes of his assailant, and an expression of relief or maybe thanks in the eyes of the woman.

"What's going on here?" Two of the hotel's uniformed security personnel approached the two men. They didn't appear to have any interest in the woman or Clint.

Clint returned to his video poker game.

"I called security on them," the waitress said as she brought Clint another Michelob. "If you don't want it, that's okay. I just thought it was nice of you to try to save your friend."

"Not my friend."

"I know. You look pretty tough, but you don't want to mess with him." Her eyes looked in the direction of the two security personnel and the two men.

"Who is he?"

"This guy," she pointed at the chair next to Clint, "I don't know. The guy who yanked him away from the woman is Roy Orlinsky. He's dangerous."

"Dangerous?" Clint asked.

"Yes, hired muscle for some people in this city you don't want to cross. They'll escort both of them out of the hotel."

"I hope not together."

"No, they won't do that. They know who Roy is. The other guy may have a room here. If so, they'll likely tell him to go take a shower and cool off."

"Do you know who the woman was?" Clint asked.

"No. Don't remember seeing her before." The waitress walked off to serve another customer.

When Clint glanced at the mirror, he saw the two men being escorted away. The woman had disappeared. Clint proceeded to lose a dozen hands in a row, left a tip on the counter, and stood to leave when a hand tapped him on the shoulder. He glanced up and saw the woman standing there.

"I wanted to thank you for stepping in a little while ago. I'm afraid Roy would have hurt Oliver," she said in an accent that Clint thought might be Australian.

"Did you know Oliver?"

"No. I don't know him and hadn't met him before tonight, but he told me his name at least three times." She shook her head like she pitied the poor guy. "Oliver from Ohio, he was a pest, but he was harmless."

"What was Roy's interest in him?"

"Long, boring story," she said.

"Can I buy you a drink?"

She looked at Clint for a few seconds before answering.

"Okay, but just a drink and not here."

"Where?" Clint asked.

"Upstairs. They have a quiet place. Plus, I need to get out of here."

She led Clint to a quiet bar and found a spot for them in a dark corner of the room.

"Call me Jenny," she said, once they were seated.

"And I'm Clint."

After they ordered their drinks, Jenny leaned back in her chair and removed her high heels. "I don't know why someone invented high heels. Women are almost required to wear them, and they're not as near comfortable as my tennis shoes."

"Guess they go with the dress," Clint said. "It is a nice dress."

"Thanks," Jenny said. "You don't look like a local, Clint. What brings you here?"

"Just some personal business."

"Filing for divorce?"

Clint smiled. "No, not married."

"A lot of people do come here to get married or get a divorce. Plus, it was an easy way to ask you if you were married."

"How about you? Are you from here?"

"For the past fifteen years. Got married and divorced here."

"Roy?" Clint asked.

"Oh God no! I pity any woman who hangs out with him."

"Then what was his interest in you?"

She looked at him for a few seconds before talking. "Will you stay and finish your drink with me if I tell you?"

"We haven't even gotten our drinks yet, but yes, I'll stay," Clint said.

"My last boyfriend isn't a nice guy. Let's leave it at that. Roy is one of his thugs. He has a lot of guys like Roy. He's told them all to chase away any guys that appear to have any interest in me."

"He doesn't want you to develop a new relationship."

"Bingo. He says it's either him or no one."

"Has he threatened you?" Clint asked.

"No. He's not like that. Don't get me wrong, it wouldn't be beneath him to have someone hurt me. He would just need a better reason than my not wanting to sleep with him anymore. He has a strange set of principles."

"Well, I guess I'll stay here for a drink or two."

"I didn't think you looked like you scare too easy," she said.

"What brought you to Las Vegas fifteen years ago?"

"My husband. My fiancé at the time, I should say. Met him in Hawaii, where I'm from. He was in the air force and got an assignment to Nellis. That's the air base just outside Vegas."

"I know where Nellis is," Clint said.

"My ex was a nice guy. Guess in most ways he still is. We weren't here a full year before he became addicted to the gambling. It ruined his career with the air force and our marriage. I pity him. He's pretty much homeless now."

"Too bad."

"Never have been too good at finding the right guy. I stayed in a relationship with a married man for five years in Hawaii before my ex came along and rescued me. Ha!" Jenny shook her head. "Maybe I should go back to Hawaii."

"You might want to at least consider leaving Las Vegas," Clint said.

"I have," she said.

"You looked like you were looking for someone earlier."

"A date, I thought. The guy never showed up. Not the first time. Tommy must have someone monitoring my calls or something."

"Tommy?" Clint asked.

"Yes, Tommy Ruffino, my former friend. I think he had someone scare off my date. Maybe that's good, because I found you."

CHAPTER 12

Clint rolled over in the large king bed. Jenny's leg quickly wrapped around him. She snuggled closer. He looked at the clock in the room. He wanted to get up and go jogging or find a place to work out, but Jenny appeared to be in a deep sleep. Yawning, he decided to give her another fifteen minutes. By then, it would be eight o'clock.

They had stayed in the lounge for an hour the night before but only had two drinks. She suggested going to his room. Clint didn't know if she had made the move to spite Tommy Ruffino, or if she had a genuine interest in him. It didn't really matter. She had to be around his age, maybe a little older, and had been around the block more than once. He didn't think she deserved any more rejection. She never asked his last name, and he didn't know hers.

At eight o'clock, he climbed out of bed. She opened her eyes.

"What time is it?"

"Eight."

"I better get going," she said.

"Shower?" Clint asked.

"Sure," she said with a smile.

Forty five minutes later she left. She kissed him at the door, but declined his offer to accompany her downstairs. She didn't say good bye. She winked at him and walked away. He still didn't know her last name or how to contact her.

Clint found a fitness room and worked out for thirty minutes before going down to the lobby where he retrieved the large manila envelope Buzz had sent him. He took it back to his room and opened it.

Clint smiled to himself when he saw what they had sent him. The envelope contained a half completed manuscript of a book. He had carried a copy of this same manuscript with him on a number of missions. He thought he still had the copy in the trunk of his car. Buzz' instructions to look at pages seventy four and seventy five inferred they must have altered something. He turned to page seventy four and saw that the two pages described the efforts of a young woman searching for her lost father. Supposedly set in some fictitious city, the trail she took in her search fit addresses in Las Vegas. Reading through the two pages, Clint could visualize the hunter's movements the last few days of his life.

The envelope also contained a wallet sized, passport-style photograph of Dick Parrot. Clint studied the picture. He had never met him. In the picture, Dick appeared to be about his age, but that's where the similarities ended. Dick had long, sandy brown hair. He also had a thin face. While Clint couldn't tell how tall Dick was, he pictured him as being wiry.

He turned the picture over and found the answers. On the back of the picture someone had written 5'10" and 175#.

Clint called Buzz. "Got your package," he said when Buzz answered. "Nice touch."

"As bad an author as you are, we figured no one would ever get to page seventy four."

"I got the picture, too." Clint ignored Buzz's comment. They both knew he hadn't written the manuscript.

"Use it when you talk to people who may have seen him."

"I will."

"All Dick was supposed to be doing there was to kill time while he waited for instructions. If he discovered something or was looking into something on his own, he never told us about it. In other words, if his movements were anything but random, we didn't know."

"Did he know about the Bilderberg connection?" Clint asked.

"Yes, but only a little. He knew we had an interest in the killings, but he also knew we didn't have much of an expectation that anything would happen anytime soon in Vegas. He had not been tasked with anything. As far as we know, no member of the Bilderberg group has been to Las Vegas in the past couple weeks."

"The odds are that his death has nothing to do with the people Deer is interested in," Clint said.

"We understand that. Your primary purpose for being there is to replace Dick. Deer wants someone there. The people behind the attacks on the Biderbergers will likely lay low for a while now, but you never know. So while you're killing time, we're interested in finding out what happened to Dick. Not at the risk of exposing you or placing you in danger, so you don't need to press the issue."

"I understand."

"I guess more than anything else she wants to know what he was doing. If you get a feel for that and nothing else occurs while you're out there, she'll be happy," Buzz said.

"I'll do my best."

He ended the call and within seconds his phone buzzed. The text read, "GPS coordinates." In addition to the two page printout inserted in the manuscript that took him through Dick's general movements in Las Vegas, someone from Section had transferred a copy of the GPS records from Dick's phone that also depicted his movements in Las Vegas.

While having both gave him redundancy with the data, he felt both had limited use. The GPS data gave him specific times and GPS coordinates where Dick spent time. The narrative provided a more general picture of Dick's movements, but included street names and some hotels.

After reading the two pages inserted into the manuscript, Clint had felt it wouldn't be difficult to trace Dick's general movements on his first full day in Las Vegas. Inside the hotel, the GPS data didn't tell him much, but it became more accurate when he left the Paris. Clint figured the reception within the building had something to do with the intermittent signal losses.

Dick had departed the hotel at ten fifteen in the morning by one of the doors on the southwest side of the building and walked onto the strip. Clint did the same and turned in the direction that his GPS took him as it retraced Dick's earlier movements. Clint found it almost impossible to match the timing on the GPS. Steady walking often resulted in his being ahead of Dick's GPS track.

Clint realized that Dick had paused at various spots during his walk, but without going back to his hotel room and plotting out the stops and brief pauses in detail, something Section had not done in their written narrative, he had no option but to backtrack now and then when he got ahead of Dick's trail.

At two locations along the route Dick had taken that first day, Clint found himself in the middle of an outdoor market with a number of small shops or tents selling items. While Clint could tell that Dick had spent some time at each open market, he couldn't tell which exact booths Dick might have seen, done, or said something. At another location next to a row of small shops, Dick had stopped for ten minutes. The store fronts were so narrow that Clint couldn't tell which one caught Dick's attention, or if he entered one of them or stayed outside. He smiled to himself as he thought about how easy they made it look on television.

He didn't talk to anyone about Dick or show anyone the picture on the first day. Clint felt certain that whatever happened to Dick resulted from something he had done on one of the last two days of his life. Clint spent hours in three of the larger casinos while he traced Dick's movements down the strip all the way to the Tropicana. By the time, he came out of the Tropicana the sun had set, and Clint felt that he had wasted the day. He decided to rethink his approach.

Clint started to walk the half mile back to the Paris when he realized he couldn't keep up with Dick's pace. He looked back to where he came out of the Tropicana and saw a row of taxi cabs. He'd rather walk, but hailed a taxi to verify his theory that Dick must have returned the half mile to the Paris by taxi. He had.

The GPS records indicated that Dick had spent the rest of the night at the Paris Hotel. Clint thought about going somewhere else, but ended up in the same chair at the same bar counter he had been at the night before.

The same waitress worked there. "Hopefully, tonight will be a little more peaceful than last night," she said as she brought him the same beer he had ordered the prior night.

"You have a good memory," Clint said.

"Only for what people drink, most times I can't remember anything else."

Clint had only started losing money to the video poker console when he felt a tap on his shoulder. He turned around to see a slim man, neatly dressed in a dark suit, staring at him with cold blue eyes.

"You're new around here, aren't you?" the man asked. His voice sounded like he might have a cold.

"Been here about one full day. Why?" Clint responded.

"My boss said to be nice, so listen good. We won't be so nice next time."

Clint stood up and looked down at the shorter man. "You either have the wrong man, or I'm missing something here. What is it that you think I've done?"

"The woman you had a drink with last night. That's his girl. Got that? She's off limits. You so much as say hello to her again, and we'll be back. Understand? Cause we won't be so nice next time."

"Who's this boss of yours?"

The man stared at Clint but didn't answer.

"Tell him I got your message, and that I doubt that I will ever see her again."

"Make sure you don't," the man said.

"Do you have a name? I might want to report your lack of manners to the police."

The comment brought a sneer to the man's lips. He didn't say anything else, but turned around and walked away. Clint watched the man leave and tried to identify who else might be with him. Despite the man's remark about the "we" in not being so nice next time, it looked like the man left the area by himself.

"What is it about this corner of the bar?" the waitress said as she walked up to Clint.

"Do you know that guy?" Clint asked.

"Not particularly. I do know he runs in the same crowd as Roy. You know the guy who threatened the man who sat there last night." She motioned to the bar stool next to Clint. "He's a scary person."

"Roy or him?"

"Both, but this guy is more like a snake. Roy is more like a pit bull. Choose your poison."

"What's your name?" Clint asked.

"Jamie. How about you?"

"Clint. I think they're mad at me because I bought that woman a drink last night. You know, the one that--"

"I know," Jamie interrupted. "What's their interest in her?"

"The guy those two work for thinks that the woman belongs to him. She told me last night that she did date the guy for a while, but she had broken off the arrangement some time ago. He wants her back and is dead set against her finding another guy."

"Men can be such jackasses," Jamie said and then smiled at Clint. "Some men, that is. This is the easiest city in the world to find a woman. I bet he's already replaced her with a new girl, and now, he's simply being a jerk trying to punish her."

"I'm sure you're right. Have you seen that woman around here before?"

"You asked me that last night. I thought about her a little more. I may have seen her a couple of times, but I couldn't swear to it. I don't know her."

"She said her name is Jenny. I didn't catch a last name. I got the impression her ex-boyfriend is some type of tough guy. Can we use the word "mob" anymore?"

"Ha! Use it. This city has more low life thugs than slot machines. Most of them don't really amount to much, but don't tell them that to their faces. We have a lot of shootings, stabbings, and beatings in this city. You just have to listen to the news."

"Sounds like every other big city," Clint said.

"Could be. The strip is actually pretty safe. The downtown area around the casinos is too. The cops and hotel security do a pretty good job. We always hear rumors of a national criminal organization policing the areas around the casinos, because they make so much money from the gambling operations."

"I thought the state had a pretty good watch over the gambling operations since they want the tax revenues," Clint said.

"They do, but that's the modern day pay off. The old fashioned bribe has just been legitimatized. I imagine there may still be a few palms that get greased, too. The city and state are addicted to the revenues from the gambling business. This hotel alone grosses over a billion in gambling revenue each year."

"You've really thought about all this."

Jamie walked over to serve another newcomer to the bar and then returned to her spot near Clint. "Not me so much as my old man. He worked the hotel side of operations at the old Landmark. He used to talk all the time at home about how the city, state, and the big guys in the mob had figured out how to best make things work. It didn't happen overnight. It took many years, and with both sides really not wanting the feds involved with operations out here."

"Sounds like your father was fascinated with all that was going on."

"He still is. These days, though, he has to read about everything in the paper," Jamie said.

"Now for a more important question, who designs your outfits?"

"Ha! Now that's a good question. Not me, that's for sure. My guess is that they were shooting for a hint of French combined with plenty of burlesque. The skirt is so short I wonder why they bothered at all. I don't have the legs for it anymore, so I like to stay hidden behind the counter."

She left and took care of the other customers in her section of the bar before returning. Clint took the picture out of his pocket. He decided it couldn't hurt to practice his spiel on Jamie.

"I know you see a lot of people every day, but do you happen to recognize this guy?" He held up Dick's picture for her to look at.

She took it out of his hand and studied it. "No. I don't think so. Why? You looking for him?"

"Yes, I'm doing it as a favor for my sister. It's her husband. He came out here a few days ago and after two days seemed to have vanished from the earth. She's sure something has happened to him."

"Is he a drinker?" Jamie asked.

"No. If he was, she wouldn't be as worried as she is. They talked by phone off and on the first two days and then that was it. He no longer answers his phone."

"Was he staying here?"

"Yes. That's why I came here. I've called his room but get

no answer. He's supposed to check-out in the morning, so we'll see if he shows up," Clint said.

"You should check his room."

"I guess, but how would I go about doing that?"

"Obviously, you're not a private detective. Do you know the room number?"

Clint pulled a scrap of paper out of his pocket. "She said he was in room 3117."

Jamie wrote down the room number and walked over to a phone. She talked into it, paused a few seconds, and then talked some more. She returned to Clint. "Housekeeping said his stuff is still in the room and everything is okay there. In other words, he's not in there hurt or worse."

"That's good, but I hate to think he may have found someone else to stay with. Don't know which my sister would rather hear: that he's in the hospital, or that he's with some other woman."

"Well if it's another woman now, he may end up in a hospital later."

"She said she called the major hospitals and the police, but they didn't know anything about him. The cops said they won't consider him missing until he doesn't return home. I guess it's not uncommon for men to come here and forget to call their wives," Clint said.

"You'd be surprised how many men and women come out here with someone other than their spouse. I hear stories all the time from a couple of friends I have in housekeeping about a husband or wife showing up and surprising their spouse. Sometimes on purpose to catch them and sometimes unaware of what's going on until they get here."

"That's probably why I never got married," Clint said.

"And probably why I've been married and divorced three times. Never again for me, but you ought to try it once. I've been told by some people that they are quite happy being married. A few of them have to be telling the truth."

Clint thought of Barbara. He had never considered himself the marrying type, but since he met Dr. Barbara White, he had questioned that.

"I've left a message on his hotel room phone. I'm sure he's going to ignore his cell phone and pretend he misplaced it. I've also left a note at the front desk. Either way, I hope to see him tomorrow."

"Ten bucks he's been with another woman," Jamie said.

Her offer to bet surprised Clint, but after all, this was Las Vegas.

"Or another man," Jamie said with a big grin.

"No bet," Clint said. "My gut says you're right. This is going to break Kris' heart." He got up to leave.

"You've got to come back and tell me what you find out," Jamie said. "I'm on from four to midnight tomorrow."

"It's a date." Clint liked Jamie. He estimated her age to be around forty five. He thought she probably dyed her hair to keep it as blond as it was, but it seemed to match her natural color. A few gray roots gave her away. He liked her sense of humor and enjoyed talking to her. However, he didn't think he'd return to tell her anything.

CHAPTER 13

"Can I join you?" Mike Grant asked.

"Sure, Mike, have a seat. I have a few minutes before I'm going up to see Amy," Theresa Deer said. She had come to one of the snack bars in CIA Headquarters to kill a few minutes between meetings. She didn't really like Grant hanging around her. The man knew too much about how the intelligence community operated and had pressed her a few times in the past to tell him what she was really doing over in the Marshal Service headquarters. However, they had known each other for years, and if not friends, they were very close to what the word meant.

"You heard the Deputy Director in analysis is retiring," Grant said.

"Of course," Deer said.

"I don't make the decision, but I have great access. I know that job could be yours for the asking."

"That's nice of you to say, Mike, but like I've told you before, I've found my little niche. It's low stress and very, very interesting."

"Come on, Terry, you're selling yourself short. It's nothing more than a small analytical office. How can you find any challenge in it? I'm surprised they haven't cut your pay grade. That office anywhere else would never support a person at your pay level."

"How's Tiff?" Deer asked trying to get the conversation off her job.

Mike ignored the question. "I know the job gives you great access. I know because I see you at places and in briefings where I don't understand why you're there. No one seems to care, because most people like you and are happy that you're not out there actively competing with them for promotion and new jobs."

"Why does it bother you that I'm happy where I am?" Deer asked.

He looked at her like he was studying her before he answered. "First, I know you. The Theresa Deer I know would never settle for a small analytical operation. Secondly, something about your office has never set well in my mind."

"One day, Mike, you too will wake up and wonder if all the stress is worth it. If at that point, you luck into an office like mine, you'll wonder why you hadn't quit working so hard before. Life's too short."

"Maybe so, maybe so, but I still wish you'd think about coming back," he said, referring to her returning to the CIA.

"This place will give you grey hair and ulcers. You're underappreciated and a target for every reporter and politician who hate America."

"Whoa, Ms. Deer, you do have some of the old firebrand in you. We do need you back and the sooner the better."

"Thanks, but no thanks. The longer I can stay hidden the better. You never did answer my question. How's Tiff doing?"

"She's doing fine," Grant answered. His voice gave away his disappointment.

They talked about his family and the weather for another five minutes before he said he had to run off to another meeting. Deer watched him leave with mixed feelings. Years earlier they had been close. They had both been assigned to the CIA field office in Athens, Greece, at the same time, and their professional relationship developed into a personal one. He returned to the States from Greece, and Deer transferred to London. A few years after leaving Greece, Grant met Tiffany Blake and the two married. Deer considered going to the wedding, but didn't.

They remained friends, and up until the last couple of years,

Deer enjoyed running into him at this or that meeting. However, he had developed a curiosity into what Deer was really doing in the bowels of the Marshal Service building. Grant could be tenacious when it came to resolving matters that mystified him. That worried Deer. Her office survived on its ability to operate invisibly and by staying outside all government oversight. She could count on her right hand how many government officials actually knew what her office did. If she used both hands, she could count how many other government officials knew only that her office was an ultra-secret operation and not what it appeared to be.

Fortunately, a number of factors helped keep Special Section out of sight. The most important was its miniscule budget. Its operating costs didn't even match what most government organizations would ignore as a rounding error in their own budgets. Personnel costs for less than twenty people in the overall homeland security budget didn't excite even the most micro-managing auditor.

The new Director of the Marshal Service had only been told that the President had a role in creating the office after 9/11 as a covert way to get feedback on how well the various national security agencies shared information. In fact, the former President himself had told the former Director, that he had authorized that the small office have access to all US community intelligence reporting. The Director understood that Deer reported directly to the National Security Advisor. As part of her role, Deer's office routinely provided high level analysis of ongoing threats to the United States. This analytical reporting provided further cover for Deer, as her office often provided analysis that supported specific Marshal Service operations.

Deer understood the importance of her office's symbiotic relationship with the Marshal Service. It gave her cover and a safe place to operate, while the Marshal Service received a source of quality threat analysis at no cost to them. She thought

Grant had already guessed that her office did more than threat analysis. He did know her that well. She didn't think his assumption that her office might be a front for something else was a problem. The practice of hiding operational activity in supposed non-related admin or research offices throughout the D.C. area had become so common it was almost humorous.

She did worry that Grant's incessant curiosity would drive him to question everyone he knew in the intelligence community until he came up with an answer he liked. Grant wouldn't do this to harm her in any way. However, he couldn't help scratching if he had an itch, and for whatever reason, wanting to know what she was really doing had become that itch.

Deer knew she would have to come up with a solution to allay Grant's curiosity, and soon. The more people he talked to in his attempt to learn more about her job, the higher the chances he'll awaken an interest and suspicion in those people. She thought about her options while she climbed the stairs to her next meeting.

She had spent years working in this building, and even though it brought back a little nostalgia, she didn't miss it. The term rat-race came to mind.

Her meeting with Amelia "Amy" Swanson developed as a follow on to the multi-agency meeting hosted by the CIA that morning. Amy had tried to voice her opinion that the murders of the Bilderberg members and associates seemed more like contract killings than activities undertaken by a terrorist group. Her comments didn't receive much support as most of those attending the meeting felt like the attacks were either the responsibility of the usual terrorist suspects using new tactics, or a new eco-terrorist organization.

There were some who speculated that a country, rather a terrorist group, might be behind the attacks. They mentioned North Korea and Russia as possibilities. At the end of the meeting, the only thing most attendees agreed to was that no one really knew whom to hold responsible for the attacks.

Deer agreed with Amy's comments and wanted to learn more about her theory. She had attended other meetings with Amy and knew her well enough to say hello, but this would be their first private meeting.

The two were about the same age, mid-to-late forties, and both knew their jobs, but that was where the similarities seemed to end. Whereas Deer still could turn a man's head when she walked by, Amy had given up worrying about her appearance a decade ago. Dressed comfortably in loose sweaters, slacks, and comfortable loafers, Amy's sole focus was her job, which she loved and did very well. If someone thought she might be fifteen to twenty pounds overweight, so be it. She didn't care. Her husband had passed away from an unexpected stroke while climbing the hills in West Virginia, something he loved to do. They had wanted children, but she had been unsuccessful in getting pregnant. They had agreed on adopting a child, but her husband died before they had gotten very far into the process.

Deer stopped in front of the open door to Amy's office and peered in. Amy saw her and smiled. "Come on in and have a seat, Terry. Am I mistaken, or are we like-minded about this new threat?"

"Yes we are," Deer said and noticed a framed picture sitting on a bookshelf behind Amy. "Beautiful dog, is it an Irish Setter?"

"Yes he is. His name is Classified, but I call him Classy. He's my best friend these days."

"Love the name," Deer said. For a few minutes, the two continued with small talk about pets and living in the D.C. area.

"So, what is your take on the killings?" Amy asked.

"I think someone has assembled a group of very talented killers. Whether the group is loose knit or tight knit, I don't know. I think the leader is a westerner, probably European. I don't think the leader has a political agenda, but I think the person who hired them may have one."

"I agree. I'm not ready to say the leader is a westerner, although the dead assassins left behind on Mallorca certainly indicate that. I'm also wary about saying there might be any political agenda. I'd be more inclined to think there might be a financial one," Amy said.

"I've studied that. I can't see how their deaths can financially change much of anything. When I say political, I admit I may be stretching the term a little. That's why I agreed with your theory over the others. Our two victims and the ones targeted in Mallorca were all old money, and all had deep holdings in natural resources of one type or another."

"So you're thinking an eco-terrorist group?"

"No, not exactly," Deer said. "I want to think a single individual, obviously a very wealthy one, hired this league of assassins, if I might use that old, overused term. He or she must have a deep seated motive, perhaps an obsession."

"She would have to be wealthy. But what? An obsession against old people?" Amy grinned when she said old people. "Or polluting the Earth?"

"I get a picture of a younger person. Even younger than us." Now it was Deer's turn to grin. "Say this person is one of the nouveau-rich. Made her money in software or social networking and is idealistic to the extreme. If she were poor, she might be out marching in the streets protesting fossil fuels or something similar, but she's got more money now than she can ever spend. Say she tried to go to a Bilderberg meeting and was rebuffed, or allowed in but snubbed by the old guard."

"She'd have to be a little crazy, too."

"Given," Deer agreed.

"So is she trying to save the world or get revenge?" Amy asked.

"Probably both."

"I like it, but it doesn't get us any closer to who's actually doing the shooting."

"I know, and that's where I'm still stumped," Deer said. "The person who assembled this group of killers did so in complete secrecy."

Amy nodded. "It's almost impossible to believe that in today's world, no one has been able to develop a single valuable clue as to who they are. Believe me, we have turned over every rock out there. So have our allies."

"I'm sure you have. My guess is that this league of assassins doesn't have a central base--"

"Like they don't have a hideaway in the mountains somewhere where they all practice kung fu all day," Amy said.

"Exactly. That's what I was going to say. However, I think that's what a lot of the others think of, and that's why they can't accept the idea. It's easier for them to lump whoever is doing this into the world they see at the moment."

"But it couldn't be that hard for someone who is wealthy enough and has access to the world's underbelly of criminals. He could develop his own list of hired killers for future use. He could use only the most secretive, since that would fit his objective, and use different ones for different events.

"I think so, too," Deer said. "I don't see him necessarily picking these targets. He could be the middle man between who wants the killings and who is actually doing the shooting."

"Like the "Broker of Death," Amy said. "It would make a great movie title."

Deer didn't mind the way Amy interrupted her with her little witticisms. She imagined Amy didn't mean anything more than adding a little humor to the conversation. "In a way, but what has me stumped is that someone like this has to have a way of being contacted in the first place. He, in turn, has to have a way to contact his hired guns. Some intel or law enforcement agency should have something on someone like this, but they don't."

"Or maybe they haven't yet recognized what they have," Amy said.

"That's possible, but I know that the FBI and Interpol are working that side of it very hard. I think maybe we should get a profiler to come up with a description of the type of person we should be looking for. We develop our theory, much like we've just been discussing, and go to him with our thoughts."

"I'm not really sure what good that would do. We know very little," Amy said. "However, I can't see how it would hurt either. Do you have someone in mind?"

"Yes, I do. He's retired from the FBI but has remained involved. It may not get us anywhere, but it's a straw we can grasp."

Deer stayed for another ten minutes, and the two discussed what information they had that could be of benefit to the profiler. Deer told Amy that she would keep her up to date with her efforts with the profiler. They both agreed to share any breaking news with each other.

She left the building feeling upbeat. Amy Swanson had very good access to what was happening in the world of terrorism. While the two agreed this might not be terrorism, the intelligence community would handle it as such, and Amy would have access to new developments in the search for the individuals behind the attacks on the Bilderberg members. Deer should also see the same reports, but some things invariably fall through the cracks, or they're discussed but never make it into the reports. She made a mental note to share some of the intelligence she came across with Amy. They had agreed to do so, but Deer knew she could get too focused on her own job, and she needed to ensure Amy knew the cooperation was mutual.

Chapter 14

At nine fourteen in the morning, Clint stood in front of the Paris Resort and Casino ready to resume his mimicking of Dick's movements from the week before. Despite his comments to Jamie, he had no intention of hanging around the front desk. He knew Dick wouldn't be returning. He had done more analysis of the GPS data that had been provided by Dick's phone and hoped his efforts would be more efficient than on his first day.

The trail took him in the direction of downtown. Remembering his few days in Manhattan, where the terms uptown and downtown had confused him, he wondered if this direction would be considered going up the strip or down the strip. New York even had a mid-town, but he had never heard of a mid-strip section of Las Vegas. The terrain in Vegas was flat so that didn't help. He guessed going toward downtown would be going down the strip and going to the end of the strip, like he did yesterday, would be considered up the strip.

By two in the afternoon, Clint had decided his efforts had no chance of accomplishing anything. While he might be following Dick's footsteps, he certainly wasn't doing it from Dick's frame of mind. He had no idea what had caught Dick's eye along the way or to whom Dick might have talked. He couldn't tell if Dick met someone while he was out, or even if someone had walked the entire route with him. At a few of the places where Dick had spent more than a few minutes, Clint asked a couple of the employees if they recognized Dick's photo. Everyone he talked to denied ever seeing Dick.

Clint stood in front of a small casino. A neon light flashed

Pappy's on a dirty window. Dick had spent nearly three hours in or very near the place. Clint looked up and down the street. While the casino was small in comparison to many of Las Vegas' huge hotels, the front of it took up enough space to give Clint little doubt that this was where Dick had spent the time.

Clint entered Pappy's Casino. The air conditioner didn't seem up to the job, and the air felt stale. The floor needed to be vacuumed. He wondered what about this place interested Dick. Most of the slot machines and gaming tables had no one at them. He felt like leaving but didn't. Finding a video poker slot machine that gave him a good view, Clint settled in and started the slow drain of money from his pockets to Pappy's. A hostess, who looked like she might have worked long enough to have completed a career at one of the nice hotels and was now working her retirement job, offered Clint a drink. He asked for a Corona and half expected to be told they didn't have any premium beers. Instead, she hurried off to get him one.

When she returned, Clint showed her the picture of Dick and asked her if she recognized him. Like everyone else that day, she told him no. Five minutes after she disappeared, a square looking man in a plaid sports jacket approached Clint.

"Excuse me, mister," the man said. "I'd like to ask you a question."

"Sure," Clint said. The man had a rough looking face. Clint pegged him as a former boxer. He didn't sense any anger in the man's voice.

"Are you with the police?"

"No," said Clint.

"What's your interest in the man whose picture you're flashing around?"

Clint pulled the picture out and showed it to the man. The man only took a quick glance at it. "You mean this man?"

"Yes."

"He's turned up missing, and I was asked by his family to

see if I could locate him. Do you recognize him?"

The man stared at Clint for a few seconds before answering. Clint waited him out.

"Yes. He was in and out a few times last week. You say he's missing? Do the cops know?"

"They've been advised, but I guess a lot of people go missing out here for a few days."

"You can say that again," the man said. "That's too bad. Hope he's okay. He seemed like a good guy. His name was Dick, right?" he asked and Clint nodded. "I'm Jake Anderson. I keep this place peaceful."

"You're doing a good job, Jake. I'm Clint Smith."

The two shook hands.

"Don't judge this place by the way it looks now. By nine o'clock tonight there won't be an empty seat here. We run a long happy hour that draws them in."

"Can you give me any idea where Dick might have gone or what may have happened to him?" Clint asked.

"No, but Ursula might be able to." Jake talked into his phone and listened to someone. "She should be in any minute. She works the shift that's coming on shortly. If you hang around, I'll tell her to come see you before she starts working."

"Thanks."

"And, uh, do me a favor. Don't mention about him having a family somewhere, if you don't mind. I think she had started thinking he was special, if you know what I mean."

"Sure," Clint said. He watched Jake walk back to the front of the casino, and wondered if his earlier pessimism had been shortsighted.

Surprisingly, Clint was ahead by ten dollars when a petite woman with short black hair dyed blue at the ends approached him. After the blue dye, his eyes couldn't help but take in the woman's breasts. Definitely enhanced, he thought. The uniform, if that was what they were called, that the hostesses wore at Pappy's took on a new light.

"I hear you're looking for Dick?" she said.

"Yes. Are you Ursula?" Clint asked. He held out his hand.

"Yes," her hand felt tiny in his.

"I'm Clint, a friend of Dick's. Do you know where he might be?"

"No. I met him here last week. He was playing black jack, and I brought him a drink. He followed me back to the bar. I usually chase them away or have Jake do it. I have a job to do, and I'm not here to be picked up."

"But Dick was different?"

She smiled. "Yes. He was a gentleman. He talked to me whenever I returned to the bar, but was polite about it. Some guys can be real pests. Vulgar, suggestive comments, you know. Dick was familiar with Romania. That's where I'm from. He could even speak a little of my language."

"I knew he travelled a lot, but I didn't know he knew Romanian," Clint said.

"Well. He didn't know it, just a few words, but he tried." She smiled at the thought. "He was supposed to meet me on Saturday. It was my day off and we were going on a picnic. Don't look like that. We were going on an actual picnic."

"What happened?"

"He didn't show up. I called his phone but didn't get anything. I really thought he was a good guy. After a couple of days, I figured I had been played by another man."

"He didn't play you, Ursula. I think something may have happened to him."

Her hand went to her mouth. "I hope not. That would even be a worse outcome."

"I'm not an expert at this, so anything you can tell me about anything that was bothering him, or something that he mentioned that seemed strange to you, might help me," Clint said.

"I can't think of anything off the top of my head."

"Any chance I can get you to think about it, and then tomorrow perhaps we can meet for lunch or a cup of coffee and talk some more."

"I can do lunch, but I'm not sure what you expect for me to remember," Ursula said.

"I don't know either, but something might pop up that turns out to be useful."

"Okay. Where would you like to meet?"

"I'm not that familiar with the area. Is there someplace around here where you and Dick went?" Clint asked.

"There's a Chinese place called Kim She just around the corner. We went there once. If you meet me here at one tomorrow, I could walk you over to it."

"Sounds good, I'll be here at one."

"I'd better get to work. See you tomorrow," Ursula said and hurried off.

Clint stayed in Pappy's another thirty minutes before he walked outside. He found a semi-quiet spot down a side road and called Buzz.

"How goes it?" Buzz asked when he answered the phone.

"Slow, but I figure you guys know I have a slim chance at best to develop something that will lead us to Dick's killer."

"We know. That's not why we sent you there, but since you're there."

"I know. I did find a woman Dick hung out with for a while during his last few days. I've talked to her a little, and we have plans to talk again tomorrow."

"Good. Think she may have something to do with his death?" Buzz asked.

"No. At least not at this point."

"Do you have her name? A picture? Fingerprints? DNA?"

"Ursula. That's all I have at the moment. I can tell you that Dick had good taste. Are you serious about the other stuff?"

Clint asked.

"Yes, but I was kidding you. I didn't expect you to have it, but anything along those lines that you can get will help us run a trace on her. I imagine you're right in your assumption that she had nothing to do with Dick's death, but we might find something interesting that could link her to someone else."

"Will do. The picture and prints shouldn't be too hard, but I doubt if she's ready to swap any DNA quite yet. Anything new with the Bilderberg group?"

"No. Strangest thing. These guys that are behind the attacks are good. No, they're beyond good at hiding their tracks, but we'll get them," Buzz said.

"We?"

"Us, the good guys, the United States and its allies. Somebody will turn over the right rock, and we'll have them."

"I hope so. I think I've already lost a hundred bucks out here. What will happen at the hotel once that Dick's time is up, and he hasn't checked out or renewed his reservation?"

"Probably not much. The hotel received their money in advance. They'll simply clean out his room and store his stuff. They might send a letter to the address he gave them. We'll see. By the way, Nye County has retained jurisdiction over Dick's body which means the pace of the investigation might pick up a little. They have less on the books and will follow the routine without too many disruptions."

"Won't that slow down any investigation in Las Vegas?" Clint asked.

"Yes. I doubt if the Las Vegas police will do anything on the matter without the victim's name or a specific lead to run. They don't know where he was killed, or if there is even a Las Vegas connection."

"That's good for me, but I feel bad about Dick's killers getting away with it."

"They won't. We've come across a couple of traffic cams

and are analyzing the footage for the times we know Dick passed through the cameras field of vision."

"Have you identified the vehicle he was in? Clint asked.

"Not yet. We're down to three or four. May be the best we can do. We're also trying to find some video of Dick walking around the area where we think he got killed."

"So can I stop?" Clint asked.

"No. In fact, we're thinking about having you skip to his last day and pick up his trek a short while before we think he was killed. We need to see if we can pick you up on any live feeds and also get you to try to locate any private security cameras in the area."

"Sounds like fun. Want me to wear my flowered shirt, so I'll stand out?"

"You have one?" Buzz asked.

"No."

For the next two hours, Clint traced Dick's movements before ending up back at the Paris. He didn't feel like drinking or gambling, so he headed up the strip a short distance to a hamburger place he had seen earlier. He was about to enter it when he saw Jenny among the crowd of tourists walking down the sidewalk in his direction.

He remained outside and called her name when she got close. She looked at him in surprise and smiled.

"Well, hello, Clint." She approached him and gave him a hug.

"Jenny, how are you doing?"

"Okay. I was just heading to my car to go home."

"Want a hamburger or something? I was just going in."

"Sure. It'll give me an excuse to have one. Mostly I force myself to eat salads. I guess this is as good a reason to splurge as any."

The two went inside and threw dietary cautions aside. They sat and talked for twenty minutes after the last of the burgers and fries had disappeared. Finally, Jenny said she needed to head home, and Clint offered to walk her to her car. The sky had started to turn dark, but the lights on the strip created an artificial daylight.

They took the first side road and walked away from the strip. When Clint and Jenny passed a part of the sidewalk that opened up to an alley to the right, a small figure came out of the alley.

"I told you to stay away--"

Clint didn't let the man finish his sentence. The man had started to remove a pistol from inside his coat. Clint jerked the man's arm out with his right hand and smashed his left hand into the man's extended elbow. The man screamed, and Clint spun the man around throwing him face first into the wall. The man hit the wall hard and slid unconscious to the ground.

"Clint!" Jenny yelled.

Clint saw the second man's shadow as the man lunged at him. Clint moved to his left avoiding by inches the knife in the man's right hand. Clint hit the man in his kidneys as he moved past. Before the man could recover, Clint kicked him in his back sending him against the same alley wall. As the man started to turn around, Clint hit the man in the back of his head with an open palm ramming the man's face against the wall. The man cursed, but Clint grabbed the man's curly blond hair and smashed his face against the concrete wall three times in rapid succession. The man cussed at Clint again.

The man tried to turn around and move away from the wall. He staggered and fell to one knee. Clint pushed him, and he fell on top of the smaller man who had started to show signs of coming to. Clint leaned over and retrieved the pistol and the knife from the ground. He grabbed Jenny's hand, and they hurried away from the two on the ground.

"Are you okay?" Jenny asked.

"Yes. Did you know they were following you?"

"No. I mean I know he has someone watching me most of the time, but I didn't see them following me. We only had a hamburger. Why would that set anyone off? I'm so sorry."

"Not your fault. Where can I find this ex of yours?" Clint asked.

"Oh, please. He might kill you. I'm not worth it."

"Don't be silly. He can't keep doing this to you or the people you meet."

"You're serious," she said.

Clint nodded.

"Where did you learn to fight like that?"

"In the military, now where can I find your ex?"

"If something were to happen to you, I would never forgive myself." Clint didn't respond to her remark, and she finally answered his question.

CHAPTER 15

Jenny told him that Tommy Ruffino owned a lounge in west Las Vegas. He hung out there most nights. In addition to his legitimate business, Jenny thought Ruffino ran unlicensed gambling operations and a string of prostitutes, but she wasn't sure. They never talked about it. She didn't think he was big time which gave Clint an idea.

Like in most legitimate occupations, there exists a pecking order among criminal organizations. That's not to say a burglar or a scammer can't be totally independent. However, if you're planning to run a criminal enterprise in a location shared by a number of other criminal organizations, you need to learn pretty quick the limits to what you can do, to whom you kiss up, and whom you can shove around. It's literally a matter of survival.

Jenny also told him that Ruffino owned a black Lexus that he kept parked in a spot behind the lounge. He loved his Lexus.

Clint had the taxi drop him off two blocks from Ruffino's lounge. He approached the lounge from the rear carrying a vanilla milkshake that he had purchased on the drive to the lounge. He spotted the Lexus right away. No other cars were parked in the small private lot that only had three spots. He saw a man walk out of the back door of the lounge and lean against the railing. The man lit a cigarette. He didn't notice Clint on the cement stairs that led up from the side to the back porch. Clint placed the milkshake on the top step.

It seemed almost unfair to Clint. The man had ear buds in his ears, and he vibrated to what must have been music. Any sympathy Clint might have had vanished when he recognized the man as Roy. He remembered him from the Paris when the man threatened Oliver for talking to Jenny. Clint looked around for any security cameras but didn't see any. Retrieving from his pocket the pistol that he had taken from the man who attacked him less than an hour earlier, Clint crept up on Roy and struck him on the back of his head. Roy staggered, and Clint hit him with the pistol again. He fell in a wad to the porch. Clint removed a revolver from a holster attached the back of Roy's belt.

He dragged Roy's limp body deeper into the shadows on the porch. He then proceeded down the back steps to Ruffino's car and poured the contents of the milkshake onto the car's hood. Using his phone, he took a picture of the car and sent it via text to the number Jenny had given him. He didn't include any message.

Not knowing who might respond or what to expect from Ruffino, Clint disappeared into the darkness behind the building next door. It took about three minutes, but Clint's patience paid off. Ruffino appeared on the back porch and walked quickly to his car. Clint didn't see anyone else with Ruffino.

"Damn it!" Ruffino said loud enough for Clint to hear. "Roy!" Ruffino shouted. He looked around, mumbled something else that Clint couldn't hear, and went to the trunk of the Lexus. He removed a towel and returned to the front of the car.

Clint left the shadows, and with Roy's gun in hand, approached Ruffino.

"Ruffino," Clint said in a steady, calm voice.

Ruffino straightened up with his back to Clint.

"Don't do anything stupid. I have a gun pointed at your back, and I can't miss from this distance. I just want to talk. Turn around slowly with your hands out to your side."

Ruffino started to turn around, and Clint saw he still held onto the towel.

"Drop the towel."

Ruffino let the towel fall to the ground.

"You get one warning. Forget about Jenny. You don't own her. We weren't crazy about your operation when you started it, but it's a big city, and you didn't seem to bother our business. I'm starting to change my mind, and unless you get your act straight, when I get back to Chicago, I'll make sure to recommend we close you down for good. If me or my friends want to have a good time with Ms. Jenny, it ain't none of your business. Tonight you got three of your boys busted up on account of you. Next, it'll just be you busted up real bad. You understand?"

Ruffino didn't have much of a choice staring into the barrel of Roy's revolver.

"I was getting tired of the bitch anyway. You can have her. I've had better."

"You can always find better," Clint said. "Don't get yourself killed over her. Now turn around and don't move for five minutes."

While Ruffino faced the car, Clint backed into the shadows of the neighboring building. He didn't trust Ruffino, but hoped his message got across. Giving him the impression that a bigger, more powerful crime family had an interest in Jenny might be sufficient. Discovering that three of his men had been put out of commission for the night should reinforce the message.

It took Clint fifteen minutes of walking before he found a taxi to take him back to the strip. During the walk, Clint disassembled the two handguns he had taken that evening and tossed the pieces in separate trash cans and dumpsters he passed. Once in the taxi, he called Jenny.

"Are you okay?" she asked as soon as he identified himself.

"Yes. Keep your fingers crossed, but I think Ruffino will leave you alone now."

"Are you serious?"

"Yes. He has to have some common sense in that brain of his. I made him think that you are now wanted by someone in a bigger organization than his," Clint said.

"Guess it's good to be wanted. That should work though. He was always paranoid about irritating the wrong people."

"We'll see if it works."

"I think I need to find a way to thank you," Jenny said.

"Maybe we can do dinner tomorrow, but I'll have to call with a time."

"Okay. Let's do it and Clint…"

"Yeah?"

"Thanks again."

Clint hoped he had put the matter to rest, but he had a few concerns. Even if Ruffino decided to move on from Jenny, any of the other three men he hurt that night might want their own revenge. They had to know he was staying in the Paris Hotel. He wondered if he should move into a different hotel. His decision could wait a day.

Clint returned to the Paris, and despite the day's excitement, he slept soundly until his cell phone buzzed at seven thirty.

"Good morning, Clint. Hope I didn't wake you," Buzz said.

"What's up?"

"We've located some footage off a traffic camera that shows Dick walking about fifteen minutes before we think he was killed. He's alone and nothing about his body language indicates he was concerned about anything."

"You can't always tell that," Clint said.

"I know. We can see him for about five minutes before he moves out of camera range. He didn't appear to be looking for anything or concerned about a tail."

Clint thought that might only indicate that Dick was good at his trade. "Did you see anyone following him?"

"No. There were other people walking on the sidewalk, but

it didn't look like he was being followed."

"So, do you all want me to jump ahead and trace his steps from there?"

"Yes," Buzz said.

"Any specific time?"

"We have him walking at four thirty. You should have the coordinates already, but to put them in English, be at the corner of Buffalo Drive and Vegas Drive at four thirty. We can walk you through his exact steps for the five minutes, and then you'll have to do your best to trace him the remaining ten."

"Okay. Anything else new?"

"No. In fact, we're sending the others home. The consensus in the community right now is that the bad guys are keeping a low profile. The Mallorca attack was a lot messier than they intended."

"How about me?" Clint asked.

"Deer wants us to do a couple more things there."

"I might be moving to another hotel today."

"Up to you. Don't you like the Paris?"

"Yes, it's great. I think I just want to get off the strip." Clint didn't feel a need to tell Buzz about his altercation with Ruffino and his crew. He wondered if Dick had said a similar thing to himself in the previous week.

"Do you have a hotel picked out?"

"No."

"Take a look at the Orleans. It's off the beaten track, but it's pretty nice and not too far from where you are now."

"Will do," Clint said.

After getting off the phone, Clint had a large breakfast at the hotel's buffet. Since he had time to kill, after his breakfast he continued his tracing of Dick's earlier movements for the rest of the morning. As before, by the time he had to stop and head over to Pappy's to meet Ursula for lunch, he was convinced his efforts were a waste of time.

Ursula leaned against the front wall, near the entrance to Pappy's. She wore tight red shorts, a black, short sleeve blouse, and black high heels that laced up above her ankles. She looked nice, real nice, although Clint couldn't help but think she also looked like a hooker.

"You look great," he said.

"Thanks," she said and reached out to take his arm. "Still up for lunch?"

"Sure."

"It's just around the corner," she led him away from Pappy's, never letting go of his arm. "I've been thinking all night what I might be able to tell you about Dick, but I don't think I know anything to help. I still haven't heard from him."

"That's okay. I need to eat lunch anyway."

When they arrived at the small restaurant called Kim She, Clint discovered it was actually a Korean restaurant, not Chinese. It didn't matter, since Clint liked Korean as well as Chinese food. He figured the name should have been a hint.

The hostess recognized Ursula, and the two exchanged greetings while they walked to the table. Ursula recommended the bulgogi, so Clint ordered it for lunch. Despite her own recommendation, Ursula ordered a salad for herself.

"I have to watch my weight if I want to keep my job or get picked up by one of the larger hotels."

"You don't need to worry about your weight, and Pappy's would be crazy to let you go."

"The competition is really rough," she said.

Clint couldn't see it. He didn't doubt the casinos wanted all their employees to look perfect, but most of the women he had seen fell short of that unrealistic goal. He couldn't see any reason why Ursula had to sweat out the competition.

"I have a list of questions that I came up with last night. Before our food arrives do you mind if we run through them?"

"Please, ask me anything," she said.

"Good. Some may seem silly, but if you don't mind. Did Dick ever have any bruising on his face or hands when you saw him?"

"You mean, like if he got into a fight with someone?"

"Yes." Clint wanted to portray himself as a friend and an amateur. He continued through his list of questions. As Ursula predicted, and Clint expected, she wasn't able to provide any information relevant to Dick's death.

Clint walked her back to the casino after lunch. They both agreed to contact the other if they learned anything new. Ursula also suggested that Clint give her a call, if he ever wanted to do something while he was in Las Vegas. Clint said he would, but he knew he probably wouldn't.

He returned to the Paris, packed his belongings, and was about to leave the hotel when he noticed his hotel phone was blinking. He listened to the message which informed him he had a package at the front desk. Leaving the suitcase in the room, he went down to the front desk where the desk clerk handed him a box that had arrived at the hotel from the online retailer, Amazon.

Back in his room, he had to chuckle when he opened the box. It contained a flowered Hawaiian shirt. Obviously, Buzz had it rushed to him after their conversation. He placed the shirt into the suitcase and left the hotel. He drove to the Orleans and checked into the hotel.

Situated about two miles off the strip, the hotel gave the illusion of being isolated. That appealed to Clint, as he wanted to keep a low profile for a few days. He took the elevator to the eleventh floor and located his room. He looked out his window and saw that he had a view of the strip in the distance.

Clint explored the hotel wearing his new shirt until he had to leave. He took a taxi to the intersection Buzz had given him. Once the taxi left, Clint tried to position himself in the same spot where Dick had stood in the intersection. As expected, his phone vibrated a few minutes after his arrival.

"We're in the process of gaining access to the traffic cam right now. You're a few minutes early so everything should be ready on time," Buzz said. "Just so you know what we're going to do, we're going to overlay your image onto his from last week. We should be able to guide you a little more accurately than the GPS."

"You should be able to recognize me," Clint said.

"You got the shirt," Buzz sounded delighted.

"Yes and besides, there's not much pedestrian traffic here today."

"Okay, we're in. Glad to see the shirt fits. Give us a few seconds to synch the two computer screens."

"No problem," Clint said and waited a few seconds.

"Start walking south on the sidewalk," Buzz said, and Clint complied. "A little slower and move over to the edge of the sidewalk closest to the road. Good," Buzz kept giving him instructions. Though the exercise only took him a little over a block before the traffic cam lost sight of him, the experience was profoundly different than his previous tracing of the GPS coordinates. Buzz had him pause a number of times and look one way or the other like Dick had done when he walked this stretch of sidewalk. The pace of the walk and occasional glancing to the right and left gave Clint a much better feeling of what Dick had been doing than his prior efforts.

Buzz had Clint repeat the sequence a second time. This time Buzz asked what Dick might have been looking at when he glanced around. At first, there didn't seem to be any pattern. The strip mall on the right and the buildings on the other side of the road were your typical variety. It struck him when he had almost completed his second walk through.

"Hey, Buzz, I think maybe Dick was looking at street numbers. You know addresses. Where you had me slowing and looking around, the only thing they had in common, was the existence of the street address, just the number of the place, not the street name. Let's walk through it one more time."

He did and became more certain that Dick walked down this sidewalk looking for a certain address. It didn't tell them much, only that it now appeared Dick had headed to a specific place minutes before he was killed.

"You'll be out of sight, but keep following the GPS coordinates for another ten minutes. We'll call you once we think you've gone far enough."

Clint kept walking. He tried to copy the pace that Dick had in the prior block and half. He also kept looking at the building numbers while he walked. Nothing of significance popped out at him. His phone buzzed again.

"You're about two minutes from the place where we think something happened to him," Buzz said.

"There's nothing of interest here. I'll keep walking."

"What's up ahead?"

"Let me get to the spot where you want me, then I can answer your question," Clint said.

"I'll send you a photo," Clint said, once he had reached the spot. He used his cell phone to snap a picture of the large storage unit facility that filled a good portion of the block. "That should give you an idea. It's a large storage operation. It's fenced in. Looks like a fair sized building plus a half dozen rows of storage units."

"It's on your side of the road?" Buzz asked.

"Yes. From my GPS coordinates, it appears to be where Dick went. There's a pedestrian gate, but I need the combo to get in. There's a sign that says vehicle access is off a different street. It's probably the road that parallels this one."

"Do you see anyone around?"

"On the sidewalk, yes, but I don't see anyone inside the fence. Do you have any idea why Dick may have gone into the area?"

"Your guess is as good as mine. Maybe he went to help

someone with something," Buzz offered.

"Could be, that would make sense. It could have been a chance encounter, or he could have come here to help someone with something, too. It wouldn't be hard to jump the fence at the gate. I could go around and try to find out if he had a storage unit here."

"Give that a shot if you don't mind. Once inside that area, he moved around only a little over the next couple of hours, before someone drove him out of the city."

"They waited 'til dark," Clint said.

"We think so. He may have been killed shortly after his arrival there, and the few movements reflected someone moving his body around."

"Like carrying him from one shed to another."

"Anything like that," Buzz said.

"Okay. I'll call you back in a few minutes."

Clint walked around the block to the main entrance to the storage facility. He entered the building he had seen from the other side of the block. Someone's grandmother sat at the reception desk.

"May I help you, young man?" she asked.

"I hope so," Clint said. "I'm trying to track down my brother-in-law. He's missing, and my sister is understandably distraught. It's a long and convoluted story, but I came across a note in his hotel room mentioning this place."

"You think he had a unit here?"

"Maybe. If I give you his name, can you check and see if he has a unit here?"

"We really aren't supposed to pass out that kind of information," the woman said.

"I understand, but I'm only interested to see if he has a unit here. Here's a picture of him." Clint showed the woman the photo of Dick. "His name is Dick Parrot. He might have used Richard, but I doubt it."

Clint noticed a jar sitting on a small table to his right that had a picture of a young boy taped to the front of it. A caption typed below the picture claimed the boy suffered from a cancer and the family was seeking donations. Without saying anything, but in a motion that ensured the woman saw what he was doing, Clint pulled a twenty out of his wallet and shoved it into the jar.

"I don't recognize this picture, but as long as you don't say anything about it, I'll check my records and see if he has a unit here. Is Parrot spelled like the bird?"

"Yes," Clint said.

The woman typed something into her key board and then studied her computer screen. "I'm sorry, but I have no record of anyone going by the name Parrot here."

"Thanks. It was a long shot." Clint turned to leave.

"And thank you for your donation. He's a sweet little boy, and there's not much hope for him."

Clint nodded at the woman and left the building. He thought of the donation as an indirect bribe that worked. Now he felt a little guilty that he had only donated the money to get the information he wanted.

CHAPTER 16

Theresa Deer sat alone in the back corner of the Panera Bread café in Alexandria. Amy Swanson had agreed to meet her there at ten thirty. Deer glanced at her phone that sat on the table in front of her. It read ten forty. Deer knew the D.C. area traffic was slow at best and could be ruthless without warning. Even those with the best intentions could find themselves running ten to fifteen minutes late.

Deer felt her anxiety build during the wait, and she began tapping her fingers on the table. She wanted to talk to Amy. She and Buzz finally discovered an anomaly that she wanted to pursue. She had called Amy to ask for her assistance, but Amy had the morning off and couldn't talk on her personal cell phone. They agreed to meet here.

A few minutes later, Deer saw a baby blue Kia Soul pull into the parking lot. Amy climbed out of the car and hurried into the café. Deer waved, and Amy walked over to her.

"I've already ordered," Deer said. "Go ahead and get something for yourself."

Amy said okay and veered to the counter. She came back carrying something foamy in a large cup.

"What's up?" Amy asked as she sat down.

"As you suspected, my profiler didn't help much. Male or female, in their mid-thirties to forties, most likely a westerner, yadda – yadda."

"I guess then that's not why you wanted to meet," Amy said.

"No. I've been trying to track the movement of funds via the Dark Net or, if you prefer, the Deep Web, and may have discovered something," Deer said.

"The Dark Net? That's a mess to weed through. Must have taken a lot of patience."

"I let the computers do the weeding. Believe me, I don't have the time. I ran dozens of different scenarios. At some point, the digital signature of any payments made to the killers had to exist. We even ran searches to see if someone used BitCoin, the digital currency," Deer said.

"Seems unlikely. Most killers I would think would want cash or gold. Never heard of one dabbling in the world of digital currency."

"I agree. Getting to the point, we discovered that on two occasions someone deposited a little over a million dollars into an internet bank named Banco Dueno that does micro-loan business in the third world. Each time, the same amount of money was withdrawn two weeks later from the bank. The money on both withdrawals was sent to the same Swiss account. From there, I have reason to believe it was split into smaller accounts."

"Okay," Amy said. "There's more?"

"The two days on which the money was transferred to the Swiss account happened to be the day after each of the two killings."

"You mean McPherson and the South American?"

"Yes," Deer said. "My problem is that while I have found several significant deposits going into Banco Dueno a couple weeks before the attack in Mallorca. I can't find any matching withdrawal after the attack."

"That attack might not have been considered a success, so payment was withheld. Have to admit, I'm impressed with your discovery. How did you do it?"

"I'm a small operation, but I have very good access and can develop my own search parameters. I don't compete for space within my own organization, and fortunately, no one reprioritizes or rewrites my parameters. I also have good access to both the intel side and the law enforcement side."

"Well, I'm jealous. I have four or five people deciding if my requests for data should even get approved. So, what can I do to help you?"

"I'll send you the data I have. I'm trying to work both ends of the money trail, and it's slow going. Anything you can do or have your people in the field do to identify who's involved with these transactions could break this wide open for us."

"I'm not familiar with Banco Dueno. I guess that means Dream Bank or Bank of Dreams. I'll do my best. Like you, I'll be happy when this gets resolved. There are a lot of important people who are getting concerned," Amy said.

"They should be."

"We've got a Greek, named Aristotle Eugeny or something like that. He's had a family trip planned to the States for some time and doesn't want to cancel it."

"So, why can't he come?"

"He was at the villa in Mallorca. He was tight with McPherson. Two days ago, Greek security stopped someone they thought had Eugeny under surveillance. The individual tried to shoot his way out of it and was killed. He had no ID on him. We don't know who he was. The Greek government doesn't want Eugeny travelling abroad, but he's insisting. The Greeks have asked our government for assistance in keeping him safe."

"For a civilian?" Deer asked.

"Yes. Naturally they're hesitant to provide any direct support, but the President and senior congressional leaders are all over Homeland Security and us to discover who's behind the killings and get rid of them."

"Get rid of them?"

"They exaggerate, but they're extremely anxious."

"When and where is Eugeny coming to visit?" Deer asked.

"In two days, he'll be here with his wife, two sons, and a

daughter. All the kids are now adults. I think one of the sons is married, but he's leaving his family behind."

"Do we have any indication they might be targeted while they are here?" Deer asked.

"No."

"Are they coming here to D.C.?"

"No, Las Vegas," Amy said.

Deer did her best to suppress a smile. "Las Vegas? I guess that makes sense. Are they meeting any other Bilderbergers while they're there?"

"Not that we know. It's apparently just what he said, a long planned family vacation. Ever been there?"

"A few times," Deer said. "Know where he'll be staying?"

"Caesars Palace, not Greek, but I guess close enough. Those places have good security. He'll bring his own, and I imagine State will find a way to enhance his security, too."

"I've looked at cash flows in and out of Vegas as part of my search for the money trail. Unfortunately, several hundred millions circulate through the city every week. There's a steady flow of dollars bouncing back and forth with Macau. A couple of their bigger casinos are affiliated with some of the ones in Vegas."

"I know," Amy said. "Think some of the money used by our group of assassins runs through there?"

"It might. I lost the trail of some of the money flowing into Banco Dueno as it bounced around between Singapore and Macao."

The two talked for another fifteen minutes before Deer said she had to go. They both agreed to further study the money trail and talk again in a few days. While Deer drove back to her office, she thought about the information that had caused her to send first Dick and then Clint to Las Vegas. If the Greek billionaire's trip had been planned for some time, his assassination may have been in the works long before the attack at Mallorca. She almost ran a stop sign in her hurry to get back to her office. She told herself to slow down and stay focused. Time to stop chasing Dick's killer, too, she thought. They had enough to share what they had with the police. She needed to get her hunter back on the trail of the real prey.

CHAPTER 17

"If the storage facility has security cameras, why can't we hack into them?" Dolly asked.

"It's an older system. The cameras are hardwired into the system," Buzz replied.

"What do you suppose happened there?

Buzz had had this same conversation with Deer more than once, but Dolly had not participated in their discussions. "We think he either responded to someone in distress or to help someone move something."

"You don't think whatever happened to him occurred out in the open, do you? If it did the security cameras, wireless or not, might have caught something. Someone from the street might have seen it."

"That's right. Since there have been no reports to the police, our best guess is that he entered one of the units and was shot by someone he never saw."

"Someone may have shouted for help. It could've been someone the killer or killers had as a prisoner. He or she may have been able to shout for help, and Dick responded," Dolly said nodding her head.

"Yeah, that's the theory."

"But what happened to the other person?"

"Might have been killed and stashed elsewhere or delivered to someone for whatever purpose that person had in mind," Buzz said.

Theresa Deer interrupted their conversation by entering the office. "Something's up. Give me two minutes and come into my office." She walked by them and into her office.

Buzz and Dolly looked at each other.

"Hope it's the break we've been looking for," Buzz said.

The two refilled their coffee cups, grabbed something on which to take notes, and marched into Deer's office.

"A Greek billionaire by the name of Aristotle Eugeny, a regular with the Bilderberg Group, is coming to the U.S. the day after tomorrow. Lucky for us, he's going to Las Vegas. Other than Clint, we've called everyone else home, right?"

"Yes. The last got home this morning," Buzz said.

"No matter. Dolly, get everything you can on this Greek, and why didn't we know he was coming?"

"We should have," Buzz said. "Do we know when he made his flight reservations?"

"Long before all this started," Deer said. "Next time we need to remember to look backwards for travel arrangements. We would have caught it when Customs processed him in, but that could have been too late."

"Sorry, ma'am, we should've done that," Buzz said.

"Well, we know now that he's coming, and that he'll be staying at Caesars Palace. He's bringing his whole family, and it's a trip they've had planned a long time. Dolly, find out when he made his arrangements to travel." She turned her attention to Buzz. "We need to find out when our mysterious friends first turned up in Vegas and compare the dates."

"Do you want Clint to move into Caesars Palace?" Dolly asked.

"No. Probably better if he's not registered there."

"He moved to the Orleans yesterday," Buzz said.

"Trying to save us money?" Deer said with a grin.

"He said he just wanted to get off the strip," Buzz said.

"No matter. In fact, he may be better hidden out there," Deer said.

"Want me to call him and update him on this Greek?" Buzz asked.

"Not yet. Let's find out as much as we can, and then I'll give him a call later today. Dolly, are you still talking to your friend, Weaver, at State?"

"Now and then, but he'll talk to me."

"Good. Try to find out what State is doing to protect Eugeny while he's here. He doesn't have any official status, but he's big time in Greece, and they have asked our government to help keep him safe while he's here."

"Will do," Dolly said.

"Let's meet again in here at four. I need as much as you can get me by then," Deer said.

The meeting adjourned and the three focused on their tasks. Once the two left her office, Deer typed a search query into her computer. Her search didn't confine itself to one search engine. The computer's software automatically sent the request out to the major public websites, such as Google and Yahoo, and to those not too public, including international and national intelligence and criminal databases. The query simply said "Banco Dueno Las Vegas."

CHAPTER 18

Clint sat up from his lounge chair by the pool. His mind continued to theorize what happened to his fellow hunter. Nothing seemed to be especially odd about the storage units where Dick had been killed. He agreed with Deer that it would have been hard for someone to get the drop on Dick and force him to go with him or them before killing him. It could've happened, but it wasn't likely.

He envisioned Dick walking by the units and hearing someone inside the compound scream or call out for help. Dick might have responded by jumping the fence and found a person injured or restrained in some way. In his mind, Clint saw a van backed up to a unit. The person calling for help could be in either the van or the storage unit. Once he found the victim, Dick's suspicions should have been heightened, yet someone still got close enough to shoot him in the back of the head. If the person he was trying to help was crying or trying to say something, Dick might not have heard the killer approach him. If the person was also blindfolded, he or she might not have been able to warn Dick of the killer's approach.

It made sense to Clint, even the fact that only one body was dumped out in the desert. The killer would have searched Dick's clothing. Once the killer realized that he had just killed a federal agent, he did his best to dispose of the body where it might not be found and tossed the gun, phone, and credentials into a lake. This would explain why the phone, weapon, and credentials had not yet been located. The second victim might or might not still be alive. Clint didn't want to think about that person. There were too many possibilities, and none of them were good.

Even for this time of year, the Las Vegas sun started to burn his already tanned body. He had expected a call from Buzz or Deer, but none had come yet. He left the poolside and went in search of lunch. He hoped when the call came, it would take his mind off Dick.

"Something's happening," Deer said.

"With the group or with Dick's murder?"

"One of the Bilderberg group is coming there the day after tomorrow."

"A coincidence?" Clint asked.

"Not likely. He's a Greek by the name of Aristotle Eugeny. He's bringing his family, and they're staying at Caesars Palace."

"Think he's a target?"

"Yes. He had a long time friendship with McPherson. He's part of the industrial side of the Bilderbergers, old money and all that."

"So are you thinking that there is an eco-terrorist group behind this?" Clint asked.

"No, not in the sense of an organization. I'm thinking there may be an individual within the Bilderberger Group who might be on his own personal crusade. I think he may have hired the killers. My interest is in the killers, not him," Deer said.

"So, what are my instructions?"

"Get familiar with Caesars Palace today, and make sure you have a full tank of gas. Other than that, I just want you to stay in the shadows. I'm trying to pin down what the Greek's security will be like. Once I have that, I'll get back with you. Buzz is sending you photos of the Greek and his family. We'll include any photos we can dig up of his security detail."

"Okay, I'll head over to the Palace after this call," Clint said.

"Gotta go," Deer said and hung up.

Clint didn't mind refocusing his efforts. He felt he was at a dead end on Dick's death anyway. He did wonder where Dick was walking to on the night of his death. He was certain it wasn't the storage facilities. If it had been, he would have entered through the front entrance. If he had time later maybe he would continue on the path Dick would've taken if he hadn't been drawn into the storage compound.

Over the next twenty four hours, Clint became very familiar with Caesars Palace. He also studied all the buildings next to it. Caesars wasn't only a hotel, it was a large complex that included a casino, theaters, shops, restaurants, pools, etc. There were a lot of ways into the facility, and thousands of people came and went from it every day. On a normal day the place employed hundreds of security personnel. He wondered how much they would increase security during the Greek's stay.

Clint could see why Aristotle Eugeny and his family might like to stay at Caesars Palace. The place exuded opulence and class, and it brought one's mind back to the era of ancient Mediterranean empires. With a little imagination or ignorance, you could think of the ancient Greeks instead of the Romans.

Clint's phone buzzed as he walked along the shops in the hotel.

"He's arriving tonight in a private jet," Buzz said. "They decided to come in tonight rather than tomorrow morning."

"Good. Keep the bad guys guessing."

"You have the photos?"

"Yes. Got any photos of the assassins?" Clint asked.

"I wish. Nice place isn't it?"

"It is. Seems older than the Paris, I guess it is though, but I like it just as much. You should finagle a trip out here, Buzz."

"I wish."

"Do you know the time of their arrival?"

"Seven thirty, but it's just them so the time could change. I'm sure a private limo will meet them and take them directly to the hotel."

"I'll stay out of the way," Clint said.

"Good luck, man," Buzz said and hung up.

Clint figured the family wouldn't pass through the normal arrival area at the airport, if they even landed at McCarran International. He remembered something about a separate terminal at the airport that handled all the very high rollers and their private jets. The Hughes terminal, he thought, named after the billionaire recluse Howard Hughes.

Clint also guessed they wouldn't have to stand in line for check-in at the hotel. He wanted to get a look at them to insure the pictures he had matched the real persona. Not necessary, Clint knew, but something he wanted to do.

The trip didn't have an announced itinerary. Eugeny and his family had come to Las Vegas for a family vacation, no business. So, unless the killers had knowledge of some excursion that he didn't, the assault on Eugeny would most likely occur in or around the hotel. Clint agreed with Deer that the other family members would only be in danger if they were near Aristotle when the attack took place.

At eight that evening, Clint found a seat in a small side bar inside the casino that gave him a good view of a main entryway into the casino from the hotel portion of the complex. There were other entrances, but this was the one Clint thought the Eugeny's would use. He bet himself that within one hour of the plane's arrival one or more of the family members would enter the casino right in front of him.

He had barely finished a glass of red wine, when he noticed a solid looking man stop a few feet away with his back to Clint.

"Jake?" Clint asked.

Jake Anderson turned around and upon seeing Clint, smiled. "Well, how are you doing tonight?"

Clint could tell that Jake didn't remember his name. "Doing well. This is a fascinating place. Are you working here now?"

"Part time gig. I'm still at Pappy's, probably always will be. They just needed extra people here for a couple days."

"Your place doesn't mind?" Clint asked.

"Are you kidding? He loves doing favors for the big boys. Say, you were looking for someone. Right?"

"Yeah."

"Find him?" Jake asked.

"No. I gave up. My sister will have to deal with the police or forget about him. I don't mean to sound harsh, but I don't know what else I can do."

"Probably best to let them work it anyway," Jake said. "Clint, right?"

"Yeah."

"Are you staying here?"

"No, just playing tourist for another day or two. This is one classy place."

"Ain't it though," Jake said. He kept glancing at the same entry that Clint had been watching.

A thin man in a well-pressed suit appeared and nodded at Jake and a second person leaning against a row of slot machines a little further inside the casino.

"I have to get back to work. Take it easy, Clint," Jake said. He turned and walked to a position a short distance into the casino.

Clint saw the thin man in the well-pressed suit step to the side, almost out of sight, and talk to someone through what looked like a Bluetooth device attached to his ear. The two sons appeared first, laughing about something as they strolled past Clint. The two wore well pressed slacks and short sleeved shirts. Large watches hung onto their wrists. They looked rich.

A few seconds later, Aristotle Eugeny and his daughter walked by absorbed in some deep conversation. They looked happy together. The old man's hair looked grayer than it had in his photo. Clint didn't get a very good look at the daughter's face, but her jet black hair and tan arms had an appeal of their own. If he remembered the information on her correctly, she was twenty eight.

Clint remained in his seat for another ten minutes to see if the wife appeared, but she didn't. More than likely, she remained in their suite to relax after the long trip. He resisted the temptation to find out where in the casino Eugeny went. If something did happen to the Greek, the last thing Clint needed was to be discovered in a review of the hotel's security video following Eugeny around.

The next day remained uneventful. To satisfy his curiosity, Clint took a cab back to the storage facility. Once there, he went to the spot where he believed Dick jumped the fence to help someone inside. From that location, he continued walking in the direction that Dick had been going. He walked another five minutes and came upon a strip mall that had a handful of shops, a sports bar, and an Italian restaurant. He thought of something Ursula had told him.

Clint walked into a small shop next door to the Italian restaurant. The sign above the door read Maria's Catering. The place looked deserted, but an older woman in an apron appeared in a door opposite the front door moments after Clint entered.

"Welcome, may I assist you?" the woman asked with a strong Italian accent.

"This may sound strange, but I'm trying to track down my brother-in-law for my sister. He came out here last week and has vanished. I think he may have come by here last week, or perhaps called in an order to be picked up."

"Do you have a name?" Something about the woman's expression gave Clint the idea that she remembered something.

"His name is Dick Parrot. I know he was planning a picnic with a friend but disappeared before the picnic happened," Clint said.

"One moment, please." The woman wiped her brow with her sleeve, turned, and walked back through the door from which she had appeared.

Clint looked around at the displays and signs on the wall. A brochure on different pasta sauces had caught his eye, when the woman reappeared.

"A man who identified himself as Dick Parrot did call in and order the Naples luncheon. He said he would come by later that day to pay for it. We prefer to collect payment ahead of time. It struck me odd at the time, because he could have given me a credit card number over the phone. I only remember it because I stayed late that day waiting for him. I finally gave up."

"I think something may have happened to him between the phone call you received and the time he was supposed to come by and pay for the order."

"Oh, I feel so sorry. I was mad at him for not coming, and now I learn that something bad may have happened to him. Have you spoken to the police?"

"My sister has," Clint said.

"And they know nothing?"

"Not yet, so we hope he'll turn up, but I'm not optimistic. It's been too long."

Clint left the catering service and headed back to the Orleans hotel. He wondered, too, why Dick didn't provide his credit card information over the phone. It would have saved him a trip and perhaps saved his life.

The call came at nine in the morning and found Clint in the buffet finishing another ample breakfast.

"The family is taking a drive out to the Hoover Dam this morning. There's been some chatter on a number of different frequencies about it. One of the frequencies is unknown to us. Very little was said on it, but you know we hate not being able to pin down something. Plus, there's too much chatter about the trip anyway, poor security," Buzz said.

"What do you want me to do about it?" Clint asked.

"There's a stretch on the road that would be a good ambush spot. We'll send you the coordinates. A little north of there you'll find a high point on a dirt road that will give you a good view for miles of everything. We'd like you to simply be an observer. Hopefully, nothing will happen, but if something does, you might be in a good spot to see things."

"I imagine he'll have a second car and perhaps a police escort. There will be plenty of observers."

"I know. This group is good though. They seem to always have more firepower than is necessary."

"Okay," Clint said, and the call terminated.

The whole plan sounded dumb to Clint. The odds were low that anything would happen. If they struck out in the open country, how in the world did they think they were going to get away? For that matter, he would be a likely suspect in any roundup of people caught in the general vicinity of an attack on Eugeny. If something did happen, it might not be easy to drive away. State troopers would seal off the few roads in the vicinity immediately. On the other hand, he didn't have anything planned for the day.

Clint left right away. He would be nearly an hour early, but it would give him time to set up and come up with an activity that might explain his being there. An idea popped into his mind that came to him from his hours of walking around. He had passed a shop that specialized in camping and fishing gear. The store had a metal detector displayed in the front window a few days earlier. He hadn't thought about it at the time.

It took him a few minutes to find the store, but once he did, it only took a minute to buy the basic model along with a battery. He doubted that he would find a penny, but there were more than enough people in the world who liked looking for buried treasure to make it a plausible reason for being out in the middle of nowhere.

The drive out of Las Vegas took him on Highway 147 through North Las Vegas and out into the desert. He drove for about thirty minutes and passed a number of intersections with dirt roads and a couple of paved roads. For the most part, however, there wasn't much on this route between Las Vegas and the Hoover Dam. When he arrived at his destination, Clint had doubts about the dirt road that Buzz had recommended. The GPS location that Section had provided put him within ten yards of an unmarked dirt road that didn't exactly intersect with the highway. The dirt road looked like it had been there a long time and might have intersected with an earlier version of the highway. Upgrades to the main road didn't include smoothing any sort of transition from the paved road to the old dirt road.

Clint drove his MKZ slowly over the rocks and weeds that now separated the two roads. He then followed the mostly single lane dirt road as it wound up a small treeless hill. After driving at a snail's pace up the bumpy road for five minutes, Clint reached the apex. The road continued down the other side. Clint drove down a short distance and found a spot where he could turn his car around. He parked it near the top but out of sight of anyone on the highway below.

From the top of the small hill, Clint could see for miles in all directions. He saw a number of other hills and a few blind spots where people could be hiding, but he didn't see any other people. On the highway, a steady but light stream of cars drove by the spot he had under observation. He returned to the car and retrieved the metal detector and a pair of small binoculars. Carrying the items to the top of the hill, he started methodically inspecting the ground with the detector. He tried to act nonchalant, something that came easy since he had little interest in what he was doing. After a few minutes, he started to wonder if the machine worked at all. It hadn't made one beep, and he hadn't found anything.

"Finally," he said to himself when he saw a three car caravan coming his way. From a distance it looked like the three were right on top of each other, but as they got closer, he could see that two of the cars were close, but the third car, a police car, was actually about a hundred yards in front of the other two. An old cream colored van drove at a steady pace a good half mile ahead of the three vehicles, but Clint didn't think it had anything to do with Eugeny's group.

He moved back to a point above his car. Suddenly, the metal detector started chirping. He looked down at the convoy and guessed they were still a mile away. The surroundings still looked peaceful, so Clint leaned down and scratched around the ground with his knife. He struck something hard, and after a few seconds of working his blade against the ground and the item, he saw the corner of what looked like a small strong box.

He stood back up and looked back at the three vehicles driving at him. Two birds appeared in the sky opposite him and made a bee line for the road in front of him. He started to turn his attention back to the cars when he realized what he had seen weren't birds. Not birds, but two drones were making a run at the road.

Clint lifted his binoculars.

"Damn," he mumbled to himself.

CHAPTER 19

Each of the drones carried four small missiles, two under each wing. The drones looked like they had a wing span of about five to seven feet, but Clint knew that was pure guesswork at this range. The cars continued their approach impervious to the threat above them.

Clint ran to his car and started driving toward the spot he left the highway. The dirt road had too many turns for Clint to drive fast, but he pushed the car as much as he dared. Additionally, he tried to keep one eye on the drones which further slowed him down. Rather than attack from the side or head-on, the drones fell in right behind the cars. The lead drone fired two of its missiles at the police car while it flew about thirty yards above the second car in the convoy. The other drone had settled in behind the third vehicle and fired two missiles at it. Both vehicles exploded almost simultaneously. The police car flipped several times with pieces flying everywhere before coming to a stop. The third car, struck by only one of the two missiles, continued down the road dragging its rear end on the pavement, but a secondary explosion caused by the damaged fuel tank engulfed the entire vehicle in a fireball that seemed to disintegrate everything in a surging mass of fire.

Seconds after firing its first two missiles, the rear drone fired two missiles at the remaining black sedan. Both missiles hit and the vehicle lifted off the ground for a few seconds before it bounced back down and came to a stop. Smoke gushed from the broken windows. Clint thought that this middle sedan had to be armored or partially armored as it somehow survived the attack. The first drone circled back and approached the disabled car from the rear.

At the same time, Clint slid the MKZ to a stop on the dirt road parallel to the smoking car. He jumped out of his car and started running toward what he now recognized as a large black Mercedes. As he ran, he saw a figure crawl through a rear window and fall to the ground.

"Here!" Clint shouted.

The person didn't appear to hear him, but she crawled under some instinct to get away from the vehicle. Clint recognized the person as Eugeny's daughter. He ran to her and lifted her from the ground. He looked back at the fast approaching drone and saw two missiles drop from its wings and race toward the Mercedes. Clint sprinted toward his vehicle carrying the woman awkwardly in his arms. The blast knocked him off his feet.

Shaken but not hurt, Clint grabbed the woman under the arms and dragged her the last few yards to his car.

"Get in! I'm on your side," he yelled, while he pushed her into the passenger seat.

She mumbled something unintelligible but managed to get into the car. Clint slammed the door and ran around to his side of the car. Before he got in he looked back at the scene on the road. The large Mercedes smoldered in a hundred pieces scattered around the spot it had been. Its armor, damaged from the first strike, did little to protect the car from the second. The drones flew side-by-side and headed due south, away from the scene. The sound of two or three motorcycles echoed from somewhere across the highway. He saw a minivan approaching the scene on the highway from the southwest.

"We've got to go," Clint jumped behind the wheel.

He gunned the Lincoln and once again steered his car up the dirt road. This time he reached the top in less than two minutes. His passenger looked at him, but her eyes weren't focused.

Grease and blood smeared her otherwise attractive face. Particles of seat cushions and ashes clung to her jet black hair. The tracks of tears lined her face, some with trails of makeup that had begun to run. Her lower lip had either been struck or she had bitten it during the blast. The lip appeared puffy with a small patch of blood trying to dry right below the sore. She wore blue jeans and boots that looked like they've seen better days. Her white blouse was anything but white anymore. She smelled like smoke.

"Elina," Clint said, "can you hear me?"

She turned her head toward him. He could tell she was trying to pull herself together. She lifted a hand and stared at it.

Clint drove the car over the top of the hill and down the dirt road on the other side. He resisted a temptation to stop and go back and look. The road flattened out and became a straight brown line in a brown world. He didn't see anywhere he could hide the car or blend in with other traffic. If a police helicopter flew over in this direction, they would certainly see him.

"What happened?" Elina asked in a slurred, weak voice.

"Your car and the other two were attacked. I'm sorry, but I'm pretty certain you were the only survivor."

"What?" She still seemed confused. She looked at Clint and rubbed her right eye.

Without taking his eyes of the road, Clint reached behind him and felt around until his hand touched something.

"Here, drink this." He handed her a bottle of water that had been rolling around behind his seat for at least a week.

Her hands fumbled at the lid but finally succeeded in unscrewing it. She took a big sip and looked around her again.

"You say everyone was killed?" Her voice sounded strained, but more natural than it had before. She spoke English with only a little accent.

"Yes. I'm sorry. There was nothing anyone could do. Was your father in the car?"

"No," she said and looked at her hands again. "I was alone. Something came up in the last minute. One of his ships is sinking in the Indian Ocean. I wanted to see the Dam, so father said to go without him. He insisted the security team stay with me, since he wasn't going anywhere. One of my brothers wanted to come, but the shipping line is actually his now, so father made him stay."

"Can you move all your fingers and toes?'

She nodded.

"How does your head feel?"

"It hurts and my ears are still ringing, but I think I'm alright."

"Do you know a phone number to reach your father?"

"Of course."

"Okay. Let me make a call first, and then I want you to send a text to your father telling him you're not hurt."

She nodded. "Why did someone want to kill me?"

"I don't believe you were the target. I think they were trying to kill your father."

"My purse!"

"Toast. Literally, it's just toast."

"Oh, I loved that purse and my phone was in it. Dammit!" She stared again at her right hand. "I'm sorry. You say everyone was killed, and I'm upset about losing my purse. It's just that none of this seems real. I didn't know any of them. There was a police car."

"Destroyed. All three cars were destroyed. I was surprised that you got out," Clint said.

"I don't remember. Why are we on this dirt road?" She looked outside the windows and back at him.

"After the explosions, I heard some motorcycles start their engines, and I believe they were coming to make sure everyone was dead. I didn't know where they were coming from, except I knew they weren't coming from behind us, this way. I didn't think it was safe to hang around there or pick a direction that might take us toward them."

"This is crazy," she said and shook her head again. She drank some more water.

Clint's navigation system silently activated, and a highlighted route appeared on the screen. Elina didn't notice. Clint smiled. He didn't need to make that call. Deer or Buzz must have realized he was trying to get away from the scene without being noticed. By now, they were aware of the attack.

"Have you called the police?" Elina asked.

"No. I don't need to be involved with the police."

A hint of fear appeared in her eyes.

"It's a long, long story, best left untold, but please believe me, I'm no threat to you or your family."

"You said I could call my father."

"Texting him would be better."

"No. You say you're no threat to me. I ought to be able to talk to him."

"Okay, but please, I need to stay out of this. No police, no reward, no nothing." Clint handed her his phone.

She took his phone. In her hands, the phone's security features kicked in, and the phone functioned like your basic smart phone. She dialed a number and someone answered immediately.

"Pater," Elina said. She listened and started to cry. She began talking in Greek.

Clint resisted the urge to tell her to speak English. She turned to him, the phone still against the side of her face. "My father says thank you. He wants to meet you."

"Tell him I promise to get you back to him safely."

She talked some more on the phone before turning back to Clint. "What's your name?"

"Max."

She looked at him waiting for a last name.

"Remember, I need to stay out of this. Tell him Max Johnson."

She nodded and talked to her father for another minute.

"My family knows how to be discreet, Max, or whatever your name is." She gave him back his phone. "Where are we?"

"A little north of Las Vegas."

"Are we heading back there?" Elina asked.

"Yes."

"Can we stop somewhere? I need to wash. I can't show up like this. I need different clothes, too."

"We should pass a mall or some place that will work. Elina, do you know why someone would want to hurt your father?"

"You mean kill him?" Clint nodded, and she continued. "Could be lots of reasons. He thinks it's because a very rich and crazy man wants him dead."

"Why?"

"He won't tell the police, but he's told me. I think now he will take his own revenge."

"Why does this man want him dead?"

"Why are you interested, Max?" Elina stretched out "Max" when she said it.

"Let's just say maybe I can help."

Elina smiled. "You are a spy! No, a secret agent." She leaned over and gave Clint a kiss on the cheek. "You are my secret agent."

"I see you've not fully recovered from the explosion."

"My head still hurts, my hands are shaking, but I'm going to be fine. It still seems so unreal, like it didn't happen. I ...., I don't feel anything." Elina took another sip of water and closed her eyes for a couple seconds. "So, secret agent Max, if I give you the name of the man, you will help us?"

"I will do my best. After all, I am your secret agent."

Elina looked out the window and finished the bottle of water.

Clint saw on the navigation display that another turn was coming up. In the distance, he could see a paved road. When the two roads intersected, he turned south onto the two lane paved road.

"His name is Christopher Little. He made his fortune in software and gaming. He also has had good timing on some of his investments. He is new money, very new money, and he does not understand the world. He would like to see all the mining, oil drilling, the heavy commerce, all of it disappear or just go away. He claims we are destroying the world."

Clint didn't challenge her. He could tell by the way she spoke that she believed what she said. She and her father had probably discussed Little in great detail.

"Look," Elina said and pointed ahead of them.

Clint had already seen the buildings that marked their arrival back into civilization.

"There should be someplace along this road where you can get cleaned up," he said.

"Wait," Elina said. Clint glanced at her, and she continued. "Do you have any more water and a jacket or something that I can wear? Maybe it would be better if I changed and washed a little before I get out where there are other people."

"Good idea. Now you're thinking like a secret agent."

The comment brought a big smile to Elina's face. Clint pulled into the parking lot of an old restaurant that had gone out of business years earlier. They were still about a quarter mile from the town or suburb ahead of them. Traffic on the road had been light.

Clint found another bottle of water for Elina and dug a semi-clean towel out of the trunk. Elina got out of the car and took the towel from Clint.

"Let me see that shoulder," Clint said. Her right shoulder had a patch of blood on it that he hadn't noticed before.

Elina peeled back the shirt from her shoulder. A superficial abrasion covered a portion of her shoulder. Fresh blood covered most of the wound, but no blood streamed out of it.

"Yuck. Not much, but I hope it doesn't scar," she said and poured water onto the towel. Using the towel, she washed her face, arms, and finally her shoulder.

Clint unzipped his gym bag in the trunk and pulled out a black San Antonio Spurs tee shirt.

"Oh, let me have that," Elina said.

He handed it to her. She studied it for a moment, and, after taking a quick glance around, she removed her blouse and pulled the tee shirt over her head. She tossed her bloody and torn blouse into the trunk.

"How do I look?"

"You look beautiful." Clint didn't exaggerate. She looked fit and much prettier than she did in her picture.

"I could use some makeup. I'm sure I washed it all off," she said. She went back into the car and lowered the passenger side visor. She took advantage of the mirror to get the last of the dirt and soot off her face. She used her fingers to remove the debris from her hair. "Have a comb?" she asked.

Clint handed her his comb. He walked around the car and got in.

"Back to the hotel or lunch?" he asked. He knew the longer he kept her in his company the more the risk he might be discovered with her. He didn't want to have to answer any questions to the police. At the same time, he enjoyed her company, and she might know something else that could help them identify and track down the people behind the attacks.

"Can we have lunch? I'm in no hurry to face all the questioning."

They drove another five minutes in relative silence before she pointed at a tall billboard advertising a Mexican restaurant.

"How about there?" she asked.

"Sure," Clint said and pulled into the restaurant.

She got out of the car, but then showed some hesitation.

"You okay?"

"I don't know. I feel like I should be ashamed. Why wouldn't I want to talk to the police? Why do I feel so little pity for the others? I survived, but they didn't. Do you know how many there were?"

"No, but don't be hard on yourself. You didn't know them, and no one behaves normally shortly after surviving something like what you went through. It will bother you for some time, but it normally takes a while to settle in."

"Will I see you again?" She asked.

"You want to?"

"Yes," she said and grabbed his arm.

They walked into the restaurant together.

At first, they ate in silence.

Clint took advantage of the silence to text D.C. She didn't seem to notice.

"You think he'll try to kill my father again?"

"I don't know. It will definitely be harder for them now. My guess is that they won't. What about your family? Will they stay in Las Vegas for a few more days?"

"We may have to, but I'm sure my mother will want us to leave as soon as possible. What should I tell them?"

"Who?"

"The police. They will want to know what happened."

"Tell them what you know."

"About you?" she asked.

"Tell them that an old man helped you after you managed to get out of the car. Tell them that you noticed two drones in the air, and that you don't remember much else."

She nodded. "I do remember seeing the drones as they flew away. At least, I think I do. I'll tell them that you're an old, fat man, going bald. Your car was brown, dirty, and old. I'll say we didn't talk much, but that you didn't want anything to do with the police or the press. Maybe I'll say you're a hermit, and your name is Max."

"You're good."

She finally smiled. "I was a teenager once. Plenty of practice. My dad and mom didn't care for any of my friends. I spent two years at UCLA here in America. You think I could tell them anything about my real life?"

"I doubt if you were that bad," Clint said. "By the way, my name is Clint."

"Thanks," she said and squeezed his hand.

"This guy, Little, does your father have any idea who may be helping him or doing the actual killing?"

"No. At least, he has not told me. Little has made comments to a few people that have gotten back to my father. That is all I know."

Not much, Clint thought, but something Deer could look into.

They agreed that she would get out of the car by the Tropicana and walk to Caesars Palace. Clint had suggested she take a cab, but she wanted to walk and to think.

"Can I see you again?" she asked.

"You have a favorite spot in Athens?"

"Of course. Do you have a pen and something I can write on?" She wrote down a name of a night club in Athens and included her phone number. She got out of the car and disappeared into the mass of pedestrians jostling along on their way.

Clint drove on and reached the Orleans in a few minutes. He sat in his car in the parking lot and called Buzz.

"Was the girl with you?" Buzz asked.

"Yes. I think she'll be fine. She was shaken up, but she didn't have any major injuries."

"When the word got out that she survived the attack, we thought you might have helped her. Did you see what happened?"

"Two drones attacked the three cars. I think her limo, a Mercedes, must have been armored because it took the first two missiles fairly well. One of the drones circled back and hit it with two more. She crawled out the window before the second salvo hit. By the time the drones left, all three cars were destroyed. If the optics in the drones picked up her escape, or if they even cared at all about her, I don't know, but they left once they destroyed the three vehicles. I heard a couple of motorcycles start up after the attack. They might have guided the strike and were leaving, or they could have been coming in to clean up any stragglers. I didn't stick around. I grabbed her and we left. Seemed like the prudent thing to do."

"Hold on a minute," Buzz said. Clint could hear him talking to someone. "Which direction were they flying when they left the scene?"

"South, almost due south."

"Okay. Did you see anything else?"

"No, but Elina believes Christopher Little is behind the attack. Apparently, her father has told her that he thinks Little is behind all the killings," Clint said.

"I suppose she doesn't have proof?" Buzz asked.

"No, she said that her dad claims that Little thinks all mining, and the rest of the so-called polluting industries, should be banned."

"Didn't expect she had any proof, but at least we have someone on whom we can focus. We'll do some work at our end. I'll call you before I go home tonight."

The call ended, and Cliff went to his room.

CHAPTER 20

For the first time in several weeks, Theresa Deer felt the adrenalin rushing through her. She had several leads she could pursue, and she was ready. Dolly would monitor any large transfers of money from Banco Dueno to Switzerland. She already had Buzz following up with Homeland Security and NSA on the drones. She personally went after Little, determined to peel back every layer of his finances and communications.

Elina Eugeny's interview with the police and the FBI had already been up-channeled, along with the results of the initial analysis of the crime scene. While both the police and the FBI would have rather kept the results quiet, there were too many people in high government positions who wanted to know all about the incident. Leaks to the press, especially out of the State Department, became a steady flow. Besides any information that would identify Clint as her rescuer, Elina and her family did hold back one additional thing, their suspicions about Christopher Little.

"Think we should?" Buzz asked Deer while seated across from her in her office.

"Yes. Marvel is a perfect way to get some outside focus on him. She pursued our last anonymous tip, and while she didn't get the scoop, she knows the information she received was accurate. I think she'll jump all over this. You know he's not our target anyway, unless we find out that he's more than just the client. We're after the team that's doing the killings and especially the head of that team."

Buzz jotted down a few lines while Deer spoke. This

behavior didn't bother her. She knew he had the rare ability to write and listen at the same time.

"How's this?" Buzz asked and held his note pad up at an angle. "Could that someone I mentioned in my last text to you be Christopher Little? He seems to have had a hatred for both McPherson and Eugeny."

"Good, but let's add something about the environmental piece," Deer said. "I don't know how smart she is, so I don't mind spoon feeding her where we want her to go."

Buzz did some edits on his note pad. "Maybe this would be better," he said and then read what he had written. "Could that someone I mentioned in my last text to you be Christopher Little? He seems to have had a hatred for the way both McPherson and Eugeny were destroying Earth's environment."

"Perfect. Send it out now. I need to make a few phone calls." Without waiting for Buzz's departure, she picked up the phone and dialed Amy Swanson at the CIA.

Buzz returned to his desk, located Mary Marvel's phone number, and sent the text. He knew Little's billions would make any newspaper hesitant to publish something tying him to the killings without tangible evidence that would link him to them. At the same time, the possibility of discovering that link and being the first to publish would have them drooling. Buzz supposed Marvel would be less concerned about any legal consequences and would be hard to hold back. Besides, from what Clint had told him, and he had since verified, Marvel already had a deep dislike for the Bilderberg Group.

While the staff at Special Section worked the phones and their computers, Clint lounged poolside at the Orleans and studied an email sent to him that morning. The email took his mind off the events of the past few days. In fact, after reading the email, he stretched out, closed his eyes, and tried to figure out how he really felt about the note Dr. Barbara White had sent him. In the past year, they had become very close. She had penetrated what Clint had long thought was an impenetrable wall around his heart. From the start, they had made no commitments to each other. Both claimed they weren't looking for a permanent relationship, and neither expected the other to "stay true." Clint remembered those were her words, but he had felt the same way.

The email said what Clint half expected. She volunteered to practice medicine in Africa; something she had always thought would be a noble cause anyway, because she had fallen too quickly and too hard for Clint. She reminded Clint that it had only been a short time since she had divorced her husband for cheating on her. She felt things were moving too fast. "My fault," she had said in her email. She went on to say that she accepted a request to stay on for a full year. She needed time. She added a lot more of what Clint thought was gibberish about it being her fault, that he had done nothing wrong, etc., etc.

The fact that the email bothered him reminded Clint how hard he, too, had fallen for her. He understood Barbara's need for space. He worked and then reworked a response. He wanted to let her know that he understood, that she should take whatever time she needed, and that he wanted only the best for her. Although not satisfied with any of his drafts, Clint finally punched the send button on the response he thought sounded the least awkward.

The hot sun eventually forced Clint to abandon the poolside. He spent nearly an hour working out before showering and taking a much needed nap. Another day passed by before the break came.

The call woke Clint at four fifteen in the morning. He saw that the call came from Washington D.C. and mumbled a hello into the phone.

"Wake up," Buzz said. "We have a break."

"And I need to know about it now?"

"Yeah, we need you to check out and head north on I-15.

You know the guy in Switzerland you sent us the photo of?"

"What about him?" Clint asked.

"He's been there and is currently driving north. We believe he's in a white Cadillac, a rental that we're tracking. We've also got a fix on his phone, but he's either got it turned off or has gotten rid of it already."

"Okay." Clint had a dozen questions, most of which he knew had already been thought about by Buzz and Deer, so he kept them to himself.

"The sooner you can get going the better. Once you get out of Vegas, I'll give you another call, and we can talk longer." The line went dead.

It took Clint only a few minutes to throw everything together and check out. When he started his car, he noticed that the navigation system kicked on, already remotely set by Buzz. The city traffic posed no problem this early, and the lights of Las Vegas had started to fade behind him when Buzz called.

"Your target is now heading north on Highway 93. He's moving fast and is about eighty miles ahead of you, but we don't need for you to catch up with him yet. We got a break yesterday afternoon. The guy whose picture you took, his name's Rafael DuPane, if that's his real name, arrived at Las Vegas International from Mexico City three days ago. The facial recognition system we've been running with Customs caught it, but we didn't get the news until yesterday. He has a French passport and supposedly is a lawyer."

"A lawyer?"

"Yeah. He stayed at the Aria. We've been gathering data on what he's been doing in Vegas. Nothing incriminating, unfortunately, but we were able to put him in the Cadillac, which by the way is rented to someone else, most likely the man driving DuPane around."

"How did you get the phone?" Clint asked.

"Glad you asked. The girl's lead paid off. After the attack, or I should say after the word got out that Eugeny was not in the car, Little made a call to the cell phone. It's the only call we can find that Little made to that number. The call was brief, but we got a fix on the receiving phone. That phone has been used twice since. Both times the GPS coordinates of the call put it in the Cadillac while the Cadillac was moving."

"How did you get onto Little's phone so quickly?"

"Don't ask and never underestimate Deer. We're digging into the names we've learned and are tracing DuPane backwards through Mexico City. It shouldn't surprise you that we're hitting dead ends everywhere."

"So maybe we shouldn't underestimate DuPane," Clint said.

"That's right. Clint, we're working on a couple scenarios to encourage the cops and the FBI to pick him up. Hopefully, you won't have anything more than a long drive home."

"I've heard that before."

"I know. We'll stay in touch."

Clint didn't expect a call back for a few hours, but twenty minutes later Buzz called again.

"The car and the phone separated. It appears they stopped briefly, probably to get gas, the phone was turned back on, and when the car drove off the phone stayed behind. Don't know if a person stayed behind with the phone, or if DuPane's wiser now and simply ditched the phone," Buzz said.

"I'd bet he trashed it," Clint said.

"Maybe so. I already put the location into your navigation system. We don't need you to go looking for the phone. We're more interested in who and what you see at the location."

The sky in the East had taken on a red hue as Clint turned off the highway and into the parking lot of the gas station and convenience store where the cell phone was supposed to be. The last road sign he had seen indicated he wasn't too far from Alamo, Nevada. Clint pulled up to one of the pumps and began filling up his MKZ. He looked around at the barren landscape and didn't see another building. A lone jeep sat parked in front of the gas station near the front door. No one else was getting gas. He saw four outdoor trash cans where someone could have dumped a phone.

After he finished filling the tank, Clint entered the station and walked directly to the row of coffee pots positioned near the center of the store. He glanced around and saw a young clerk playing a game on a tablet he held on his lap, impervious to the world around him. A man, about his age, with less hair on the top of his head than on his face, sat at one of the two small tables drinking coffee and looking out the front window. Across from him sat another cup of coffee in front of an empty chair.

He decided to postpone the coffee and entered the restroom. Once inside, Clint went directly to the nearest urinal, while noticing that someone occupied one of the stalls. As he zipped up his jeans, a toilet flushed behind him. He moved to the sink to wash his hands, when the man came out of the stall and started to walk by him. Their eyes met in the mirror in front of Clint. Recognition came instantly to both of them.

The man reached inside his lightweight jacket. Clint didn't wait to see what came out. He spun and punched the man, striking the man's nose and doing his best to drive his fist through the man's head. The man staggered backwards against the wall. Clint thought he broke the man's nose and saw that the man's eyes looked out of focus. Despite this, the man's hand managed to come out from under the jacket holding a short barreled revolver.

Clint stepped to his left as the man fired the revolver. The round tore into the sink. The man tried to turn and face Clint, but he had not regained control of his senses. Clint grabbed the revolver with his right hand. At the same time, he struck the man's nose again with a straight left using his open palm. A gasp escaped from the man's lips, and after bouncing off the wall, he started to collapse into Clint. The man's nose had turned into a bloody mess, so Clint spun the man's body to face the sink.

Suddenly, the door to the restroom flew open, and the man who had been sitting at the table charged in with a pistol drawn and ready. Not having much choice and little time to think about options, Clint pulled the limp man's body closer to him a split second before the second man fired. Clint had no time to aim, and in close quarters with a limp body pressed against his, he could do little but reach around the man and pull the revolver's trigger. The second man's momentum carried him into the room despite the nasty hole that suddenly appeared in his throat. Clint stepped back and let the first man collapse to the floor. The second man fell next to his friend.

Clint saw a hole in the front of the jacket of the man whose nose he had broken. He lifted the edge the jacket and verified the presence of a bullet wound that had torn into the man's chest right where his heart should be. He grabbed a paper towel and rubbed the revolver with it. Using the paper towel to hold the short barrel of the revolver, he pressed the gun back into the dead man's right hand. He put the paper towel into his pocket.

A quick inspection disclosed that both individuals had stopped breathing. He took pictures of both men, and for a second, he thought about searching them for the cell phone but decided against it. Clint checked himself in the mirror to ensure there were no obvious signs of blood on him, washed his hands, and left the bathroom.

The clerk still sat in his chair focused on the tablet in his hands. Clint noticed the young man's head also swayed back and forth. Clint poured himself a cup of coffee and went to the counter to pay. The clerk looked up, put down the tablet, and pulled a pair of ear buds out of his ears.

"That will be a dollar forty five," the clerk said.

Clint gave him exact change.

"Did you hear something? It was like a loud pop or something. I thought I heard it a minute ago," the clerk asked.

"I'm not sure. The man who was sitting over there was arguing with another man in the restroom and slammed a stall door in the men's room. That made a loud noise."

"Are they fighting?"

"Not while I was in there. They were just arguing," Clint said.

"Good."

Clint left, and as he walked to his car, he looked back and saw the clerk putting the ear buds back into his ears. The clerk's head started to sway. It might be an hour or so before someone discovered the bodies. The sun blazed low in the horizon, but it was still early, and this was a long way from nowhere.

Clint sent the pictures to Buzz and drove off. Once the car reached the speed limit, he called Buzz.

"I ran into some trouble at your gas station," Clint said.

"Not much, I hope," Buzz said. "We got the pictures. You're okay?"

Clint explained what had happened to include recognizing one of the two men from his encounter in Switzerland.

"I wonder if one of them had the phone, or if they were there to see if anyone came looking for the phone?" Buzz asked.

"Could be either way. I imagine you'll learn about it after the police discover what phones they had on them. Any way you can delete my presence from the service station's security footage? I'd rather not get sucked into the investigation."

"We'll see what we can do, but no promises. It might be easier to deal with this in other ways."

"These guys are smart, Buzz. If I hadn't recognized one of them, things might have gone a lot differently. If they were there to see if someone was tracking the phone, it means they have learned a lesson from Switzerland, and left it for bait," Clint said.

"That might be why they left someone who could recognize you."

Clint imagined if the man had been at the table when he arrived, rather than in the restroom, he could have seen and recognized Clint before he even entered the building. Things could have turned out a lot worse.

"Are they still driving north?" Clint asked.

"Yes, and keeping the car at the speed limit."

"Won't be long before they discover something's up. They probably expect the two to check in every hour or so."

"We're monitoring all the police frequencies in the area. Something should pop soon. By the way, the Greeks are cutting their vacation short by a couple of days. They're heading home, and if you're interested, the medical report on the daughter is that she only suffered minor injuries."

"I figured she was okay," Clint said. "She said her mother would insist that they go home. Have you picked up anything that might indicate the old man is plotting his revenge?"

"No. Deer thinks he won't make a move until he's safely back in Greece. He'll be careful not to leave any trail that might connect him to whatever action they might take."

"Does Deer think Little is behind the killings?" Clint asked.

"Yes. He's paying someone to do them. How he knew of this group of killers is what she'd love to know. We've started to peel back a few layers of the onion, but we still have a long way to go. These latest two bodies should help."

The call ended. Clint kept the car on the trail of the white Cadillac some one hundred miles ahead of him. He looked around and didn't see a cloud in the sky. He also didn't see another car on the road. Glad he didn't leave without getting the cup of coffee, Clint found an old Johnny Dollar radio show on the Radio Classics channel, and put the car in cruise control.

CHAPTER 21

Throughout the rest of the day, Clint followed the Cadillac's trail. The route took him north on US Highway 93. He passed through towns he had never heard of like Pioche and Jackpot. Always staying at least eighty miles behind his prey, by mid-afternoon, he found himself in Idaho.

His phone rang for the first time since his morning conversation with Buzz.

"Hey, it's me again," Buzz announced.

"What's up?"

"A lot, the Cadillac has stopped about fifty miles ahead of you in Buhl. It's been there for a while, but we don't want you there. We're trying something else. There's a small town just outside of Twin Falls called Filer. We want you to go there and find a place to get a bite to eat. Do whatever you need to do until our plan with the Cadillac pans out."

"That's fine with me," Clint said. "What happened when the two bodies were discovered?"

"That's moving slow, but after all, that place is pretty isolated. The bodies were discovered about a half hour after you left the place. It took fifteen minutes for the first police to show up, and another half hour before anyone who could process the crime scene arrived. Another thing, you can quit worrying about the security cameras. They haven't worked there for six months."

"You would think as remote as that place was that they would have functioning security cameras."

"People are cheap. The system broke down, and the owners never got around to fixing them. Anyway, from what we've been able to get, the clerk hasn't yet mentioned that you were even there. Everyone seems to be willing to accept the possibility that the two shot each other."

"At some point, a smart investigator will wonder how the one man's nose got broken," Clint said.

"Maybe, but from what we've been able to learn, by the time they were discovered, they were laying in each other's blood. The scene was contaminated by the first couple of responders. I guess they felt obligated to ensure they were both dead. Anyway, the good news is we have two new names to work with, and law enforcement will soon have fingerprints and DNA. They'll also be working the car and the phones the two had."

"Has anyone linked them to the attack on Eugeny?" Clint asked.

"We already suggested that possibility to the FBI. They'll be closely monitoring the investigation. They may even take the case over from the locals. We'll see," Buzz said.

After the call, Clint drove another thirty minutes before he pulled into a gas station with a Subway sandwich shop. Unless it had started moving again, the Cadillac should be some fifteen miles ahead of him. He topped off the gas tank and went inside to get a sandwich.

The station had seen better days. A handful of the ceiling tiles had holes in them, the entire place needed a good cleaning, and the air smelled like the walls had mildew in them. Clint didn't see any other customers in the place. No one occupied the space behind the counter to the gas station, but a woman, fortyish, with dyed blond hair, and too much make up on, leaned against the Subway counter and chatted with a woman of similar age wearing a Subway apron. This second woman seemed nondescript until Clint got close enough to see she sported a black eye.

Both women stopped talking when Clint approached. The two smiled and looked at him like they were sizing him up for their next meal.

"What would you like?" the Subway attendant asked.

Clint ordered a Black Forest Ham sandwich and tried not to stare at the woman's black eye.

"Don't worry about Liz," the blond said. "She gave worse than she got. What brings you way out here?"

"Driving up to Canada to scope out a few fishing spots," Clint said.

"By yourself?" Liz asked from behind the counter.

"Yeah, just me."

Clint paid for his sandwich and walked around a bunch of Cheetos that someone had spilled on the floor between the counter and the two small tables provided for the rare customer. He wondered how many days the Cheetos had been there. The two women resumed their conversation, every now and then giggling and looking his way.

His phone rang shortly after he sat down.

"They've left the Cadillac," Buzz said.

"What do you mean?"

"They've abandoned it. We left an anonymous tip with the Buhl police that the vehicle was used to transport a minor across state lines for illicit purposes."

"Big words, did they understand what you meant?" Clint asked.

"Our tip was a little blunter. Anyway, the locals checked it out, only to find out that the Cadillac had been left there. The three men in it climbed into a black sedan, possibly a Toyota Avalon, and drove off."

"Any tag number or other way to trace the Avalon?"

"Washington state tags are all we know at the moment. We were lucky to get that. They parked the Cadillac off the main road. An old man lives in a house across the road and about a hundred yards away. While they left the Cadillac just inside the city limits, they chose a spot where there's not much around."

"How'd the old man see it?"

"When he saw the police inspecting the Cadillac, he walked up to them from his house and told them what he had seen. He had been inside looking out his kitchen window. He said it gave him a clear view. The white Cadillac pulled off the road, and its occupants got out and fiddled with the engine for a few minutes before the black sedan arrived. The old man was just about to go out to offer his help when they all got in the sedan and drove off. When they left, they drove right by his house."

"So where does that leave us?" Clint looked at the two women staring at him. "I'd just as soon get back out on the road."

"For now, we'd like you to head up to Boise. I'm not too sure what will happen next. Unlike a few days ago, we're in information overload right now. It should take you a couple of hours to get to Boise. By then, hopefully, we'll have a new plan."

Clint finished his sandwich and left. He wasn't surprised to see a new route in his car's navigation system. He drove off into the afternoon sun.

CHAPTER 22

"We got a break," Dolly said as she stuck her head into Deer's office.

"What did we get?" Deer asked, looking up from the two computer screens on her desk. She noticed the clock said they only had five minutes until six. Another long day, she thought.

"Police in Buhl discovered that the man who rented the Cadillac called the rental company and told them he was leaving the Cadillac, and where they could find it. He claims it broke down, and that he wasn't going to pay any pick up fee."

"Do you think the Cadillac broke down or that they simply wanted to ditch the Cadillac?"

"My bet is that they wanted to change cars. The good news is that we identified the phone number of the phone that called the rental agency. We verified that the call was made from Buhl, Idaho. We also have the name and address of the phone's owner, and the best part is that we now know the phone is moving northwest on I-84."

"Good work, Dolly. Set the new coordinates into Clint's navigation system," Deer said.

"Should I call him?"

"Not yet. Let's find out all we can about this guy. Run the same background routine we used on the two men this morning. Let me know of any commonalities."

"Yes, ma'am," Dolly said trying to not show her disappointment as she left.

Deer stared after her. She had no problem discerning the disappointment in Dolly's voice. Deer wondered how she should handle this fixation Dolly had developed concerning

Clint Smith. The small office had an unwritten rule that forbade fraternization between the staff and the hunters. The staff had to make decisions that sent the hunters into harm's way. They didn't need a lot of emotional baggage that might affect good decision making.

Deer considered making light of the whole matter, even joking with Dolly about it, but that might send her the wrong message. If the rule had been set in writing, she could simply tell Dolly to read the rule and the rationale behind it. However, the office didn't have any rules set in writing, so Deer's solution wouldn't be that easy. She would have to talk to Dolly about it, one on one, woman to woman, and if necessary, boss to subordinate. Deer knew though, that telling a grown woman to get over her crush on someone would be about as effective as telling a teenage girl to do the same thing.

Deer's desk phone rang.

"Theresa, this is Amy. Thanks for giving us the tip on Little. Our analysts looking into Banco Dueno have been able to definitely link him to the bank, both as a user and as one of the unlisted owners. Secondly, our person inside the Bilderberg group has verified that Little has been extremely vocal on the environment and the damages that many of the older industries do to it."

"Great, Amy. I'm more confident than ever that he or someone on his immediate staff is behind the murders, but most likely as the person who hired the group that's doing the shooting."

"Agreed, he's definitely our best link to the group."

"Link is the right word. We can't find any evidence that either Little or someone from his staff were anywhere near the attack locations," Deer said.

"What does Homeland Security have on all this?" Amy asked.

"They have what I have. They may have developed more on

the drones, but if they have, they haven't shared it with me yet."

"I don't think they have anything yet. I mean I think they've been able to verify drones were in the area, but that's all. Our analysts think that this second failure in a row should cause the group to go to ground somewhere and try to stay hidden for a while. Plus, Little may be tired of throwing money away after two setbacks," Amy said.

Deer didn't necessarily agree with her, but she kept her thoughts to herself. Despite what she had told Amy, she had not passed on Little's name to Homeland Security. The two agreed to stay in touch before saying their goodbyes.

She glanced up and saw Buzz look into her office.

"Got a minute?" he asked.

"Sure."

"I think we've found a common point to all of these guys."

"Fantastic!" Deer said.

"Well, at this point it's still a long shot. The biggest problem we've had is that all these individuals seemed to have operated under various aliases. That's why we kept running onto dead ends. Once we get their fingerprints, however, we can link them to their real names, but only if they have a police or other traceable record."

"Okay."

"Interpol got hits on two of the four dead attackers in Mallorca. They were able to work the history of the two back to when they were your basic street thugs. They developed some info on the other two but not as extensive. The two Clint shot this morning were also in the system. Got their real names and have been working on their travel histories."

"Quick work," Deer said.

"Only have a partial return, but we've got a great relationship with Australia. In the past three years, all four who have been identified have spent time in Australia. Not all together, but the fact that all four visited Australia is interesting. All four do not have another country in common that I know of yet."

"May not be much to go on," Deer said, but she, too, felt it was too much of a coincidence to ignore.

"I know. I've gone to the Australians with a request to let us know where these four may have gone while in country," Buzz said.

"It would be a good coincidence if they all visited the same city. Share DuPane's photo with them and see if they can come up with anything from it."

"Will do."

"Amy Swanson has developed information that indicates Little may be one of the owners of Banco Dueno. She also verified something I suspected. The CIA has a person in the Bilderberg Group."

"I would kind of hope so," Buzz said. He imagined the CIA also had someone inside the Trilateral Commission and the other international organizations that are at the heart of so many conspiracy theories.

"Me, too. Going back to DuPane and the car that we have Clint following, I like the fact that we can track the phone, but I'm getting a little paranoid. We burned this guy once using his phone. I think he left the next phone at the gas station as bait. Now we're tracking a third phone. I can't believe he's not thinking about that possibility," Deer said.

"You think he may not be with the guy with the phone?"

"That's one guess. Could also be that he's setting a trap. Could be that the car, the phone, and a person will drive off a cliff, and we're supposed to believe DuPane is suddenly dead. I don't know, but this is a hunt where I'm no longer sure if Clint is the hunter or the prey," Deer took a sip of cold coffee and grimaced.

"I'm sure Clint has thought about all this," Buzz said.

"I'm sure he has, but our job is to be one step ahead of our prey. The odds are right now we aren't."

"Should we have had the cops pull them over sooner, while they were still in the Cadillac?"

"No. We might have learned a little more about them, but what would the police have held them on? I didn't like sending in the police when we did at Buhl, but I wondered at the time if they had abandoned the Cadillac," Deer said.

Buzz nodded. He also had thought that at the time.

"I was also concerned that we might be sending a cop or cops into a situation where they would have no sense for the real danger they were in," Deer said.

"Want to call Clint off?" Buzz asked. Deer stared at Buzz for a few seconds before answering. "No."

Buzz returned to his desk not nearly as excited about their progress as he had been when he went in to tell Deer about the Australia coincidence. He would be calling Clint in a little while, and, despite his own reassurances to Deer that Clint already realized that his target might be setting traps for him, he would caution Clint.

"We received an initial trace on John Blaine, the guy who owns the cell phone," Dolly said.

"That wasn't the name of the man who rented the Cadillac," Buzz said.

"Nope, and that's probably why we came up with nothing on his trace. This guy Blaine has done time. Not much, but he has a record of transporting stolen items. He's a wheelman, but he doesn't own a Toyota Avalon."

"Doesn't matter, we're only calling it an Avalon because that's what the old man called it. Wonder how DuPane met Blaine?"

"Don't know that. This Blaine guy has an address on Whidbey Island," Dolly said.

"That's just off the coast by Seattle," Buzz said, and Dolly nodded. "Think they could be going there?"

"Up in that area, yes. Not to the guy's place, it's a one room apartment, but there are a lot of islands off the Washington coast. A person could hide out there quite easily," Dolly said.

"I imagine you could get a sea plane in and out of there, and no one would know the difference. Very very interesting, Dolly."

"And with a small fishing boat, you can bounce from one island to the next. I imagine you could work your way all the way to Canada. Bring your boat in at a private dock and avoid customs. I bet it's not very hard."

"You think he's working his way up to Canada?"

"It makes sense to me," Dolly said.

"Yeah, me too."

CHAPTER 23

Clint's route took him past Mountain Home and through Boise. Buzz had called and told him that they were tracking another phone. He told Clint his concerns that DuPane might be playing them with the phone and to be careful. Clint didn't need the warning. He had been thinking the same thing even before the morning's encounter with the two men. They also agreed that as more than one person traveled in the Avalon, and they could alternate drivers, that Clint should stop for the night whenever he felt like it.

The scenery during the drive through Idaho and into Oregon fascinated Clint and made it easy to stay awake. However, once the sun went down, and the only scenery that changed was the number of headlights coming at him, he decided he'd done enough driving. He checked into a hotel that sat adjacent to I-84 in northern Oregon.

He woke early and armed with a banana and a large mug of coffee hit the road again. It surprised him that no one called him during his drive northwest on I-84 through Oregon and then north into Washington on I-82 before picking up I-90 south of Ellensburg. When he stopped for a lunch a little south of Seattle, the call finally came through.

"Bet you're tired of driving," Deer said.

"Yes, ma'am. Anything new developing?"

"A lot, finally. Most of it is finally allowing us to figure out who these guys are, but one thing has developed that you need to know. One of the men you ran into yesterday morning took your picture while you were pumping gas and again while you were inside the gas station. He sent the pictures to another cell number. That number belongs to a burner phone, and that phone has not been used since. It's either turned off or destroyed."

"The cops discover that?" Clint asked.

"Yes. You're now on the police's radar, but at a low level. They're focusing more on the new phone number. The man had taken pictures of three other men who obviously were at the station before you."

"So, they were definitely using the phone we were tracking as bait."

"Looks like it. Worse thing is that if the picture was sent to DuPane, he knows you're on his trail."

"He also has a general idea what my car looks like," Clint said.

"Yes. If you want to back off this, we can send someone else in to stay on DuPane's trail. Your call."

"How long would that take?"

"A day, possibly two," Deer said.

"Let me stay with this, at least until we have a fix on where it leads. It might work better if he has reason to believe that I lost his track. He might not expect someone new showing up so fast," Clint said.

"Okay. We'll keep you several miles away from the phone and have someone new come in after you. That means in forty eight hours you head home. I don't want any overlap."

"Not a problem."

"With any luck we'll be able to sic Homeland Security on the whole crew by the time you leave," Deer said.

"Good."

"The phone we've been tracking has gone home to Whidbey Island. It made a couple of short stops on the island before it reached its final destination. Our guess is that if DuPane was still traveling with them, he got off at one of those locations. Of course, he could have left the crew in the Avalon at any of the short stops they made in Oregon or in Washington before they ever reached Whidbey."

"Okay. I'll stay in the shadows," Clint said.

"Good. It's been a long couple of days here, and I expect the next few won't be any quieter. I hope things stay peaceful out there for you, but stay alert."

"I will."

"Your weather won't be as nice as it was in Vegas, so feel free to buy what you need on us."

"It's not so bad now," Clint said.

"There's a front that has already reached Whidbey. It's supposed to linger in the area for a few days before moving on."

"Okay," Clint said. His original trip took him from south Texas to Las Vegas where his main weather concern was the heat. Now it looked like he would be in a chilly, wet climate for a couple days.

The call ended and after finishing his lunch, Clint returned to his car and headed further north on I-5. He ignored signs about a ferry to the islands. He would be a sitting duck on a ferry, if someone was watching for him. By the time he took the US-20 exit west off the interstate, the low clouds and light rain had replaced the sun. Although the sun wouldn't set for at least two hours, Clint turned on his car's headlights. Visibility had dropped to about two hundred yards.

Clint had visited Seattle on a few occasions, but he had never been to this part of Washington. The winding road and poor visibility made driving a chore. He kept the vehicle about five miles per hour below the designated speed limit. Something about driving slowly and almost blind into a high threat area made the hairs on the back of his neck itch. Around every bend he half expected an ambush. He tried to think about something else, but at the same time he knew better than to ignore these feelings. How did that saying go? Just because you're paranoid doesn't mean someone isn't following you.

He slowed even more when he saw two men working along the side of the road a couple hundred yards ahead of him. Clint noticed a white pickup truck parked near them. The two men had shovels and were shoveling gravel onto the ground alongside the edge of the road's shoulder. Clint placed the Beretta on his lap and drove past the workers. Nothing happened, but Clint felt certain they both stared at him as he went by.

The precipitation changed from a thick mist to a steady, light rain. The wind picked up and Clint could see the branches sway in the smaller trees by the road. Definitely a day to stay indoors, he thought, and he hoped any would be ambushers had the same feelings. He drove for a few miles without seeing anyone outdoors and almost no other traffic on the road with him. As the highway turned south, Clint started to feel his tension dissipate. Then, he came to the bridge.

The bridge connected Whidbey Island to the rest of the world. Clint figured most people would be fascinated with it. The bridge crossed the quarter mile, open air gap a few hundred feet above the ocean below. The rocky cliffs on both sides dropped nearly straight down. Even with the limited visibility, Clint felt the view from the bridge had to be magnificent.

He also knew the bridge would intimidate a lot of people. Someone suffering from vertigo would not enjoy crossing it. Heights didn't bother Clint, but he still found himself a little intimidated. He couldn't shake the instant feeling of danger he got when he first saw the bridge. Once on it, he would be an open target. He would be like one of those ducks that crossed in front of the shooting gallery at the carnival. If an attack came while he was on the bridge he could do little to evade it.

His mind went through the list of options in the twenty seconds it took to reach the beginning of the bridge. He could stop, turn around, and come back to cross the bridge at night. Of course, if the two men he saw alongside the road were spotters, they could be following him right now in the white pickup. Turning around would bring him right back to them. He couldn't see to the other end of the bridge, as the bridge curved, and there appeared to be two parts to the bridge. A jeep came off the bridge as he reached it. He saw nothing that might be used to block his crossing or trap him on the bridge. Someone could be sitting in the trees waiting for him to drive onto the bridge for an open shot at him, or on the outcropping ahead, but in this weather it would definitely take someone very motivated. He saw a sign with the name of the bridge, Deception Pass Bridge. That didn't help. He had to do something unexpected, so he did.

He entered the bridge with his headlights off, the accelerator pressed to the floor, and the MKZ's wheels spinning wildly on the wet road. Clint concentrated on keeping the car in the middle of the bridge's two lane road. He almost didn't notice the sound of the high powered round as it ripped through the MKZ right behind his head and exited the back passenger side window. The second round hit the front windshield at an angle and tore a golf ball size hole in the glass right in front of Clint's face. The entire front window became a spider web of a thousand cracks. The shooter had to be up in the trees on the side of the hill to his left.

The MKZ started fishtailing as the speedometer hit ninety. Clint willed himself to stay off the brakes until the MKZ left the second part of the bridge. As it did, Clint stepped hard on the brakes despite the conditions. He barely had any visibility out the front window. The front end started to slide to his left, and Clint's effort to control it led to a skid to the right. The car's deceleration provided a false sense of security, and Clint decided to not fight the car's momentum as it slid off the road onto the right shoulder.

Even at thirty miles an hour, a car leaving the road onto slick grass and moss covered, muddy ground can be impossible to control. Add a slight downward slant, and Clint soon found himself trying to dodge trees as the MKZ slid a good seventy feet farther into the bushes and trees that paralleled the highway. To his surprise, the only tree he hit was the one that ultimately stopped his car.

Clint opened his door as far as he could and squeezed out of the car. It took him a second to get his bearings. He knew where he was, but he couldn't see anything to corroborate his location. The car had squeezed into a thick patch of bushes and small evergreens. Clint made his way to the rear of the car and followed the path the car had taken into the woods. It only took a few steps for Clint to break clear of the bushes. When he did, he quickly took a step back and crouched to look around.

He didn't see anyone, but he heard the sound of a large truck approaching the bridge. For a brief second he thought about waving down the truck. The sniper might still be out there, though, and he might have a friend or two. Stepping out in the open could be a quick way to let the sniper make up for his missed shots.

The truck, a moving van, drove by. For whatever reason, it surprised Clint how close he was to the road. It may have taken him over two hundred yards from the bridge to come to a complete stop, but only about fifteen yards separated him from the road. He stepped behind a tree and stood up. Three cars drove by following the moving van.

Clint decided to back away from the road and circle around toward the bridge. He wondered if someone might come looking for him to make sure the attack was a success. He kept the Beretta in his hand and edged deeper into the woods. The ground sloped downward from the road, and Clint knew somewhere soon he would run into a steep drop off to the ocean below. After moving as cautiously as he could while trying to stay concealed, Clint decided that he had gone far enough, and that any further movement might attract attention to him.

He found a spot where the natural contour of the ground along with the bushes and a tree provided good cover and some protection from the rain. The clouds seemed to be lowering. He saw a wispy patch of cloud settle in among a section of trees across the road. The sound of another approaching vehicle broke the silence, and Clint saw the white pickup with the two supposed workmen slowly leave the bridge and drive onto the island. They drove past him a short distance and stopped. Clint immediately thought they had seen his car or the tire tracks it must have left as it drove off the road. Rather than get out of the pickup, the two men stayed inside. The man on the passenger side appeared to be looking around for something or someone.

Clint didn't see the grey sedan approach the pickup until it was almost upon it. It paused as it came alongside, then it drove by before making a u-turn and parking right behind the pickup. One man climbed out of the sedan, and the two men got out of the pickup. The three huddled for a few seconds, and Clint could see the man from the sedan shake his head. The three separated. One man walked toward the bridge studying the ground along the side of the road. Another walked away from the bridge and the third crossed the road and walked away from the bridge.

Suddenly, the man walking away from the bridge on Clint's side of the road shouted, and the other two men started running in his direction. They must have discovered the spot where Clint went off the road. He guessed the man who arrived in the sedan had been watching to see if Clint made it over the bridge and further down the road.

Clint knew that a prudent man might take advantage of the moment to escape. Clint, however, didn't feel like being very prudent. He knew the men would be focused on following the tire tracks, and while they might be cautious as they approached the car, he didn't think they would worry too much about their rear.

Clint quickly retraced his steps to a spot near his car and arrived only moments after the three started shoving the bushes aside to get a better look at it. Two of the men stepped back and watched the third force his way into the thick bushes. Clint could only see the back of the man's legs as he tried to peer into the MKZ through the rear window.

Clint had studied the area along the road while he approached the three men and had seen no signs of anyone else. The sniper had most likely left the area and now awaited word on his results. Sunset couldn't be far off, and with all the trees and bushes in the area, visibility would soon be down to a handful of yards.

"He's not here," the man who had been looking through the car's rear window stepped back and said loud enough for Clint to hear.

Their reaction, delayed by no more than a second, would have been the same if he had shouted ambush. Suddenly, the three spun around looking for the person they had expected to be in the car. Despite Clint's attempt at concealment, one of them spotted him.

"There!" the man shouted and raised his hand that now pointed the end of a pistol at Clint. Without any hesitation, the man made a dumb decision and pulled the trigger.

Clint had the better position. Partially protected by a tree, he fired back at the men standing in the open. Five loud shots later and the three men lay on the ground. Two made no sound or movement. The third man groaned and his right arm moved back and forth across the ground like he was trying to grab something.

Keeping the Beretta pointed at the groaning man, Clint checked the other two for signs of life. He had fired three times, once at each man's chest. The two motionless men had already stopped breathing. Clint looked at the third man and saw the man staring back at him.

"Help," he gurgled.

Clint kicked the man's revolver out of his reach and kneeled over him.

"Help," the man gasped again. From the sound of the man's voice, Clint knew his third shot had struck one of the man's lungs.

"Where's DuPane?" Clint asked.

"I don't know. I really don't. Call an ambulance."

"Who's in charge of the group you belong to?"

"I don't know. DuPane tells me what to do. I don't know who he takes orders from. Please," the man's voice weakened.

"I will. Just a couple more questions. Where can I find DuPane?" Clint asked.

"Hotel, Oak Harbor." The man coughed up blood, his eyes widened, and the life went out of them.

"Damn," Clint said to himself.

A couple cars drove by on the road. Kneeling, he couldn't see the cars. He knew they couldn't see him either. Per his routine, he used his phone to take a picture of each of the men and each of their driver licenses. He then dragged the bodies one at a time to a spot deeper in the underbrush about twenty yards from his car.

Clint fought his way through the bushes and crawled into his car. He started the engine and slowly backed out. The stronger branches of the bushes scraped the sides of the car. His back window had not been damaged and the rearview camera worked fine, so keeping his speed steady, Clint had no problem following his tire tracks. He managed to return to the road despite the slight incline and slippery conditions.

Once he started going forward, however, he faced a more difficult situation. He had to lower the window and lean his head outside to see. Fortunately, the rain had turned back into a light mist. With his flashers on, he drove about a half mile before he found a spot to pull off the road. The spot was perfect, as it looked like an unofficial parking area used frequently by hikers and other nature lovers. Clint parked facing the trees next to an old Volkswagen Beetle that had seen better days. In fact, the poor VW looked abandoned.

He called D.C., and Buzz answered.

"You okay?" Buzz asked right away.

"Yes. Did you get the pictures?"

"Yes. Already working them. Do you need help?"

"My car does. They were waiting for me at the bridge. A sniper ahead of me on the island tried to take me out as I crossed. The shooter was good, real good. I floored it once I got on the bridge, and visibility was terrible, but he, or maybe she, still put two rounds within inches of my head. My car needs a new front windshield and other cosmetics. I need to get it towed and fixed."

"No problem. Are you leaving it there?"

"Yes."

"Okay, hold one second," Buzz said. The line went silent for a few seconds. "I'm back. How'd the other three men show up?"

"Two of them I passed shortly before the bridge. They were pretending to be working alongside the road. They were the spotters. The third man came from the other direction. He must have been placed there to let everyone know if I made it through and perhaps to follow me if I did."

"I moved the bodies about thirty feet farther from the road. Hate to leave you with the mess. I moved the car to get a little more separation from the bodies. One of the three said they worked for DuPane, and that he was on the island."

"Anything else?" Buzz asked.

"No. The other two weren't speaking, and that was about all the third guy had to say."

"Will you need a ride with the tow truck when it comes?"

"I don't think so, but I'll let you know if I do," Clint said and ended the call. Through the mist, he saw a figure wrapped in a rain poncho come out of the trees about fifty yards away. The person turned toward the parking area.

CHAPTER 24

The person didn't look threatening. Clint thought of the sniper, but he had fired from the other side of the road and much closer to the bridge. Still, he didn't feel like taking any chances. He climbed out of the car, walked around the front of it as though he was inspecting his windshield, and stopped by the front passenger side wheel. He looked up at the approaching figure like this was the first time he noticed him.

Clint nodded at the person. "How are you doing?" When the person didn't immediately answer, Clint said, "Not the best day to be out walking in the woods."

"Afternoon," the man said. He had gotten close enough for Clint to see his features. He looked to be in his late sixties or early seventies. A grey beard covered the bottom half of his face. He wore round, wire rim glasses and had eyebrows that had started growing wild years ago. When the man reached the Volkswagen, he stopped. The man's eyes took in the MKZ's windshield.

"Any possibility you can give me a ride into town?" Clint asked.

"Jeez, man, what happened to your windshield?" the man asked.

"Something fell off a truck as it went by me. It hit so fast, I'm not sure what it was. I never saw it until it struck the window in front of me. Might have been a brick. I went off the road and through some bushes, but got it back on the road without doing much damage."

The man walked over and pulled a twig with a few leaves still attached out of the MKZ's grill. He shook his head.

For the first time, Clint noticed the damage the tree had done to the MKZ's front bumper.

"I'm Griff," he offered his hand.

"I'm Clint."

"Makes sense. You look like Clint Walker."

The name didn't ring a bell at first with Clint.

"You know the movie star. You're as big as him," Griff said.

Clint smiled.

"I know. I'm more the Gabby Hayes character."

"I tried driving with my head out the window, but that was a miserable idea," Clint said.

"Good way to lose an eye. You want to put some tape over that big hole in the window? It will keep this rain out. Supposed to get harder as the night goes along," Griff said.

"You have some?"

"Hell, does a duck have feathers?" Griff walked to his old car and opened the passenger door. He fiddled around going through a bunch of stuff piled up behind the passenger seat before finally turning around with a roll of duct tape. He tossed the tape to Clint.

Clint used his small pocket knife to cut three foot-long sections of tape and placed them over the hole. The tape didn't want to adhere to the wet window, but after rubbing the tape a number of times with his hand the strips finally stayed in place.

"Not sure if they'll stay on," he said.

Griff had come over and watched Clint work the tape. He nodded. "Well it's better than nothing. Did you already call a tow truck, or are you going to try to get it yourself later?"

"I'm having it towed, but I'm not optimistic that they can get to it tonight. They wanted an extra fee to give it priority this evening, and I didn't want to pay it."

"Crooks," Griff said. He said it with more conviction than Clint expected.

"I'll gladly pay you gas money for taking me to the closest

town in whichever direction you're headed."

"Don't need your money, Clint. You're welcome to ride with me. I'm not exactly going to a town, but I can get you close enough to Oak Harbor."

Clint didn't know what close enough meant, but he figured anything would be better than standing out in the rain.

"Thanks."

Griff pulled another twig out of the MKZ's grill before walking back to the VW.

"Give me one second," Cliff said. He hurried to the trunk of the MKZ and transferred a clean golf shirt and a few other essentials from his suitcase to a gym bag.

Griff stood by the VW's driver's door while Clint got the items out of the trunk.

"Just throw that stuff behind the seat somewhere," Griff said.

Clint opened the passenger door and discovered a pile of dirty clothes on the passenger seat. A pair of wet, muddy boots with white socks stuffed in them sat on the floor in front of the seat. He moved the clothing and shoved the boots to one side. He placed his gym bag on top of the pile of junk behind the seat.

Griff took off his poncho, rolled it up and tossed it behind his seat. He had a camera slung around his neck on a strap. He placed it on top of the wet poncho.

They both got into the car at the same time. Once the doors were shut, Clint noticed the unpleasant odor that permeated the inside of the car. He couldn't pin the scent down to anything specific, but guessed if Griff kept wet boots, dirty clothes, and other trash in the car for extended periods of time the odor should be expected.

Griff started the engine, but before backing up, he took a rolled cigarette out of his shirt pocket, put it in his mouth, and lit it. He sucked hard on the cigarette and held his breath before exhaling. Clint figured years of marijuana smoke in the car probably didn't improve its odor, either.

"Would you like one?" Griff asked.

"No thanks. Are you a photographer?"

"Yes, been doing it for years. I love it, although I have to admit it's more of an addiction that a profession. Do you do any?" Griff asked as he backed the car onto the road.

"Some, but not much," Clint said. He thought of the five faces he had photographed in the last two days. "How long have you lived up here?"

"Moved here nearly forty years ago. Lived down in the Bay area until it became too commercialized. A lot of us moved up here when the culture changed. We've been able to preserve our life style on this island."

Clint figured the reference to the Bay area meant San Francisco and its surroundings.

Griff took another drag, "Yeah, it was really sad to watch what was happening back then. We lived free. Some of us in communes, some right in the heart of the city. Damn, those were good old days, but this is fine up here. You know, it was the dollar. Suddenly, that's all most people wanted. Not happiness, not freedom, they wanted more money. Property values began to shoot up, and the land prices, rent prices, even the food prices shot up. Hell, they even drove the weed prices sky high. That's when I knew it was time to leave." He chuckled to himself.

"It must be beautiful here," Clint said.

"Couldn't tell today, but it is. This rain supposed to be around for a couple of days. What brings you up here, Clint?"

"Taking a break between jobs, and thought I'd visit part of the country I hadn't been to before."

"Well, don't let the man get you down, son. Not having a job can be a blessing sometimes. Hell, you'd be surprised how many of my friends came here after the system tossed them out. You know, it's all a software program."

"What do you mean?" Clint asked only to be polite. While he listened to enough of what Griff was saying to be able to respond, his mind had turned to the fact that Buzz had not asked him why he had killed the three men rather than simply try to hike out of the woods and avoid any confrontation. Deer and her staff had been good like that. They didn't challenge his decisions.

Shortly after she hired him, Deer had told him that she wouldn't tolerate indiscriminate killings. She had a responsibility to help protect the United States and its citizens, and only those who posed a serious threat to the U.S. should end up dead or harmed at the hands of her hunters. She had made a point of explaining why she used the term hunter instead of killer. His job would be to track down his target. At that point, if it was at all possible, the proper authorities would be notified and would take over. The local authorities would never know of the hunter's existence. If circumstances prevented the locals from making the apprehension, then the hunter would be given the green light to terminate the target.

Clint knew from experience that once she sent him on a mission, she didn't second guess him. He thought that after each mission she might look back and analyze the decisions made and actions taken. If she did though, and what she did with that analysis, he didn't know.

"It's all a software program," Griff said again. "The whole system is geared to get as much out of you and put as little back in as possible. The machine lets them know when they can get someone else to do what you're doing for a cheaper price. When that happens, they get rid of you. Business men and politicians, I don't like either of them. Don't matter what business they're in or what political party they belong to."

"You don't have to worry about me," Clint said. "I'm not in politics and certainly don't own a business."

"Good," Griff said.

Clint noticed the two wiper blades were no longer wiping the windows in synch with each other. A drop of water had work its way through the seal at the top of the window next to him and slid down the inside of the window. As he watched it, he saw a second drop develop and follow the first. He wondered how old the car was.

"Is this an antique?" Clint asked.

"Thirty years old, does that make it an antique?"

"I'm not sure," Clint said.

"Well, it's paid off," Griff said and grinned. "Where's home?"

"Right now, Texas.

"Texas? Hell, I've never been there. Actually, I never wanted to. No offense."

"None taken. Have you ever lived anywhere else besides here and the Bay area?"

"No. I've travelled up into Canada. I've been to Alaska, and of course, Oregon. That's about it. I don't think I would fit in most other places," Griff said. "Hell, I wouldn't even want to live in Seattle anymore."

Clint was about to tell him he would fit in in Austin, when his phone buzzed in his pocket. He took it out and saw that Buzz had sent him a text message.

"Your car is being towed into Oak Harbor tonight. Heinrich's Towing and Auto repair will work on it tomorrow. Paid him extra to be discreet and quick," the text read.

Clint sent a short text back. "Thanks. I'll follow up with them in the morning."

"Any problems?" Griff asked.

"No. Surprisingly, the tow guys are getting it tonight."

"Good."

"I'll need to get the windshield fixed, but I wanted to spend a couple days here on the island anyway."

"Just the windshield?"

"It'll need a lot more touching up, but that can wait. I just can't drive it until I get a new windshield," Clint said.

"My place is right ahead," Griff said. He pointed his index finger ahead while he kept a tight grip on the steering wheel.

Clint looked ahead but didn't see anything but trees and fields. Griff drove about a half mile farther before turning off the highway onto a narrow paved road that led down a gentle slope toward an open field surrounded by five houses. The paved road turned left, but Griff drove straight onto a dirt road that took a loop around the front of all the houses. The houses were only about twenty yards apart in an arc that formed a semi-circle in the middle of the field.

Griff stopped at the second house. "This is it."

Clint climbed out the VW and stretched himself. He studied the houses. The one in the center had a yellow sunshine painted on the front wall. The next one down had a number of flowers painted across the front of the house. The front of Griff's house was painted a solid sky blue. Twenty to thirty small pinwheels adorned his front yard.

"We all moved in about the same time. I'd been up here on the island three years by then. Cassy and I lived in it for about five years before she moved in with Beau over there." Griff pointed at the last house in the arc. "I've been living here with Mel ever since. You'll love her, she's totally laid back. Come on in," Griff started walking toward his front door.

Clint didn't have much of a desire to spend any more time with Griff, but he also didn't have any options. He followed Griff into the house.

"Mel! I'm home, and I've brought in a stray," Griff shouted.

"You better not have," a voice came from a back room.

Griff turned and smiled at Clint.

Clint returned the smile, but the interior of the house had already captured his attention. The house didn't look dirty, but to describe it as cluttered would be an understatement.

However, the clutter didn't grab Clint's focus. The photographs did. Photographs covered all the walls. Most in simple frames, but in some spots, a tack held a picture without a frame against the wall. From where he stood, it looked like every wall had been totally covered. More significantly, though, the quality of the photographs amazed him.

He approached the closest wall and studied the pictures. One picture of the coastline after another adorned the wall. Some were close in shots and others from far away. Some had to have been taken from a boat off shore. Some caught the coastline at sunrise or sunset and others in storms.

"You like them," a woman asked.

He turned and saw a tall thin woman with long, wavy grey hair smiling at him.

"I'm Mel," her eyes seemed to smile along with her lips.

"Nice to meet you, Mel. I'm Clint." It looked to Clint like she was wearing pajamas.

"Don't mind me," Mel said as though she could read Clint's mind. "On days like these I sometimes wear my pajamas all day."

"Actually, I think those are mine," Griff said. "So, Clint, what do you think of the pictures?"

"They are really, really good," he said and looked back at the wall.

Griff beamed.

"Are they all taken of this island?" Clint asked.

Griff looked at Mel like she might know better than he would know. She shrugged.

"I think so," he said.

Clint walked to a different wall and studied the pictures. "These are good, too. These might be as good as those." The pictures on this wall consisted of photographs of people. Most were close up facial shots, but some were group photos. "How can you get people to look so natural when you take pictures of them, especially the kids?"

"It's not hard," Griff said. "Besides, I get rid of most of my shots because they aren't good. Only one in a dozen make it to the walls."

Cliff looked around the room. "You must have taken a lot of pictures then."

"It's what I do."

"May I get you a beer or a glass of wine?" Mel asked.

"Oh, thank you, Mel, but I shouldn't stay."

"Nonsense. I have plenty of stew already fixed. We were just waiting for Griff to get home."

"We?" asked Griff.

"Why Missy, of course," Mel said.

"Oh, yeah," Griff said. His expression gave Clint the idea that Griff hadn't expected Missy. "Clint, let me give you the rest of the tour."

He took Clint to the next wall. "This is my plant wall. Mostly, they're flowers, but I've included some pictures of fields and trees on it, too."

"I bet a number of magazines would pay you a lot for some of these pictures."

"I don't sell them," he said.

Griff took him around a corner and into a hallway. Both sides of the hall were lined from floor to ceiling with pictures. Most of these were black and white rather than color.

"I call this my human body collection."

"Incredible," Clint said, and he meant it. "Amazing detail. What? You have a portion of the wall dedicated to the foot?" He looked at Griff, who simply grinned. "Here's the hand."

"Behind you is my ear collection. I think they might be my favorite, not counting the nudes. It's funny how people are much more willing to have me take a close in picture of their ears than they are of their feet."

Clint turned around and looked at the photos. "How long

have you been doing this?"

"Forever."

Griff took a couple steps down the hall and pushed open a door. "My cloud and storm collection is in there."

Clint looked in and saw a bathroom with its wall covered with photographs.

"And in here," Griff opened the next door, "are my nudes."

Clint looked in the room and saw it was a bedroom.

"Go on in, I want you to see them."

The bed was unmade and clothes were scattered about on the floor. Once again, though, the pictures took his mind off the room. Both color and black and white photographs of naked people adorned the walls. Many of these pictures were larger than the eight by tens that covered the other walls. Most of the pictures were of individuals, but some were pictures of couples or small groups. Some of the people had posed for the camera, but a lot looked he had caught them doing something and unaware of the camera. One picture caught a much younger Mel from the side as she washed dishes in a sink. Her head faced the camera, like Griff had called her name a second or two before he took the picture.

"Again, very high quality, Griff. I'm impressed."

"Our little group has always preferred fewer clothes to more."

"Some of these pictures were taken a long time ago, unless people are still driving cars like these on the island." Clint pointed at a picture of two couples sitting naked on the hoods of two Chevy's that dated back to the seventies. A Mustang from that era could also be seen parked behind them.

"That does go back thirty some years," Griff said. "Here's the only one that almost got me shot." He touched a picture of a young woman who could have still been in her late teens. She stood sideways to the camera with a slight turn towards the camera at the waist. Her eyes stared right into the camera and seemed to fix at Clint when he looked into them. Her red hair hung straight down her back past the shoulders.

"She's beautiful."

"She and this one," Griff pointed to another young woman about the same age in a similar pose, "were taking my photography class. They wanted me to take their pictures. It was their idea, not mine. So I did it, and this one's dad got his hands on the picture and went through the roof. He came out here waving a gun around. For a moment or two, I thought he was going to shoot me."

"It's a good thing he didn't, or I wouldn't have gotten a ride tonight."

"Mel had to talk him down. He was super pissed. We finally convinced him that I don't sell the pictures or put any of them on line. I do hang them on my walls, but we didn't tell him that. I gave both girls a copy of their pictures, and we discussed the lighting, the angles, their postures, etc., etc., etc."

"So you teach a photography class?" Clint asked.

"Yes, at the local junior college."

"Missy's on the way over. Do we want to sit down and get started?" Mel said from the bedroom doorway.

"I really shouldn't trouble you," Clint said. "I can call a cab."

"Don't be silly," Mel said and walked away.

"No use arguing," Griff said. "She's a damn good cook. Why don't you use our bathroom to dry yourself off a little? There's a clean towel or two below the sink."

Clint would have preferred changing out of his wet clothes completely but settled for washing his hands and face and drying his hair. After leaving the bathroom, he found Mel and Griff in the kitchen. A small round table sat off to the side and had been set for four.

"I poured you this," Mel said and offered Clint a large glass of red wine.

Griff had a glass of wine in his hand and raised it slightly in a gesture of a toast. Clint accepted the wine and returned the gesture to Griff before taking a sip.

"Clint, I do appreciate your staying for dinner. I don't get to host many people outside our group up here, and I'm always curious if my cooking is still any good. You'll have to give me some honest feedback," Mel said.

"Mel! I'm here," a woman's voice rang out from the front porch.

CHAPTER 25

Her appearance surprised Clint. Not her arrival, as Clint knew Mel invited a person named Missy, but she didn't look how Clint imagined Griff and Mel's friends would look. Their behavior, appearance, the setup of the five houses, everything suggested to Clint that Griff, in particular, couldn't let go of his 1960's hippie roots. Mel fit right into that picture.

Missy, however, didn't have that look. She wore a new pair of jeans and a light green blouse. She had her long, curly brown hair pulled back in a pony-tail. Clint couldn't tell if she was mixed race, from the islands, or maybe the Mediterranean, but he could tell that she was nice to look at. He also figured her to be only a few years older than himself. That would place her twenty five to thirty years younger than Griff and Mel.

"Missy, this is Clint," Mel said. The way she said it gave Clint the impression that Mel might have called Missy to join them for supper only after Clint arrived at the house.

"Hi, Clint," Missy extended a hand. She had a nice smile.

"Dinner's ready, so I suggest we all sit down and eat," Mel said.

They did, and Clint discovered why everyone told Mel that she was an excellent cook. Fortunately, the conversation stayed away from his personal life and focused, for the most part, on the Texas coast versus the Washington coast. Clint admitted that for sheer beauty the Washington coastline whipped the Texas coastline, but for swimming, sunbathing, and relaxing Texas came out ahead. Griff didn't agree with the relaxing part, but gave in to the rest. After dinner, Mel insisted Griff stay in the kitchen to help her with the dishes. She pushed Clint and

Missy into the living room.

"Mel the matchmaker," Missy said with a smile, once they left the kitchen. "Sorry if you feel trapped."

"No, not at all," Clint said, despite feeling the opposite. "How'd you end up here on the island?"

"I was born here. Mel, Griff, and the others helped raise me. I didn't have the most normal childhood, but for the most part I can't complain."

"Was this like a commune?" Clint asked.

"Not hard to tell, is it?" Missy said and grinned.

"Did your parents have one of these houses?"

For the first time, Clint could see a little sadness in Missy's eyes.

"Yes, at first. My father never got over Viet Nam. I don't remember too much about him. I can see him, and I can remember him holding me. He died when I was five. Today, I imagine he would have been diagnosed with PTSD. My mom kind of fell apart. The war affected more than only the vets. It affected their families. I can remember that my mom said she had to go and take care of her sister. She said that she would be back, but she never came back. No one knows what happened to her."

"I'm sorry."

"Thanks, but don't be. The group here raised me. I don't think the authorities ever realized I wasn't still living with my parents. Old Sally signed everything for me using my mom's name. She passed away with a heart attack about eight months ago. Now that was sad. To me, she was my second mom, but everyone chipped in to raise and protect me."

"Have you lived here since?"

"No. I actually moved to Seattle and worked there for nearly twenty years. I got married, but that only lasted eight years. My fault, after living with this group of free spirits, I found married life too confining."

"What brought you back?" Clint asked.

"Sally's funeral. After that, I decided to stay for a while. A few of them could use a little help now."

"Are all the houses still occupied by the original group?"

"For the most part. I'm by myself in Sally's house, so I'm new. The Griffins lived here until I was about seventeen. They moved away. I think she had to take care of her mother in Pennsylvania. Jack and Jill, and yes, that's their real names, moved in right after the Griffins left. They were friends with everyone out here and were a natural fit. There were a lot of people on the island that were envious of the little enclave they created here. I remember gatherings out here when there had to be a couple hundred people partying."

"Sounds like you have a lot of good memories about this place," Clint said.

"I do, but I don't think I would recommend my childhood be used as a model to raise children."

"You look like you turned out okay?"

"There weren't many rules I had to follow, and I watched a lot of behavior by the grownups around me that aren't accepted by most of society. Drugs, alcohol, and sex were pretty much the norm out here. What I found interesting was that the larger group seemed to coalesce in a subtle intervention to help those with problems."

"Did it work?"

"I think more often than not. Hey, did you see my picture on the wall? You probably didn't recognize me."

"I don't know," Clint said.

"Come on," she grabbed Clint's hand and tugged him to follow her. She pulled him into the hall toward the bedroom.

Clint's initial thought was that she wanted to show him a picture of her in the bedroom. She surprised him by stopping abruptly and pointing at one of the pictures of an ear.

"There. That's me." Missy pulled her hair away from her right ear and posed for Clint.

"A beautiful ear," Clint said smiling.

"Oh, give me a break. Ears, like feet, are never beautiful. I've always given Griff a hard time about his hall. Now the rest of the pictures, the ones of the coastline, the storms, the people, even the nudes can be beautiful, but not the feet or the ears."

"Okay," Clint said and nodded.

"Did you see my picture in the bedroom?"

"I don't think so."

"It's not there." She looked past Clint.

Clint looked behind him and saw Griff. He grinned at Missy.

"Because, Griff said I didn't make the cut," Missy pursed her lips in a pout.

"Be careful with that one Clint, she lies a lot. Did so ever since she was a kid," Griff said in a tone that gave Clint the impression he didn't really mean it.

"He said I was too fat," Missy said and smiled. "He said the only pretty part on me was my ear, and only one of those."

"I may have said that." He winked at Clint.

The four ended up sitting in the living room talking for another hour about life on Whidbey Island and how it had changed or not changed since Missy was a baby. The rain had picked up and sounded loud against the roof. When the noise from the rain finally faded, Mel made the suggestion that Clint figured was part of her plan all along.

"Clint, we don't really have a place for you here tonight, and I think it's too late to call a cab," Mel said.

"I'll give you a ride into town," Missy said.

"I don't mean to be any trouble--"

"No trouble," Missy interrupted. She stood up. "It's going to start pouring again, so I suggest we get going. Do you have a bag or something?"

Clint thanked Griff again for the ride, Mel for the dinner, and followed Missy out of the house. He grabbed his gym bag out of Griff's car. The two walked next door to her house, the first one in the semi-circle. They walked into the house without unlocking the door. Unlike Griff's house, Missy's looked neat and clean.

"Does anyone lock their doors out here?"

"I do when I go to sleep at night," Missy said. "I'm going to have a coke, but if you'd like some more wine, Clint, I have some."

"No thanks. I've had plenty of wine."

"Ice water?"

"Sure, that would be fine," Clint said. He sat down on an old stuffed chair in the living room and looked around. He could see most of the kitchen. A small dining room occupied the end of the same room he sat in. The furniture looked old, but the walls looked like they had been recently painted and the laminate flooring looked new.

"You've been fixing the place up," Clint said when Missy came back into the room.

"It's been fun," Missy said. "The bathroom is next." She fished her car keys out of her purse that had been sitting on the counter. "If you're ready, we can go."

"Ready."

For the next fifteen minutes, Missy drove in the dark and told him stories about her adventures as a teenager among the old hippies. He enjoyed the stories, and the two laughed together.

On the outskirts of a town, she turned into the parking lot of a Best Western hotel. "You know Griff and Mel were trying to set me up, again. They think I need a man in my life and have no hesitation in doing what they just did."

"I thought the whole thing had to be a bit embarrassing for you."

"I was more embarrassed for you," she said. "If you're in town tomorrow night and want to do dinner or something, give me a call. While they might not see the need to get to know someone before starting a relationship, a number of years back I finally realized it might be a good thing to do."

"Dinner sounds great, but a lot depends on when I can get my car back. If I'm around, I'd be happy to call."

Missy jotted down her phone number and gave it to him. She drove off.

"Strange night," Cliff said to himself. He hoped the hotel had a room.

CHAPTER 26

"Still no sign of the drones, but a lot of other things are coming together," Buzz said to Deer moments after she had arrived at the office. He had waited for her to pour herself a cup of coffee and turn on her computers.

"The drones can be dismantled and driven away in the back of a van or large SUV. They can be hidden in a backyard shed. Find the people. Then we'll find the drones. What's the good news?"

"The Aussies raided a remote ranch house. Found a ton of weapons, ammunition, explosives, and training manuals. The place is not licensed as a business, so they believe it was being used to train some type of militia. You know, the Aussies can be easy going with ranchers and weapons, but they take this type of stuff seriously."

"Have they gotten back with us, or is this from an intercept?" Deer asked.

"An intercept, but I think they've given a preliminary report to the embassy. This raid was in response to the info we shared with them," Buzz said.

"I better give Amy a call and see if she'll take lead on this. We don't need the Australians contacting the FBI thinking that was who sent them the initial information."

"This raid could bust our modern day league of assassins apart, if it's related, and I'm willing to bet it is."

"I'm sure it is. Let's hope they've retrieved the names and locations of any people who have gone through their training."

"What do you want to do with the hunters?" Buzz asked.

"Call them both off the hunt. Let's give the authorities the opportunity to do their thing now. We've done enough already," Deer said.

"Viv hasn't left for Whidbey yet. Her plane leaves at noon, so she'll be easy to stop, and Clint already knows he was heading home today or tomorrow. I'll let him know that the hunt is over. Once his car is good to go, he's to head home, too."

Buzz left, and Deer called Amy at her office in the CIA. After a very brief period of small talk, Deer got down to business. "Amy, I need you to do a small favor for me. The Australians busted a ranch house last night that I believe is connected to our group of killers. Can you follow up on it and leave me out of it. In my enthusiasm, I may have overstepped my charter."

"Well if you're right, and it blows open this whole thing, I doubt if anyone will care," Amy said.

"Maybe, but I'd rather you take the lead and get whatever credit there might be. Would you?"

"Sure. If you want to keep your name out of it, it's all right by me. What do you need me to do?"

"Have your people in Australia contact the Australians and express an interest in the results of the raid. Have them go at it with the goal of seeing if any of the dead attackers from Mallorca had ever been there. Then you may want to see if either of the two men found dead yesterday at a Nevada gas station had ever been there."

"What?"

"I'll fax you their names and whatever else we have. Also, I'll include another name, DuPane. I'll send you everything we have. Your people may also want to ask the Aussies if they found any evidence of training people how to fly and operate drones at the ranch," Deer said.

"Can do, but if the Australians raided the ranch, they must already be in coordination with the FBI or State."

"That's where I need your help. I may have sent them

something that piqued their interest and used a rather vague return address. If you know what I mean."

"Damn. You've got guts. Now I understand."

"If your people follow up with the Australians, it might preclude the Australians from trying to figure out whom to respond to on this side of the ocean."

"If this pans out, there'll be a lot of kudos flying around. Sure you don't want to be in the celebration?" Amy asked.

"Believe me, I'm just glad that we may have busted a nasty group of people."

"Who's the ring leader?"

"I'll leave that to you, NSA, and the FBI to find out," Deer said.

"I guess you don't want me to info you on any of my correspondence."

"That's right. Leave me out of it. In a couple days, we can do lunch at that barbeque place you like and talk about what you find out. If it pans out, you can buy. If it's a flop, I'll buy."

"It's a deal," Amy said.

"The fax should answer all your questions, but call me back if you have any." After the call, Deer walked out of her office.

"Amy will take the lead with the Australians, Buzz, who do you think is our best contact at the Bureau to get them interested in Whidbey?"

"Your guess is as good as mine. How about Wicks?"

"Maybe," Deer said. "We haven't used him before, but he is at the Counter Terrorism Center."

"The better question is how do you intend to get him thinking about Whidbey? It's not like anything we have has been gathered legally."

"I have an idea," Deer said.

She executed her idea an hour later by routing a brief email through a server at a Starbucks in Seattle. The email read: "Special Agent Rochester Wicks, I got yr name off the NCTC website. I overheard John Blaine, who lives on Whidbey Island, WA, tell my husband that he drove the mastermind of the attack on that Greek billionaire in Las Vegas to Whidbey from Las Vegas. He said the dude was super scary. I don't want my man mixed up with Blaine or this other guy. Can you arrest them?"

Deer used a sanitized Kindle Fire to send the email. The email had a bogus registry and email account. She knew the FBI would want to speak to the sender and would attempt to identify her. However, the information in the email pertained to a high priority investigation and would get fast tracked. Any check on a John Blaine from Whidbey would disclose Blaine's past record as a wheelman, and that should be enough to get some follow up and focus on Whidbey Island.

Dolly stuck her head into Deer's office. "I reached Viv and cancelled her flight."

"Good. I think we can back out of this feeling good about how everything turned out. Has Buzz reached Clint?"

"I think so. You want me to have him come see you?"

"Only if he hasn't made contact. Thanks."

Deer spent the rest of the morning studying international terrorism updates. During her lunch break, she drove twenty miles into Maryland to a library that took donations of kindles, nooks, and other e-book readers to pass out to the less fortunate in its community. She gave the library four fairly new kindles and declined a receipt. She had already deleted all record of her email to Special Agent Wicks from one of the four.

Her cell phone rang on the way back to the office.

"Perfect timing this morning, my friend," Amy said. "I don't have anything yet, but we made contact with our office a few minutes before our friends showed up looking to discuss it. Prevented a lot of confusion and embarrassment."

"Great. Must be burning the midnight oil over there."

"They should be. Our friends are excited about what they've found."

After the call, Deer felt more confident that she could leave the matter to the more legitimate agencies. She had no remorse that she didn't get to bask in the glory. Other than the people who worked for her, only one other person ever discussed her operations with her. She hadn't talked with him for three months, and now wondered if she should give him a call. Leon Thomas had filled the senior, permanent civilian position on the National Security Advisor's staff for ten years. While the majority of the people who filled the other positions around him came and left with each administration, the political appointees from each party had the sense to know they needed someone with continuity.

Thomas had been on the staff during 9/11 and the reorganization afterwards. He knew what Deer's office had been created to do and how critical its mission was. He also knew that her activities had to be conducted in absolute secrecy. This not only protected the country's leadership from embarrassment, a goal Thomas could actually care less about, the secrecy also protected Deer's activities from compromise. The modern day popular fiction that depicted the President and other senior politicians routinely having an active hand in covert operations was just that – fiction. While activist or paranoid Presidents might want to control everything, the involvement of senior politicians invariably led to delays, inefficiency, and compromise. Thomas hated the way some Presidents put US troops and civilians in danger, and then tied their hands even in their own self-defense.

There had only been one new administration since 9/11. Fortunately, incoming Presidents and their new National Security Advisors receive way too many briefings when they first come into office. Thomas had no problem inundating the Advisor with so many briefings on black programs and sensitive plans that were politically "hot", that almost nothing needed to be said about Deer and a couple of other projects that

Thomas wanted to protect.

The Advisor whittled down the briefing for the President to fifteen major topics, and Deer's activities were included in the many others that the Advisor would keep the President informed of as needed. Thomas maintained a list of all projects briefed to the Advisor, along with corresponding dates. If the project was briefed to the president, the list was annotated. Since the President agreed to his Advisor briefing him later as needed on the less significant government operations, Thomas had checked off Deer's mission as briefed to the Advisor and acknowledged by the President.

CHAPTER 27

"What the hell happened to this thing?" the young man wearing a denim work shirt with the logo Heinrich's over the buttoned pocket asked. A small red tire dotted the second "i" in Heinrichs.

"Something smashed into the front window, and I went off the road," Clint said.

"These are bullet holes," he said. "You should report this to the police."

"You're pretty observant. Most people wouldn't recognize them as bullet holes. Ever thought of going into forensic work for the police? You know, CSI?" Clint actually thought most anyone could have recognized the bullet holes, but he didn't need this to get reported to the police.

"Nah. I don't want to have a full time job. This place belongs to my aunt. She lets me work here as much as I want, or as little as I want," he smiled as he said this last part. "It's a good setup. I got certified when I was only nineteen, although I helped out here all through high school."

"How long will it take?"

"I can have the windshield and the two side windows replaced as soon as the replacements get in, which should be around noon. I can buff out most of the minor scratches while I wait for the windshield and windows. You need a front bumper and grill, but that will take more than a day to get the parts in. I understand you're in a hurry. The engine and radiator are fine, so if you want to drive it away today, you can."

Clint walked to the front of the MKZ and looked at the damage. "I can get this fixed later."

"You know you have a lot of broken glass inside your car. Our normal policy is to remove the most obvious of the pieces, but I'll be happy to give it a thorough cleaning. May cost a little extra," his grin reappeared.

"If you can get this fixed, cleaned, and ready to go by four, in addition to your company's bill, I'll make it worth your while."

"I'll be here at four, and your car will be spotless, except for the front and maybe a couple of the larger scratches I can't touch up. My name's Dennis. If you don't see me, just ask anyone, they'll know how to reach me."

Clint tossed his gym bag into the MKZ's trunk and left the car with Dennis. He thought about calling a cab, but as he had over six hours to kill, Clint decided to take a walking tour of downtown Oak Harbor.

A few historical markers indicated that Oak Harbor's roots went back to the mid 1800's, and despite it being on the Pacific Coast, Europeans such as the Dutch and Scandinavians played important roles in the city's early history. He also saw signs to a nearby Naval Air Station.

Clint found a small coffee shop thirty minutes after leaving the garage and took a break from his walk. He had received a text from Buzz and had not yet sent him a response. The text simply read, "Mission over, suggest you leave the area as soon as your car is fixed." Clint started to send a reply by text, but called Buzz instead.

"I got your text," he said once Buzz answered. "I should be out of here late this afternoon. I take it from your message that you're not replacing me."

"Correct. Things have finally been resolved to the point we can back out of this whole matter. In fact, there will likely be something happening in your area today. May go down quietly, except they'll likely have to use a Greyhound bus to get all the reps in from all the federal agencies that want a hand in this."

"Going after DuPane?"

"Only if he happens to be there. They're going after the driver, the guy who rented the Cadillac in Las Vegas. Admittedly, a relatively small potato, but it's their first chance to get at someone alive with links to the group."

"Well, I wish them luck," Clint said. "I'm tired of these guys, plus they damaged my car."

"Can they fix everything there?"

"My car?"

"Yes. Will they be able to do all the repairs there today?" Buzz asked.

"Enough so I'll be able to get out on the road. I'll stop in Seattle at a dealer and get the front bumper and grill replaced."

"Ouch. I don't think your insurance company will cover shootouts."

"You're my insurance company," Clint said. "And, I don't think there's even a deductable."

"All kidding aside, we're just going to be reading the wires today. Want us to get in touch with a Lincoln dealer in Seattle and give them a heads up on tracking down a bumper and grill for you. I imagine there's a whole package of stuff that they have to replace."

"Sure, if you don't mind. I was going to do that later, but you know my route home. If you could find a place that wouldn't take me too far out of my way, I'd appreciate it."

"Consider it done."

Clint finished his coffee and continued his walk. About forty five minutes later, he discovered the public library. He hadn't spent much time in a library since college and enjoyed spending the next couple hours reading newspapers, magazines and doing some more research on the Bilderberg Group. This time he skipped the numerous conspiracy theories and tried to hone in on the members. His research yielded very little, but he hadn't expected much.

After his visit to the library, Clint stopped at a small

restaurant for a late lunch before heading back to Heinrich's garage. As he approached one of the busier thoroughfares in the small city, he saw two unmarked, black SUV's and a city police car drive by with their lights flashing. They weren't using their sirens, but they moved with a sense of purpose that gave Clint the impression they were heading toward, not away from, whatever mission they had been sent out to do.

Dennis came out of the small office as Clint approached the garage. "Everything's ready for you," he said.

"Good. I'm ready to move on," Clint said as the two walked over and inspected the MKZ. "I'm impressed, Dennis. I can see some of the damage, but considering all the scratches and the damage to the windows, this looks really good."

Dennis opened the driver's door. "Look inside. I think I got it looking like new again." He opened the rear door on the driver's side, too, to allow for Clint to inspect the back seat area.

"Looks good, so what's all this going to cost me?"

"The bill is up front in the office. I'll go up there with you, but I think fifty would be fair for my extra work." Dennis didn't make eye contact, and when Clint didn't answer right away, he said, "maybe thirty."

"Dennis, you need to work on your negotiation skills. Here, keep it," Clint said and handed Dennis a hundred. "You not only did a good job, you did it very quickly."

"Thanks!" Dennis said and led him to the cashier.

As Clint drove off, Dennis wondered who he really was. Who gets shot at and doesn't want the police to know about it? Who hands out one hundred dollar tips? He figured Clint was a gangster, but a nice one. He meant to tell him about the man who had appeared in the garage at two o'clock. The man claimed that he wanted to check out the place, since he was looking for a local garage to use. However, Dennis noticed the man's interest seemed to be more focused on the MKZ than anything else.

CHAPTER 28

Although darkness had not completely taken over, the sun had long set by the time Clint parked in front of the Holiday Inn Express in Seattle. He could see the Lincoln dealership's lights from the hotel's parking lot. Buzz had told him the dealership's service department could take the car first thing in the morning. They didn't commit to when he could have it back.

Before he entered the lobby of the hotel, Clint studied the parking lot and the access road that led to it from the interstate. He felt uneasy, and he didn't like the feeling. Glimpses of what he thought was the same blue Chevy Silverado in his rear view mirror on the drive down from Whidbey Island had worried him. The Silverado never got very close, and it didn't follow him off the exit he took to the hotel. Clint knew anyone traveling from Whidbey to Seattle would take the same route he did, unless they came by ferry, but he still didn't like it.

His cell phone buzzed before he reached the front desk. He expected the call to be from Buzz, but Deer's voice came to him through the phone.

"How's your car?" she asked.

"It drives fine, but it still needs a face lift."

"The raid in Oak Harbor went well. The idiot still had his contract for the Cadillac from the car rental agency in Las Vegas. They also found some notes that have the FBI excited and a weapon they can use to yank his parole status."

"Any news on DuPane?" Clint asked.

"No, not yet. The Australians have some stuff on him they're sharing, and we've hit the mother lode on the group's finances. You can't imagine how many different agencies and how many different countries are going after this group. I think it's safe to say that our League of Assassins will have a difficult time ever reforming."

"That's good news. Any link to Little, the rich guy who may have hired them?" Clint really wanted to know if the Greek had bumped him off yet.

"No, and I doubt that we'll we find anything on Little, unless we get our hands on DuPane or someone else high up in the group. DuPane appears to be the boss of this outfit, or at least the field boss. There may be someone sitting back in an office somewhere who is pulling the strings, but if there is, we still have no clue to who she might be."

"DuPane could still be up here somewhere," Clint said.

"He's not our concern anymore. Homeland Security and the FBI are both pulling out the stops to catch him. For today, he's their number one priority, and I think there might be a little rivalry going on."

"Well, once my car is ready, I'm heading home. I may swing by the place in Colorado."

"No problem, things should hopefully stay peaceful for a while now."

They ended the call, and Clint proceeded to check into the hotel. He didn't feel as optimistic as Deer had been, but he looked at everything from a different perspective. He didn't doubt that the collective resources of the free and not-so-free world could and would crush the organization behind the attacks, but he still saw DuPane as the threat. He was the lead assassin, the head of this snake, and if the body was removed, Clint felt that DuPane could generate a new body. Until DuPane's arrest or death, Clint didn't think the threat would be gone.

At two in the morning, while Clint slept, a blue Chevy Silverado drove into the hotel parking lot and stopped behind

Clint's car. The driver got out for a mere ten seconds before getting back into the pickup and driving away. The driver knew he should be a thousand miles away, but this had become personal for him.

Clint spent the next day touring Seattle in a loaner car provided to him by the Lincoln dealership. The day turned out uneventful with two exceptions. First, the service department told him that his car would be ready by noon on the following day. He had worried that he might be stuck in Seattle for three or four days. Clint had nothing against Seattle, but he was ready to head home. The second exception came in the form of a phone call from Buzz updating him on the status of the international effort to crush the group behind the attacks.

"Major breaks have come from efforts in Australia, France, and in the U.S. The ranch in Australia yielded a dozen or so names and identified two bank accounts used by the group. The three men dispatched on Whidbey were on the list, as were the two from the service station in Nevada. The names of the four killed in Majorca weren't on the list, but we know from Australian customs that they've been to Australia."

"Are they going after the others on the list?"

"Yes, and by the way, DuPane's name wasn't found on any document there," Buzz said.

"That doesn't surprise me. The guy's sharp."

"He's probably out of the country by now and will stay in hiding for some time."

"I agree. We may not hear anything from him for a long time."

"That would be fine with me," Buzz said.

"What are your plans for the three bodies on the island?"

"Once you're on the road tomorrow, we'll get the word to the sheriff's office. Some anonymous hiker will be calling in the report."

"Good. Let's hope my car will be ready like they said."

While the dealership didn't have the car ready by noon, Clint only had to wait an extra ninety minutes. The car almost looked new again. He pointed the car southeast and didn't stop driving until he hit the outskirts of Boise. He didn't see the blue Silverado on his tail at any point during the drive. He slept more soundly that night.

The next morning, Clint took the interstate southeast into Utah. Near Salt Lake City, he took the I-84 bypass before getting off the interstate and taking a route that led him through a remote stretch of the state. Once he got on US 40, it didn't take long until traffic thinned out to only the occasional car. He stopped at a truck stop that included a restaurant and had a late lunch.

"Where you headed?" the waitress asked while she refilled his water glass.

Clint looked up at her and couldn't help wondering how the place, so far from anywhere, found employees. The waitress had a pleasant, round face surrounded by dark brown hair that didn't look quite right. A wig, he wondered.

"I'm going to Colorado," he answered.

"Nice place, but too crowded for me."

Clint smiled, but before he could come up with some witty remark, the waitress moved on to another table. The restaurant did pretty good business considering its remote location. Of course, it didn't have much competition, and regular travelers through this area would find it a convenient place to stop.

Back on the road, he had driven another hour before he saw the car on the side of the road. He didn't think much about the car, but the woman standing next to the car and waving at him to stop made an impression. He hit the brakes, but had gone by the woman a good fifty yards before he got the car to a complete stop.

Clint put the car in reverse and stayed on the shoulder of the road while he backed up. He didn't see another car on the road, but a caution flag had gone up in his mind. Stopping the MKZ a few yards in front of the Toyota Avalon, he glanced around, but didn't see anyone else in the area. He stayed in the car, and the woman walked up to him. In the side mirror, he could see that she carried a cell phone in her left hand.

"My car died on me. My brother will be out here in about twenty minutes. He swears he can fix it, but I kind of need to get to my place in a hurry. It's only a mile straight up this road. Can you give me a ride?" the woman asked.

"Sure," Clint said.

She didn't appear to be a threat, but something about her signaled a little alarm in the back of his mind. Although no expert on what women wore, she didn't appear to be dressed for a casual drive to town. In her sunglasses, tight shorts, and sleeveless white blouse, also tight, Clint thought she had expertly dressed to stop a guy driving along the highway. The coincidence that she drove an Avalon with Washington tags hadn't escaped his mind either.

"My name's Bee, like the honey bee. I really, really thank you for the ride. I have to go to the bathroom bad," she made a face when she said it. "I couldn't wait for my brother."

"Not a problem," Clint said and started driving. The area around them didn't contain anywhere for a person to hide until you reached the trees a good forty yards off the highway, but Clint still had memories of the sniper. That time they knew the area and suspected that he was on their trail. This time it didn't make sense that they could be ahead of him, yet his gut insisted something was up.

"There's a dirt road up here to the right. Just past where the trees close back in on the road," she said. "It's my driveway."

Clint glanced over at her and realized she stared ahead of them, looking for the turn off like a person who had only been there once or twice before.

"Better slow down," she said. "Just after we get off this road there's a gate. I'll have to get out and unlock it."

"There," she said with too much emotion.

Clint sensed the tension in her voice. He started to turn off the road, but then shot past the dirt driveway another twenty yards before stopping. As he did, he saw a man near the gate duck down behind some shrubbery. Bee stared at him wide-eyed.

"Stay here. If you get out of the car, you may accidently get shot." Clint said it like a threat rather than a warning. He made sure she saw the Beretta in his hand as he got out of the car.

"He'll kill you," she said. "Please, let's drive away."

"Is it just him? DuPane?"

"Yes."

"You know he'll think you warned me."

"I know," she whispered.

"Then let's hope he doesn't kill me," Clint closed the door.

Through the trees he could see the spot by the gate where the man had been waiting. He would have been hidden from view to anyone pulling off the main road and stopping in front of the gate. Two tall trees and a clump of thick bushes provided ample concealment, only five yards from the driveway. Clint envisioned that if he would have turned onto the driveway and stopped at the gate, Bee would have gotten out of the car and distracted him, and the shooter could have walked toward the car firing away with lethal accuracy at the side or back of his head.

Once Clint had driven past the driveway, DuPane's hiding place did him no good. He moved around the trees and bushes, but too late not to be seen. The trees still provided some protection, but DuPane had lost the element of surprise. A number of trees provided similar protection for Clint, and he fired four rounds into the bushes while he closed in on DuPane. He stopped firing when he reached a thick tree about ten yards from DuPane.

"It's over DuPane. The cops are coming right now. There's nowhere for you to go, and your lady friend has already started talking." Clint hadn't called the police, but he knew DuPane would believe that he had. It left DuPane no choice but to surrender or take some action that would bring him out into the open. Clint didn't expect DuPane to surrender or wait for the police.

Clint didn't have to wait long. When DuPane moved, he did so with speed and the experience of someone who had been in similar situations before. He didn't charge or attempt to run across the open driveway. He fired once and then sprinted along the barbed wire fence that lined the front of the property. Clint fired, and DuPane went down. Clint realized instantly that DuPane dove to the ground and rolled when he saw Clint raise his arm to fire the Beretta. He had missed. Clint fired a second round as DuPane disappeared behind a clump of bushes surrounding a small tree. This time he thought he saw a puff of red fly off DuPane's left arm.

DuPane fired twice from behind the bushes. One round smashed into the tree inches from Clint's head. Splinters of wood tore into his temple. Clint instinctively crouched, keeping most of his body behind the tree.

DuPane dashed again along the fence line toward a larger cluster of trees. He fired blindly in Clint's direction as he ran.

Clint knew DuPane needed to keep him from firing for the five or six seconds it would take him to reach the next patch of trees. From there, it could become a foot race as DuPane would be in thicker woods and would be running away from him. He didn't like leaving himself exposed while DuPane fired off rounds in his direction, but he knew it would be more dangerous chasing DuPane through the woods.

Clint leaned out, took aim, and fired two rounds at the moving target. He couldn't tell if the first, second, or both rounds hit the target, but DuPane spun sideways and fell back against the barbed wire fence only a few feet from the cluster of trees. One of the barbs must have snagged DuPane's shirt, because he slumped over in an awkward position while his shirt stretched tight keeping him in a partial sitting position. Clint cautiously walked up to DuPane. When he noticed DuPane's right hand moving up his leg, Clint fired another round into DuPane's head.

He removed DuPane's wallet and photographed everything in it except the cash. As he walked back to the car, he sent a text with the photographs to Buzz. He half expected to find his car empty and to see Bee sprinting down the road toward her car. However, he found her where he left her more frightened than before. Her wide eyes had already shed a tear or two, and her hands trembled in her lap.

"Is he dead?" she asked.

"Yes," Clint said while he made a U-turn and started driving back the way he had come.

"What are you going to do with me?"

"That depends. My plan is to take you back to your car and let you drive away, but there are conditions," Clint said.

"I'll do anything you want, just don't hurt me."

"What's your real name?"

"Laura Richards."

"Ok, Laura," Clint said while he slowed down. "Here's the deal." He stopped the car across the road from the Avalon.

She stared at him. The fear in her eyes had become less obvious.

"I have your picture, your fingerprints are on the door handle, and I have your DNA if one strand of your hair fell out. I've got a picture of the car and its tag number. By the way, is that your car?"

"No, it's his."

"I want you to go home, wherever that is. I want you to have a drink, a hot bath, whatever you need to calm down. I want you to forget today ever happened. Understand?"

"No."

"What don't you understand?"

"Why you want me to do that."

"I want you to do that, because I don't think any of this was your idea. But, I want you to walk into the police station nearest to your house three days from now and tell the police there everything you know about DuPane and his activities. However, I don't want you to mention anything about today. Okay?"

"I don't know much about him," she said.

"So, he picked you to come along this ride with him just for fun?" Clint asked.

She looked at him for a few seconds. "No."

"How did he know where I was?"

"He put a tracker on your car back in Seattle," she said.

"Damn. The guy was good."

"He's scary, but very, very smart. When he told me to come along, I couldn't exactly say no."

"I believe you," Clint said.

"Why don't you want me to mention today?"

"I'd like to stay out of the official investigation. I'm a very secret Australian agent, and it would be embarrassing for me to be compromised. So, Laura, our deal is I don't go to the police and have them press charges against you for conspiracy to commit murder, and your part is to tell the police, in three days, all you know about DuPane and his now defunct organization. Don't mention me or what happened today. Do we have a deal?"

"Yes," she said.

Clint couldn't read her. He knew she felt trapped and would probably agree to anything in order to get away.

"Now, if you don't go to the police, I'll make sure the FBI gets an anonymous tip about your involvement. By then, I'll be out of the country."

"Will the police be interested in DuPane?"

"I think by then they will be," Clint said.

CHAPTER 29

Three days later, Clint sat on the back porch of the Little Fawn Bed & Breakfast in Breckenridge, Colorado, drinking coffee and reading the Denver Post. Although some guests had already left the Little Fawn looking for lunch, Clint had slept in. Renters occupied his Dillon Lake condo, so while he had gone by the condo and checked on it, he selected the Little Fawn to spend the week he planned to be in Colorado. He had seen the bed and breakfast on a few occasions, but he had never spent the night there. He liked the small town of Breckenridge, and the Little Fawn hadn't disappointed him.

A short article on the bottom of the front page caught his attention. "Chris Little Missing and Presumed Drowned" read the headline, and the article carried a caption that identified it as late breaking news. The article indicated that Little disappeared while surfing off his semi-private beach in northern California. His two personal security personnel, one had been surfing with him, and the other observing from the beach, claimed that it looked like Little simply slipped off the board, went under the water, and never reappeared. His body had not yet been found. Initial speculation blamed a large shark, but the article did note that no body parts or even traces of blood were spotted in the area where he disappeared.

He took out his cell phone out of his pocket. He had not heard from them since he had briefed them on his confrontation with DuPane. He had talked to both Buzz and Deer at the time, and had gotten the impression from Deer that she had some concerns with the way he had handled Laura Richards. DuPane's body hadn't been discovered until the day after the confrontation, and Clint believed the discovery occurred without Section's involvement. He dialed Buzz.

"Hey, I hear there may be an early snowfall coming your way," Buzz said, rather than a normal hello or how's it going.

"I hope it does," Clint said. "Have you seen the news about Little?"

"Sure. Think our Greek friend is involved?"

"It would be my first guess. I also think the body will never be discovered."

"I agree," Buzz said. "No body makes for no evidence."

"How's the roundup and the rest of the investigation into DuPane's group going?"

"Good. I'd say there was no more group, but we do think there is another person behind the scenes who either masterminded the whole group or was right under DuPane and took care of finances and logistics. DuPane was definitely a field man. He ran the operations, but no one has found any evidence that he oversaw the training in Australia or the organization's finances. He may have had some hand in the recruitment process, but he wasn't the only one," Buzz said.

"So we've got someone out there who still needs to be found."

"Yes, but they're no longer of interest to us. There's enough people trying to track them down, and they don't pose a threat anymore."

"Did anyone ever pin down where the helicopter that was used in the attack in Mallorca came from or find the drones?" Clint asked.

"No to both. DuPane didn't leave us a paper trail. The stuff that they have found has been great, but it's mostly logistics and financial stuff. Plus, they've identified a handful of other suspects that are being rounded up."

"Do we know anything more about DuPane?"

"Not yet, I know we've said it too much, but the guy was

good. The whole DuPane alias disappears eight years ago. The guy took covering his tracks to a new level, and not only for himself. All the people he had working for him had sequentially used a couple of aliases in the past few years to hide who they really were. Luckily, fingerprints and DNA have helped us determine the real identities for most of them."

"But nothing on DuPane?"

"No."

"Anything for me at the moment?" Clint asked.

"No. Take a vacation."

"Anything ever pop on the investigation into Parrot's murder?"

"Maybe. A woman's body was discovered locked in an abandoned U-Haul van south of Las Vegas. Turns out she was a part time employee at the same storage operation where we believe Dick was killed. No one had seen her since that same day someone killed Dick," Buzz said.

"Could be who Dick was trying to help."

"We'll possibly never know, but that's a good assumption. The police will be going through the security camera videos from the storage facility. Even if it doesn't show who did what to whom, it may show that Dick was there. Linking the two investigations could help," Buzz said.

"Have they learned his real identity yet?" Clint asked referring to Dick.

"No, but Dick had a close friend, an older woman, a widow, who was his neighbor. She looked after his place when he was on the road. We're going to have her learn about his disappearance and have her contact the sheriff's office."

"I hope they find out who did it."

"We all do," Buzz said. "By the way, if you haven't done so yet, get rid of the Beretta. I know you like it, but the cops will be discovering the three dead men on Whidbey later today. We held off because of everything else going on. When they discover the same gun used to kill them also killed DuPane there's going to be a never ending search for that weapon."

"Already taken care of," Clint said. He had taken the pistol apart and left the pieces miles apart in western Colorado.

"Good. The FBI has a team doing its best to put all the pieces together. Their main goal is to make sure they understand how DuPane and anyone in cahoots with him put the team of killers together. However, I'm sure they're also going to do their best to discover who killed DuPane and five of his henchmen. They may even start wondering how Little's disappearance fits in to all this."

"I'm sure you'll let me know if I need to fly off to Brazil or somewhere else to hide."

"That may not be a joke," Buzz said. "The real test will come when and if your Ms. Laura Richards walks into the Seattle PD today."

"Is that her real name after all?"

"Yes, but what's interesting is that we haven't been able to find any connection that she had to DuPane or the others."

"Well, he didn't pick her up hitchhiking," Clint said.

"I know. I'll call you tonight, and by the way, you did good. This group of killers needed to be stopped," Buzz said, and they ended the call.

Clint knew a lot of loose ends still needed to be tied up. Once the police had Dick's identification, they would discover that Dick stayed at the Paris Resort and Casino. The murder and the police investigation would be a conversation topic among the hotel staff for a few days and someone like Jamie could remember him. He knew not to obsess over the ultimate outcome of the investigation into Dick's death, but it would be difficult to control his curiosity. Buzz might tell him one day. From the shadows, Theresa would stay on top of the investigation, and without a doubt, she would be an invisible factor in its solution.

Dick's involvement with Section had most likely already been sanitized. To even the most dedicated investigator, Dick's trip would appear to have been made for personal reasons.

He made a mental note to stay away from Las Vegas for several more years, and then remembered his discovery with the metal detector on top of the hill above where the drones attacked the three cars. Clint had planned to go back and check that out. He wanted to believe that he had found a strongbox, the type used on stagecoaches to transport valuables. With his luck, though, it would only be the lid to a box, and the box wouldn't be there. Whatever it was, if it had been buried there for the past hundred years, it could stay hidden a few more.

He didn't think he had much to fear from Missy, Mel, or Griff. When and if the press reported on the discovery of the dead bodies on Whidbey, the news announcements would likely identify the three as suspected members of a group of international terrorists or something similarly sinister. Clint hoped that would be sufficient for Griff and Missy to keep their thoughts to themselves.

Still, he thought maybe a trip out of the country would be a good idea. He wondered if the airlines had any sales going on for flights to Athens. Now where had he put that phone number that Elina had given him?

Acknowledgement

"I couldn't have done this alone. Some of you also deserve the blame.

Thanks."

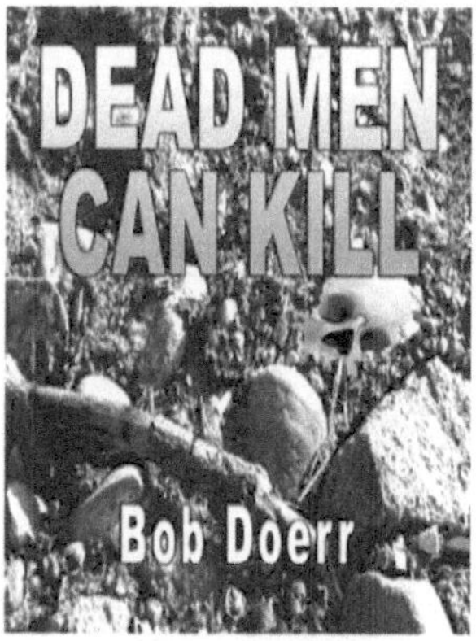

Title: ***Dead Men Can Kill™***

- Author: Bob Doerr
- Publisher: TotalRecall Publications, Inc.
- Format: HARDCOVER, 6.14" x 9.21"
- 13-digit ISBN: 978-1-59095-758-5
- Paper Back: ISBN: 978-1-59095-759-2
- Book: ISBN: 978-1-59095-761-5
- Number of pages: 320
- Publication: December 8, 2009

When Jim West, a former Air Force Special Agent with the Office of Special Investigations, moves back to New Mexico, his goal is simple: start an easy going second career as a professional lecturer on investigative techniques to colleges and civic organizations. He never envisioned that his practical demonstration of forensic hypnosis on stage with a state university student would stir up memories of an 18-year old murder mystery. When the student is murdered three days later, West finds himself ensnared in a web of intrigue that pits him and the small town's authorities against a ruthless, psychotic killer.

An aggressive reporter for the town newspaper seeks out West for help with the story, but after one of her co-workers is murdered, she quickly aligns her efforts with West and the Sheriff. As West works closely with her, he begins to wonder if this could be the first real relationship for him since his devastating divorce a few years earlier.

The killer, though, has other plans for the reporter and the story takes fascinating twists and turns, leading to an inevitable, riveting confrontation.

Look out for a new hero on the mystery/thriller landscape! Jim West, retired military investigator, is resourceful, intuitive, pragmatic and always competent. All of West's abilities are tested when he matches wits with psychopathic serial killer William White, a man whose appreciation for murder is surpassed only by his delight in domination. Bob Doerr has crafted a must-read addition to the genre in Dead Men Can Kill, which evolves from absorbing story to absolute page-turner as West closes in on a killer who is supposedly dead. Highly recommended!

--Dallin Malmgren, author of...

The Whole Nine Yards   The Ninth Issue   Is This for a Grade?

A Jim West™ Mystery/Thriller

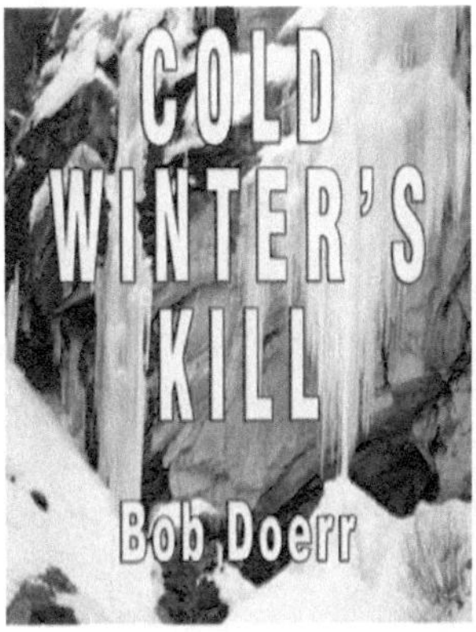

Title: *Cold Winter's Kill*™

- Author: Bob Doerr
- Publisher: TotalRecall Publications, Inc.
- Format: HARDCOVER, 6.14" x 9.21"
- 13-digit ISBN: 978-1-59095-762-2
- Paper Back: ISBN: 978-1-59095-763-9
- Book: ISBN: 978-1-59095-764-6
- Number of pages: 288
- Publication: Dec 8, 2009

Cold Winter's Kill is a fast paced thriller that takes place in the scenic mountains of Lincoln County, New Mexico and throws Jim West into a race against time to stop a psychopath who abducts and kills a young blonde every Christmas...

It was one of those phone calls former Air Force Special Agent Jim West never wanted to receive--an old friend calling to ask if he could drive down to Ruidoso, New Mexico to help locate his daughter who has disappeared while on a ski trip with friends. Jim found himself heading to Ruidoso even though he believed, much like the local authorities, that if she had gone missing in the mountains in December, her survival chances were slim. He didn't want to be there when they found her, but still he drove on.

Once in Ruidoso, Jim discovers a sinister coincidence that changes everything. It appears that someone is abducting and killing one young blond every year around Christmas. The race is on--can Jim locate his friend's daughter in time? But why is this happening and who's doing it?

Jim can't wait for the local authorities to raise the priority of their search, or for the pending blizzard to pass. In his haste he puts himself in the killer's sights. Will he, too, suffer from a cold winter's kill?

"GREAT SUSPENSE! In ***Cold Winter's Kill*** Bob Doerr grabs your attention from the beginning and holds it until the last sentence. Hard to put down!"

--Shelba Nicholson
former Women's Editor, *Texarkana Gazette*

A Jim West™ Mystery/Thriller

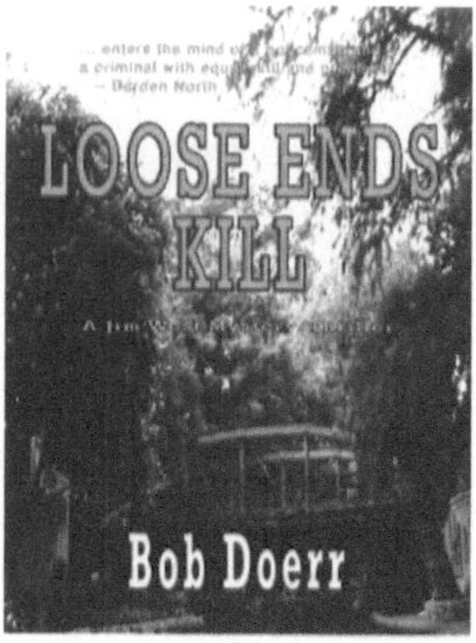

Title: Loose Ends Kill™

- Author: Bob Doerr
- Publisher: TotalRecall Publications, Inc.
- Format: HARDCOVER, 6.14" x 9.21"
- 13-digit ISBN: 978-1-59095-717-2
- Paper Back: ISBN: 978-1-59095-718-9
- Book: ISBN: 978-1-59095-719-6
- Number of pages: 288
- Publication: Oct 27, 2010

***LOOSE ENDS KILL* is a fast paced mystery/thriller** that takes place in the historic city of San Antonio, Texas, and throws Jim West into the middle of a police investigation of the murder of an old friend's wife. The police already believe they have the killer in custody – West's friend.

West is drawn into this mystery by a call from the old friend who requests his assistance. West agrees to help his friend and digs deep to try to find another suspect. In the process he soon discovers that he is being followed and targeted for harassment, but by whom?

West quickly discovers that he didn't know his old friend's wife as well as he thought. To his surprise, he learns that she has had a number of affairs dating back for more than a decade. In fact, while investigating the murder, he realizes that his friend and he may be the only two people unaware of her philandering behavior.

Theorizing that one of her lovers could have had just as much motive as her husband, West starts turning over the rocks identifying one lover after another. In doing so, West unintentionally ignites an outbreak of more death and mayhem. The police and his friend's lawyers want West to go back home. The police even threaten to arrest him.

Soon, West believes the real killer wants him gone or dead. Deciding the only way to resolve the case before the outside pressures force him to leave, he sets a trap for the killer using himself as bait. However, he soon learns he may have only outsmarted himself.

A Jim West™ Mystery/Thriller

Title: ***Another Colorado Kill™***

- Author: Bob Doerr
- Publisher: TotalRecall Publications, Inc.
- Format: HARDCOVER, 6.14" x 9.21"
- 13-digit ISBN: 978-1-59095-784-4
- Paper Back: ISBN: 978-1-59095-785-1
- Book: ISBN: 978-1-59095-786-8
- Number of pages: 288
- Publication Date: September 06, 2011

It was supposed to be a short, fun golf outing, but when Jim West and his friend Edward "Perry" Mason stumble across a dead body in a restroom at a rest stop along I-25, things turn bad and then only get worse.

With the golf outing shot, West intends to stay in Colorado Springs only for a day or two. However, when two more murder victims turn up – one with West's name handwritten in her notebook - the heat on West skyrockets. The police instruct him to stick around, and soon he discovers that while the police may want to pin the crimes on him, the killer wants him out of the picture. Way out – like dead.

West's only ally is Lieutenant Michelle Prado, a tall red head with large green eyes that captivate West. Assigned to keep an eye on West, Lieutenant Prado decides the best way to do so is to keep him close. West and Prado do their own digging into the investigation. In the process, Jim wonders how close their relationship will evolve.

It seems to West that as the police focus less on him, the killer intensifies his focus on him. Barely surviving an initial confrontation, West realizes he must take the initiative. If he doesn't, or perhaps even if he does - he may end up as just another Colorado kill.

A Jim West™ Mystery/Thriller

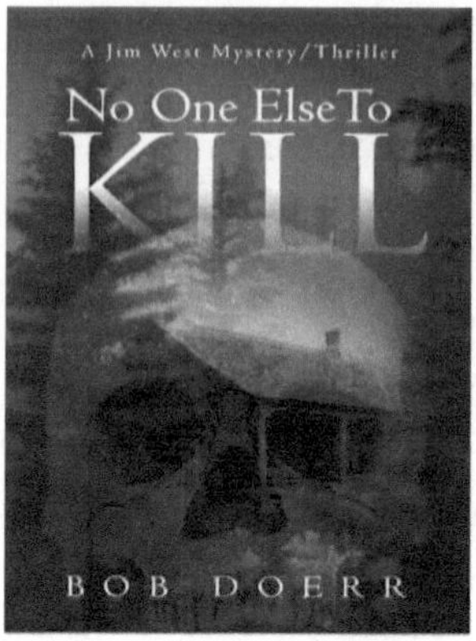

Title: *No One Else To Kill*™

- Author: Bob Doerr
- Publisher: TotalRecall Publications, Inc.
- Format: HARDCOVER, 6.14" x 9.21"
- 13-digit ISBN: 978-1-59095-422-5
- Paper Back: ISBN: 978-1-59095-423-2
- eBook: ISBN: 978-1-59095-424-9
- Number of pages in the finished book: 352
- Publication Date: December 4, 2012

No One Else to Kill, **Bob Doerr, TotalRecall Publications** - In this newest book in the popular Jim West series, Mr. West finds himself stood up and out of town. Looking forward to some R & R he keeps his reservation at the remote hunting lodge. Located in the Pecos Wilderness area in New Mexico it's a hunter's haven. Expecting to do nothing other than relax, he has no idea what the rest of the weekend holds for him. When a murder takes place, the hotel guest are detained and no one is beyond suspicion. The sheriff is called in, and while the investigation is underway, a second murder takes place. Both crimes are clearly related, but by whom and why? With time running out and unable to find a motive, the legal experts seek Jim's help.

The cover for *No One Else To Kill* **is a 2013 finalist for the da Vinci Eye award.**

Bob's four previous novels in the series are titled *Dead Men Can Kill, Cold Winter's Kill, Loose Ends Kill,* and *Another Colorado Kill.* The latter two were selected as Eric Hoffer Award finalists for 2010 and 2011, respectively.

Bob Doerr's *No One Else To Kill* was awarded the Grand Prize in the "Books With Out Publishers" writing contest at www.ultimateherocontest.com

A Jim West™ Mystery/Thriller

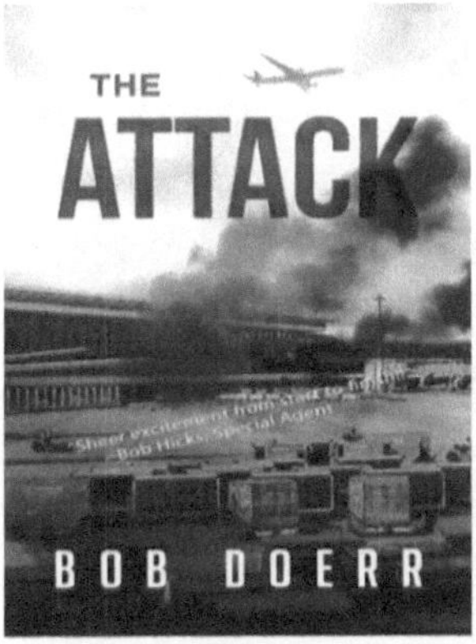

Title: ***The Attack***™

- Author: Bob Doerr
- Publisher: TotalRecall Publications, Inc.
- Format: HARDCOVER, 6″ x 9″
- 13-digit ISBN: 978-1-59095-145-3
- Paper Back: ISBN: 978-1-59095-146-0
- Book: ISBN: 978-1-59095-147-7
- Number of pages in the finished book:
- Publication Date:

A terrorist team has just set off four explosive devices in an international airport close to New York City. The leader of the terrorists, Ahmad Khalin, survives the attack and plans to attack a second U.S. airport within the month. As Khalin makes his escape from the New York area he is involved in a shooting in Connecticut. Clint Smith, a U.S. government agent assigned to an ultra-secret agency, is at a restaurant across the street when the shooting occurs. He responds to the scene to see if he can help, but Khalin is gone. On a hunch, Teresa Deer, Smith's boss, sends Smith after Khalin. Smith's pursuit takes him to Bar Harbor, Maine; Wiesbaden, Germany; the Costa Brava, Spain; Northern Scotland; Lake of the Woods, Ontario, Canada; and finally into Saskatchewan, Canada, where the final confrontation takes place. Throughout the pursuit, a number of interesting characters add to the subplots and try to survive their involvement in the chase.

A Clint Smith Thriller™

Author Bob Doerr Uses his special knowledge to provide authentic details in his novels about how law enforcement agencies do their work.

www.bobdoerr.com

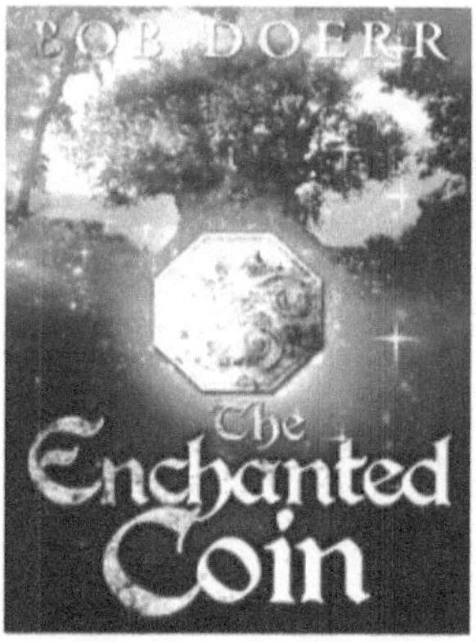

Title: *The Enchanted Coin*™

- Author: Bob Doerr
- Publisher: TotalRecall Publications, Inc.
- Format: HARDCOVER, 6.14″ x 9.21″
- 13-digit ISBN: 978-1-59095-083-8
- Paper Back: ISBN: 978-1-59095-084-5
- Book: ISBN: 978-1-59095-085-2
- Number of pages in the finished book: 130
- Publication Date: September 17, 2013

We have all heard of tales of UFO's, ghosts, people who say they can talk to the spirits, ancient curses, and magical talismans. Most of us automatically dismiss them as false, figments of people's imagination, and understandably so. However, might not just a few of them be true? I don't know, but I heard this story from a young man the other day who swore the fascinating tale I have set forth in this book really did really occur, because it happened to him. You be the judge.

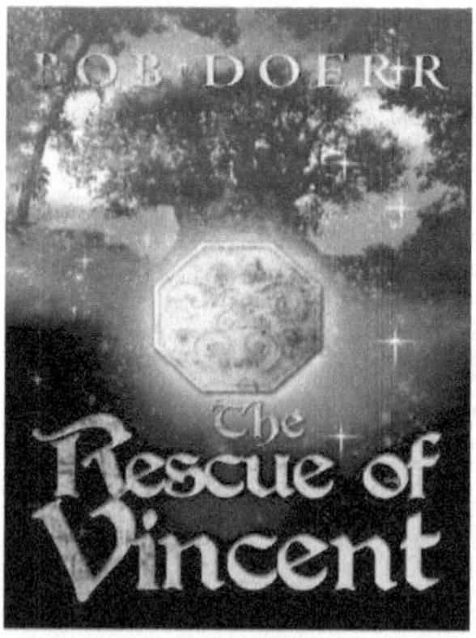

Title: *The Rescue of Vincent*™

- Author: Bob Doerr
- Publisher: TotalRecall Publications, Inc.
- Format: Paperback, 6″ x 9″
- 13-digit ISBN: 978-1-59095-279-5
- eBook: ISBN: 978-1-59095-280-1
- Number of pages in the finished book: 160
- Publication Date: October 28, 2014

The Rescue of Vincent: Book 2 in The Enchanted Coin Series is a 31,000 word fantasy adventure targeted at Middle Grade readers. Imagine being a fourteen year old again and finding a coin that seems to give off a light of its own. The coin has your name on it, and instructs you to toss it into a fountain next to the Tree of Life. That's what happens in The Rescue of Vincent, and what starts my protagonist off on a magical adventure that many young boys and girls would love to have. This book is "G" rated.

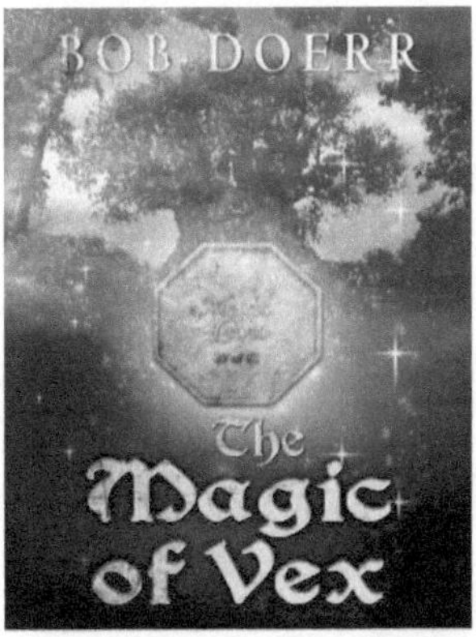

Title: ***The Magic of Vex***™

- Author: Bob Doerr
- Publisher: TotalRecall Publications, Inc.
- Paper Back: ISBN: 978-1-59095-309-9
- eBook: ISBN: 978-1-59095-280-1
- Audio ISBN: 978-1-59095-281-8
- Number of pages in the finished book: 140
- Publication Date: August 4, 2015

Samantha Gillespie's discovery of a magic coin results in her transportation to the strange world of Vex where magic is real and where she has to overcome a number of challenges if she ever hopes to return home.

What happened to Samantha was totally unexpected and quite frightening. It led her to an adventure that many might think impossible to believe, but it did.

You be the judge.

For a complete list of books by Bob Doerr, a previews of upcoming titles and more visit his website www.bobdoerr.com or find him on Facebook.

Titles by Bob Doerr

Mystery Detective Suspense Thrillers

Dead Men Can Kill

Cold Winters Kill

Another Colorado Kill

Loose Ends Kill

No One Else To Kill

Caffeine Can Kill

Action Adventure Series

The Attack

The Group

Mouse Gate Series

The Enchanted Coin

The Rescue of Vincent

The Magic of Vex

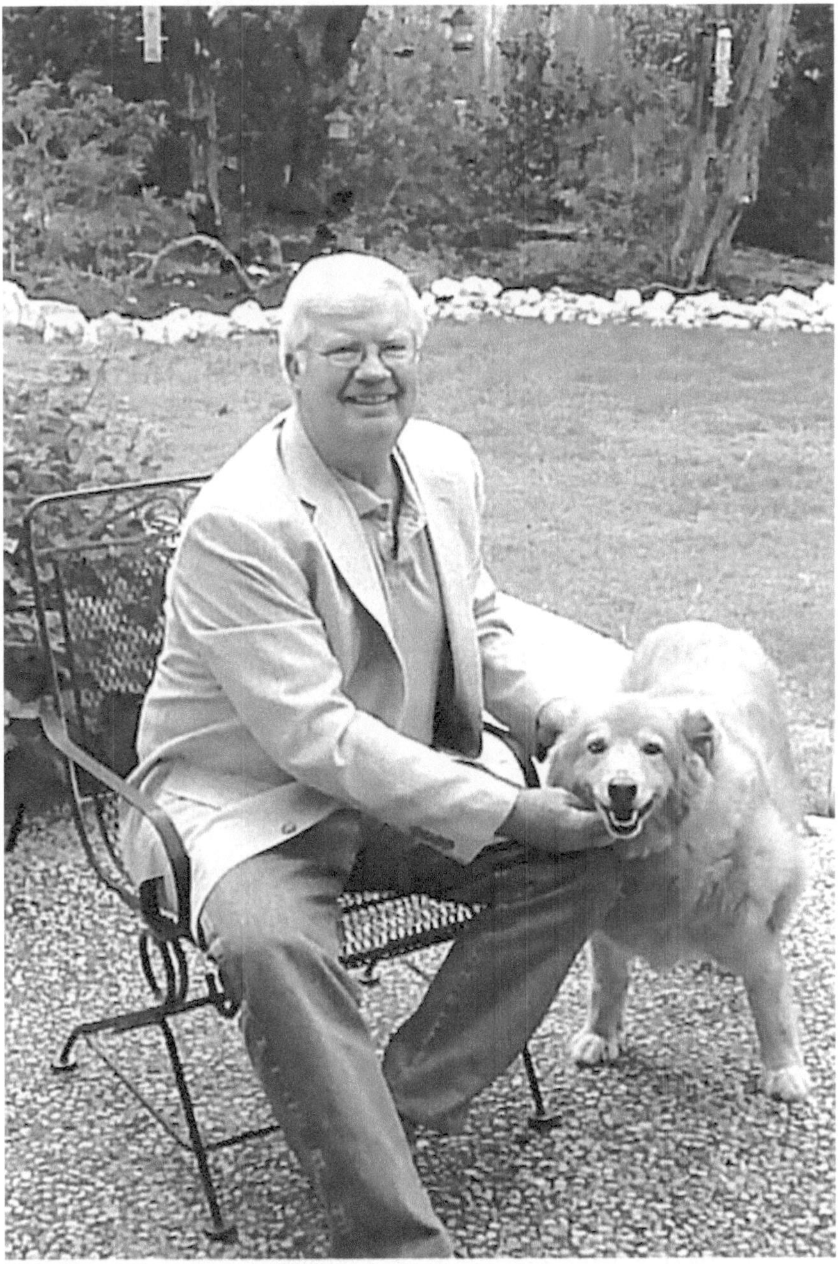

For a complete list of books by Bob Doerr, visit his website and preview his upcoming titles and events. Locate Bob on Facebook and let him know how you like his books.

www.ingramcontent.com/pod-product-compliance
Lightning Source LLC
Chambersburg PA
CBHW020404120726
47904CB00002B/698
* 9 7 8 1 5 9 0 9 5 5 6 9 7 *